BOUND
IN
BLOOD

BOUND IN BLOOD

Printed by Kindle Direct Publishing, an Amazon company.

Requests for permission to make copies of any part of the work should be emailed directly to m.runte25@hotmail.com

Cover design and interior artwork: Jon Stubbington
www.jonstubbington.com/book-covers
Formatting: Lindsay McDonald
www.helpingauthorseveryday.com

Text set in EB Garamond, 11 point

Summary: Tristan never forgave his brother for leaving but Aran's return heralds a curse, one he never expected to resolve. Susannah resents a move away from Kingston and her parents' ambitions for her. Neither thought mythology was more than stories until a man from Aran's past stepped into their lives.

PROLOGUE

Tristan

His side burned from the graze that the bullet had left behind and he could smell the blood stink on the air. Smears of it stained the worn wood of the pier that extended over the Sound. Tristan gritted his teeth against the pain as he lifted his gaze to look at her. She smelled human, a fear scent clinging to her skin as much as the distant smell of rain. She was terrified despite the rock steady grip she had on the gun. "Irene..."

Irene spat on the wood between them, taking a step back, closer to the end of the dock. "Don't. I know what you are. My father warned me about shapeshifters, how dangerous they were to people. He also said they had no place in a modern world."

If she believed that, she was a long step past bigotry and deep into something no one should believe in. And if she had witnessed his change from human to German Shepherd, how long had she been tracking him? The choice, more than a month ago had been death or running on four paws to escape something that lived deep within Seattle's forgotten tunnels. Whatever the monster had been, its only thought had been to trying to eat him. "Please. You don't—"

"I think I do." She took the safety off her weapon and aimed it at his chest. "You broke the rules your kind tries to enforce. If it wasn't going to be me, it's probably going to be one of them. At least—look at me."

Irene's voice went as brittle as ice as she touched the trigger on the gun again, finger closing around it but not tightening yet. "It's over."

She didn't know how right she was. And how wrong. Tristan went to his knees, seeing his brother behind the hunter. Aran's arms were folded across his chest, he was dressed in his usual uniform of a loose-fitting white tunic. His expression gave little away as he looked on, sandy blonde hair plastered against his scalp.

Tristan swallowed, pressing his arm against his shirt. The light gray cotton was stained dark but there was no one nearby to see the blood on the fabric. "Irene."

Her name came out as a croak as he fumbled for any explanation that would delay and defuse the tension. And draw Irene's attention away from what she hadn't yet seen behind her back. "You don't—whatever thing your dad has with my brother, we're not—fuck!"

Irene's first shot had grazed his side, the second was better aimed and her grip was steady on the trigger. Tristan gaped, sinking to his knees wide eyed as he pulled his hand away from his side. "Look out!"

Aran had always had an uncanny way of being quiet until he wanted to be acknowledged. And Irene's distraction had only benefitted him. Irene smirked, bitter until she caught a glimpse of Aran standing behind her. Her jaw dropped in disbelief, and she faltered, gun wavering in her grip at the sight of the older, stronger shapeshifter.

Tristan gritted his teeth, forcing himself to stand as fire seared through his side. Anyone human would have succumbed to shock by now or bled out on the dock but he wasn't human. Mortal but definitely not human. Too bad for either of them though. Aran was something... more than that, whatever it was. There was no denying the danger that his brother was, not with that look in Aran's eyes. Or the way he looked tonight, faded. Half in the real world, half in whatever place he called home. The lights of a passing cruise liner swept through the insubstantial outline of his brother's body, only making him seem more uncanny, not less.

Tristan bit back on the Welsh expletive that threatened as he took a step closer. Irene's first shot had been made in warning, skimming across his side, rather than into it. If she wanted to kill something—someone, she would have. She was playing with him, but she hadn't counted on a bigger threat showing up or how Aran's temper ran when he was willing to show it. "Aran, don't. It isn't worth it. Fight Irene's dad over a book refund or whatever but let me get her out of the way."

The feud was a bit bigger than a bad business practice but he was trying to navigate the situation as discretely as he could, and praying that the police wouldn't become involved over shots fired. Irene was innocent, even if she was holding the gun.

You called me, little brother. Aran signed his words, never speaking aloud. *I answered.*

Even gestured, the warning couldn't be missed. Tristan swallowed, seeing the impassive mask in his brother's eyes. There wouldn't be much mercy tonight. It wasn't in his brother when he was like this. "Not like this. She—"

Irene's gun went off, point blank into Aran's chest as she retreated away from the danger of the edge, what little confidence she had been trying to summon looking like it had evaporated into nothingness. Aran snarled, showing touch too sharp canines for a moment before he seized her arm and used the momentum of her stumbling steps to send her headfirst over the edge, pinwheeling wildly before she hit the water with a splash.

Tristan swore, following after Irene before thought could catch up with impulse. His dive was better than Irene's fall but water was like concrete if a jump wasn't timed right. He surfaced gasping in the cold, trying not to acknowledge how the saltwater felt like acid against the raw gunshot wound. "Fuck!"

He squeezed his eyes shut against the pain, shifting form and using the smaller shape to escape the restricting jeans and t-shirt. The brown fur of his otter form was warmer than clothes, anyway, better suited to the Pacific's chill, but not for speech or persuading his brother to release Irene. Jeans could be replaced or borrowed from his father. The almost abandoned t-shirt less so and he needed hands, not paws for this. Tristan let the otter form slide away, shifting back to human and seized the shirt, ignoring how it was inside out and backwards as he pulled it over his head. Some things were more important than how a t-shirt was worn.

Aran was kneeling on the silty ground, hand at Irene throat as she thrashed against his hold. Tristan choked, inhaling water before he surfaced, gasping for breath. He dove again, trying to tug at his brother's arm away from her. His hand passed below the surface of Aran's wrist, and he backpedaled a foot or two away, swearing silently as he signed his next words for the older shapeshifter. If touch couldn't work, sign language would have to. "Let her go, Aran. Please, for my sake."

It wasn't worth another life, not tonight. Aran's gaze met his and he flinched at the washed-out blue that nearly turned the color from clear Mediterranean water to a silver-white. "Aran, please."

She tried to kill you. That's not something I'll tolerate. Aran said.

Not could tolerate but would not. Tristan pulled at Irene's arm, wrapping his own below her underarms. She was unconscious in his hold, head resting against his shoulder. The consequences of getting between a kelpie and his prey could wait for a time when there were bubbles coming from between Irene's lips. He didn't give himself time to worry about that, or the fury that flashed across his brother's face.

Tristan dragged her onto Alki beach, swearing again as sirens sounded in the distance. Someone would have seen the confrontation and the jump off the dock. Luck had only traced them here.

5

He pressed down on Irene's chest, pausing for a moment and placed his mouth at hers. "C'mon, breathe, damn it!"

If there was any chance of resolving this peacefully, Irene's life would be a good start to calling a truce to Aran's disagreement with her father. "Please..."

She remained too still under his touch, unresponsive to the CPR as he sat back on the balls of his feet. "Damn it!"

Damn Aran for drowning her as well. The older shapeshifter had acted in his defense but there could have been another way to handle this. Irene hadn't had to die tonight. A scent of burning paper and ink filled his nose before he saw Irene's father stride out of the darkness. "I didn't do this..."

If anyone was to blame, it was Aran, but his brother was out of the witch's reach. There weren't many people capable of leashing a kelpie and Martin wasn't one of them. The vise that tightened around Tristan's chest, cut his words off before he could finish his sentence.

"She's dead." Martin's tone was as black as it could come as he cradled Irene's body in his arms. "You and yours are responsible for this and I'll make sure you pay for it."

The pressure on his chest redoubled, sending him to all fours as he gagged on the taste of salt water. Tristan lifted his gaze, trying to force the plea and apology from his mouth as darkness wavered at the edges of his vision.

Martin was beyond listening, left hand clenched white knuckled. "It doesn't matter, boy. Irene's dead and you, or one of yours was responsible. Someone must pay for this.

No. Aran stood in the water between the open ocean and land, this time dressed in a dark blue shirt and black jeans though his hair was still wet, falling loose around his shoulders. *He won't pay, Martin. Hurt my brother and I'll kill you as easily as I drowned your pup.*

Martin scowled and drew back, slashing his forearm open with a pocketknife. Blood scented the air and Tristan flinched, gaze dragged towards Aran as the older shapeshifter took a step forward, drawn by the scent. "Don't!"

Aran probably wouldn't do anything, but it was hard to be sure of anything where his brother was concerned. A lack of an appetite didn't mean Aran failed to occasionally find the scent of blood appealing. Tristan scrambled to his feet, attempting to grab for his brother's arm.

He ended up on his knees, winded as his control slipped and he gagged, retching onto the sand as the familiar soft light surrounded him. The light may have been gentle, but its touch wasn't, prickling—burning against his skin as he fought the change from human to otter. The shirt was once more too loose, tangling around his new form until he wriggled his way out of it, remembering nothing of the hours until the sun peeked over the horizon.

ONE
Tristan

ONE YEAR LATER

The towel fell over his head, blotting out the early morning light before Tristan dragged it off, drying his hair. Towel dry and brush wouldn't make him completely acceptable later, but it was the best he could do on such short notice. Circumstances were rarely within his control these days. "Thanks. For the towel."

Modern life and the lights of Seattle never felt as distant as they did now. More for his brother than him, but he understood Aran in a way he hadn't before. Tristan pulled his jeans on, following them up with a wash abused black t-shirt. The phone was on its last twenty percent. He glanced at it and tossed the device into the knapsack he'd cached before looking at his brother's back. He could count on one hand how often he'd seen Aran, and this was still just as disconcerting as it was a year ago. "Aran?"

Tristan stood, reaching for his brother's hand and let it fall back to his side, resisting the urge to shiver at the lack of substance that should have been there under his touch. Aran wasn't dead or a ghost, but he did leave a good impression of one with the way the weak sunlight and the little wavelets lapping at the beach front were visible through his body. "Could you, please?"

Aran was impossible to read, listening to some song only he could hear before he shook his head, expression clearing. Regret or longing briefly seen in his eyes before he sighed, signing his answer. *Forgive me.*

There was nothing to forgive now, and the thing between them was unrelated to his question. Tristan balanced on one foot, pulling the shoe on before he found the other one beneath the trunk of a driftwood tree. "That wasn't what I was asking for and you know it. You're still doing the ghost thing or whatever it is."

I see. Aran glanced down at himself, making a face before the eerie effect faded.

Tristan tilted his head slightly, relieved at the appearance of solidity. It wouldn't do much for what his brother preferred clothing wise. A knee length Greek tunic was more costume than proper clothes to him, but Aran liked it, for whatever reason. Nothing was going to change the older shapeshifter's mind. "That's better."

So long as he resisted the temptation to reach out and take his brother's hand, he could pretend that Aran was a flesh and blood critter, not whatever he really was. "I've got to get to work."

Something as mundane as that might not occur to Aran but it was a necessity for the rest of the world, curse or not. "So meet you back at the house later?"

I suppose. Aran's expression flickered, briefly pained as he flexed his hand and let it fall back to his side. *For you, not the man you call father.*

"Dad." Tristan gave in and poked a correction into his brother's answer. "You're always so formal, Jesus."

And you're still a pup. Aran cast him a wry look, signing his countering answer back at Tristan's complaint. *Wait until you've lived over a couple thousand years and then tell me what you think.*

"Pass, thanks." Tristan shuddered at the prospect of that time involved. It couldn't be pictured and anyone who lived that long was either crazy, or so far from human that they could 'cope' with it. Maybe the two were the same in the long run. "Let me be happy with a normal, human view of life for the time being."

Aran's laugh was more of a thin rasp, abruptly cut off as the color drained from his face and he went to his knees on the rocky scrap of beach. Tristan swore, ignoring the untied shoelaces as he went down next to his brother, resting one arm across Aran's shoulders. "Shit!"

The older shapeshifter rarely welcomed physical touch and only tolerated him at the best of times but now wasn't the time to quibble about nicety now. Tristan shifted position, angling himself to get a better look at Aran. And followed it up with a softer, milder curse. "Hell."

There were no words in his vocabulary for what he was seeing. The gray of his brother's eyes was so pale it was nearly white, and the pupil was almost lost beneath the film. Tristan sat back, ignoring the pain of scraping his knees up on rough stone as he passed a hand in front of Aran's face, watching as his brother tracked the motion. "That's good, I guess."

It was something at the very least. If Aran could see the gesture, track it, he wasn't blind despite the haze washing the color from his eyes. Tristan flinched, trying and failing to pull away in time as Aran's hand tightened on his wrist, the small bones in it grating against each other. "You're fine, Aran. You're fine."

Speaking as though his brother was a young puppy in need of reassurance and not currently in human form. He brushed a hand through Aran's hair, sweeping a still damp strand behind one ear as he kept up a low murmur in Welsh. "I'm here, I don't plan on leaving you."

Aran's grip eased as the haze gradually faded from his eyes and he sat back on the balls of his feet. *I'm better now. Thank you.*

If this was better, he didn't want to know what worse was. Tristan rubbed at the fading bruising on his wrist as he glanced into the trees bordering the small beach and parking lot beyond them. "Yeah, you're welcome."

Aran coughed, brushing a hand across the base of his throat, and looked away. *For now, anyway. I hurt you.*

"Not much. It's only a bruise and we heal faster than humans." Tristan covered the fading mark with his

12

other hand. "I'll just say I banged it badly against something if anyone asks."

That doesn't make it right. Aran said. *If I'd...*

"It doesn't matter." Tristan sighed, pointedly signing his words this time. "Trust me, it looks worse than it hurts. Six hours and it'll be gone."

Aran's mouth tightened in distaste as his gaze followed the sign language Tristan used. *Let me help, kit.*

"Fine." Tristan held the bruised wrist out, relieved when Aran's gentle touch came with combat worn skin and warmth, and not a ghost light touch over his arm. "Help me."

Refusal wasn't an option when his brother didn't know the meaning of no. Aran glanced at him, fingertips lingering over the bruise for a moment. It faded to blue and then yellowish green under his touch before healing completely. Tristan pulled away, wiping his hand on his jeans. "Thanks, but I've really got to go now, or I'll be late for work. And Aran."

He shouldered his backpack, wishing for a moment that he could kick his shoes and socks off, go barefoot across the stoney ground but time had run out for that. Job obligation might not matter for Aran, it did for him—even if the small parking lot smelled of gasoline with a fainter undertone of sunblock and fish. A party of tourists in brightly colored clothes chattering with a leisure fisherman or two as they passed by him on the narrow path. Tristan paused at the trail head, calling over his shoulder. "You might want to change your tunic. No one does the Greek warrior thing unless they're into those damned costume parties."

The light breeze teased through his hair and he gave an exasperated sigh, shaking his head. A few more stolen moments wouldn't put him too far behind schedule if he was going to throw caution to the wind and risk trouble with his boss. "Fuck you, too."

If this was how Aran chose to show how badly he wanted him to stay, he'd listen to his brother. Tristan pushed the backpack into a little hollow off the trail and turned back the way he'd come—keeping only the dark peppermint chocolate bar in his hand.

He sat on the driftwood log without invitation, resting his head against Aran's upper arm and shoulder. Between the ocean breeze, the feel of the worn wood under his hand and the slight warmth of the midmorning sun—he could almost pretend nothing was wrong. The only thing that would complete it was a broken off square or two of his chocolate bar. Tristan savored it, enjoying the taste before he rationed the rest for later. "You want?"

Aran shifted position, pulling away from him with a look of distaste at the offered chocolate. *You know I don't eat.*

"Your loss. It's good." Tristan placed the remaining chocolate at the bottom of his backpack where it was less likely to melt on him. He flipped his phone open and sighed, dropping it back inside the bag.

Aran's expression was always difficult to read but the warning edge in his eyes had Tristan swallowing, remembering too late what their father had told him. "Okay, fine. Just don't bite my head off. You don't make it easy for me not to be scared of you sometimes."

His brother looked human, but Aran was so far from humanity that it was looking at him in the rearview mirror. It was easy to forget until he got *that* look in his eyes. Like he was and never had been mortal. Tristan shoved an agitated hand through his hair, fidgeting in his

14

seat before he pushed the fear away. This was Aran, brief and obvious lack of kindness aside. They were family, even if it wasn't by blood.

The moment passed as Aran glanced down, preoccupied with the cloth wrapping around one forearm. Tristan let out a sigh of relief, grateful for no longer feeling like a mouse trapped under the gaze of another predator. Until he caught a glimpse of his brother's forearm and the red flush starting at his wrist. Washington wasn't the warmest state in the country but that didn't make sunburns impossible for the careless.

Aran wasn't careless. All thoughts of making it on time to the Blue Cat diner vanished as he caught his brother's hand in his own, reversing the care Aran had given him earlier. Tristan hesitated, biting the inside of his cheek as he looked on. The damage was slight but noticeable now that it was no longer hidden by wrapping. It looked flushed and beginning to peel from exposure. Aran flinched at his touch and snarled, baring his teeth in displeasure.

Tristan pulled his hand away, tucking it out of sight behind his back. "No touching, alright. I get it but that isn't a normal sunburn. I know the difference between someone forgetting lotion and what it means for you."

This scared him more than the blank, impassive mask Aran usually wore. He'd lost his brother once, losing him again would be more than he could bear. "Is this... your kind of shapeshifter thing or just some other shit I'll never have to deal with?"

Some other shit. Aran said. *So to speak. Just because I chose flesh and blood for you, doesn't mean*

I am but it doesn't make me one of those shadows either.

Whatever logic Aran thought was in the signed words went over his head. Tristan made a face, looking out towards the water lapping against the beachfront. "Sure, I'll—I think I'll just humor you and pretend to understand here. Either way, that sunburn doesn't look good. Just be safe, whatever you decide to do with your day."

Aran drew a leg up to his chest, resting his chin on the arm he placed on top of his knee. *I can match Coyote or the one named Sieh for power but that comes with consequences I have to live with. They can no more travel further than half a day from the coastlines than I can spend longer than a few months on land. It's been four months since I last went swimming and last night was only a taste of what I need.*

"So soon?" Tristan shifted from one foot to the other, glancing towards the water's edge. "We only just found each other last year and you're planning on leaving. Again."

Little things like working as a dishwasher were less important than family. And family stuck together no matter what. "You can't go."

Aran snarled softly, fury showing through the neutrality before he regained control over his temper.

I have no choice, Tristan. I promised you that I'd be back, not that I would stay, kit. I kept my promise. We're done, so far as the fates are concerned.

Tristan glared at him and turned on one foot, striding towards the vehicle illegally parked in the small lot. If there was nothing more to say, then nothing more needed to be said. He was late enough for work as it was. Aran could make his own way home.

He retrieved yesterday's shirt and jeans and stuffed them roughly into his backpack. With a three-hour drive back to the city, it was best if he left before he was late for his shift at the diner. "See you at Mom's, later."

It was going to be an interesting family dinner tonight one way or the other. One he wasn't completely looking forward to though he never would have said aloud. It was rude and Aran was family, his past or power didn't matter. That still counted for something regardless of origin.

TWO

Aran

Tristan was hurting, anyone could see that, but he was acting like the same spoiled child he had been at five, instead of the twenty-two-year-old he appeared to be. Aran sighed, making his way halfway up the narrow trail just in time to see the ten-year-old Nissan start and skid on a patch of gravel before the engine faded into the distance. His little brother still couldn't understand how strong a tie had on his soul for the lack of a better word. Or how dependent he was on the Pacific for his survival. Mortality made Tristan lucky.

His brother might deny it to his face but that didn't make it less true—Tristan had their father's Welsh stubbornness and less patience.

Aran stumbled over an exposed root, using a nearby tree to support himself as he tried to catch his breath. Even a short walk as this one was leaving him exhausted and his vision swimming in front of him. He blinked back the sparkles, forcing himself to stand. The gang of tourists and the sport fishermen were gone—onto the water or elsewhere, as far as he could tell, he was alone.

Nausea twisted at his stomach as he took another couple faltering steps and went to his knees in the dirt. He retched between his hands, sweat dampening fair hair to his forehead. It was only bile but still nothing he cared to see in front of him, or taste in the back of his throat.

He closed his eyes, searching for the innate ability to change and taking to the sky in osprey form. It was a coastal raptor but that was all he could say about the bird shape. Pain made his flight wobble, nearly falling before he found the wind to carry him home.

Tristan couldn't know but he was more ill than he was willing to let on and concealing it from his adoptive family. Instinct, not conscious choice led him to a ramshackle bungalow rather than the safety of his own apartment. The habit had dragged him towards Chinatown, not the modest place he kept up for the pretense.

The wind was gone from under him and he was falling with less grace than he might have managed if he'd been in good health. Aran shrieked, skidding in the dirt of a patchy back lawn as a dark-haired woman left the screen door open to the elements and mice that might be hoping for a way inside. They never would, Mariko changed the traps daily, occasionally feeding the nearby foxes she had an affinity for. The neighborhood cats had long since learned to stay away from a kitsune's home.

He stirred in her hands as she held his osprey shape gently, wrapping a small towel around him for warmth. If it had been anyone else, he would have lashed out to leave bleeding scratches on their arms and hands, but he lacked the strength for even that much.

It could have been hours or mere minutes when he finally woke again in a small bedroom with a scent of cherry blossoms and roses in his nose. An unfamiliar coverlet lay over his legs and there was a pair of jeans and t-shirt folded neatly on an oval backed antique chair in the corner of the room. *Mother?*

He'd never been comfortable with his brother's less formal use of mom to address Mariko though he used it to keep appearances up.

His vision was still blurred, black spots dancing before his eyes until he blinked them away, bringing the small dark-haired woman sitting at the foot of his bed into focus. Tristan's room, not the mattress on the bare floor of the apartment he rarely used.

Mariko offered him a sad smile as she touched the damp cloth wrapping his forearm before she signed her answer. "So far from home, child."

She brushed a strand of dark hair behind his ear, letting him catch her hand in his before he released it.

Aran swallowed back on the dry, aching feeling in his throat and tried to sit up, accepting the teacup full of water she offered him. He drained it in a few mouthfuls before signing his words back to her. *So are you.*

"Not in the same way. I don't have the connection to nature that you have. I could return to Japan if I'd wanted to, if I hadn't lost my family seventy years ago." Mariko went through the motions of the words before folding her hands in her lap.

The world swam around Aran as he levered himself up into sitting, resting the back of his head against yellowing wallpaper. He pressed his palm against his chest, exhausted, panting from the small exertion before he spoke once more.

Grief keeps you here, not some power of your own binding you to the sea.

His adoptive mother nodded tiredly, pouring a little tea from the pot sitting on a tray for herself. "Yes. And your brother."

Sickness briefly overwhelmed him before he forced it away, arranging the pillow against the bedroom wall so it cushioned his back. Even that small motion had him wincing and sucking in a pained breath as he shifted position. *Tristan wasn't begging me to stay but he's not happy with me either, from the sound of it.*

"You were gone for long enough to leave him a child and come back to a young man." Mariko said.

Her tone lacked the small warmth he remembered from the time he'd spent posing as her son in San Francisco. Love wasn't in doubt, in its own way, but it would take time to heal the rift he'd created seventeen years ago. If it could be healed. Mariko wasn't the sort of

22

woman who forgave easily, no more than her son or husband.

I filled my promise to Tristan when I came back last year but he still isn't happy with that. What more can I give him? Aran asked.

Fire knotted in the pit of his stomach, and he choked on the sharp intake of breath he took before the spasm passed. Aran wiped his mouth with his hand, seeing the traces of dark blood stark against his skin. *What more does he want of me?*

Mariko fixed him with a look that was somewhere between severe and displeased as she dabbed at the blood at the corner of his mouth with a damp cotton handkerchief. "Family, a connection. He's been alone for too long. You left your brother a five-year-old on Alki beach with nothing more than a note. You came back last summer to find him twenty-one. Tristan knew you, recognized you but you barely knew him as your brother. Not everyone has the luxury of being untouched by time."

You haven't either. Aran said.

She smiled flatly, giving him enough grace to fold his hand in hers for a moment before releasing it. "In spirit, no. In appearance, I've had to pretend to it. You're fortunate, you have so little interaction with humans."

Aran passed a hand over his eyes, cursing the migraine forming behind them as he squinted at her. Mariko looked no different to him, still the sleek black haired Japanese woman she appeared to be. A little silver in her hair, maybe—a few lines of age around the eyes but nothing that said she was aging like a human might. He shook his head, burying his face in his hands. *I don't see it.*

Mariko sighed, shaking her head. "I dye the worst of it dark, for the pretense but I'm not the same mother you left seventeen years ago."

Her mouth thinned, the only outward sign of her anger beyond the severe tone she still had in her voice. "Steffon isn't inclined to regard you as our son. I'm prepared to take that chance, for the sake of the history we have as a family—he no longer is."

Has he ever? Aran signed dryly, glancing at her. *Even when we were in North Carolina at the outbreak of the war, he only ever saw me as something to be leashed, chained to him. I may not know mortals well, but I know what family is—I had one a long time ago. I've been a father and husband myself. He hides his possession well, but it's all he sees. I know his kind... well. Too much of the dragon in his heart.*

He wrung out the damp cloth in a chipped basin on the nightstand, grimacing a little before he balled it up and placed it against his forehead for a moment, signing one handed. *I needed to leave, yes. But if I'd stayed, tried to defy my nature—it would have still turned into a fight between your husband and I. What then? Your adopted son against Steffon? No one should be made to choose between family, so I took myself out of the situation—until Tristan's call for help dragged me here last summer.*

Mariko sighed, worn down by his logic. "I suppose not. But don't mistake this for forgiveness, child."

Child? He managed a weak attempt at sarcasm, letting the handkerchief soak in the basin again. *I'm over six thousand years old. When were you born again?*

24

Her laugh still had a bitter edge to it but at least the sound was genuine. "A good man never asks a woman her age, you should remember that much."

She strode to the bedroom door, standing beneath the frame. "The washcloth may ease the headache, enough to sleep at least."

I don't— Aran cut his sentence off before it could finish, quailing a little under Mariko's look. There weren't many people who could silence him like his adoptive mother and when she turned that look on him, it was wiser to listen to her. The only other man who had been capable of such a thing had been Poseidon and he had long given the impression of being locked in Tartarus, guarded by his brother's allies and servants.

"Try at least. There's water in the bathtub if you need it." Mariko placed her hand on the doorframe, the blunt tone of voice hiding most if not all of the worry in her words. "Your control is slipping, Kaito. I'd suggest getting something to eat but I know how you feel about food."

Thanks. Aran teased the damp cloth between his fingers, undecided in how he felt about her use of a name he'd had and abandoned a long time ago. *How are you…?*

The look she cast his way was now bleak as she folded her arms over her chest. "I am, no one should have the power you do but I'm also your mother. Call it more fear *for* you than of you, for now. I love both my sons, not just Takara. Sleep, and rest if you can. I've left water in the pitcher on the nightstand."

Still water wouldn't do much for him, but Mariko was being as kind as she could be. Aran tried for a weak smile in return, settling down beneath the light flannel coverlet, head pillowed on his arm. *Thanks. For helping*.

Mariko flipped the switch next to the door, casting the small bedroom into shadow as she closed the door behind her. The darkness helped some of the headache behind his eyes but only a little. Sleep wouldn't come despite his attempts to let himself drift off into it. Peace and rest could only come when he let himself go, settling in the half-ruined halls and columns of Poseidon's domain. Not in the physical world that his mother and her husband claimed as home.

He rolled over, trying to a cool spot beneath the thin coverlet and cursed it as he gave up on the endeavor. Try as he might find what his mother wanted of him, everything felt too tight—too itchy. His throat was too dry, sandpapery. Aran rasped, struggling to draw enough breath in to breathe as he went to all fours on his hands and knees on the floor. It felt like his body was on fire, either from the fever or from the raw, painful rash visible on his arms. It went further than that, hidden beneath the cotton pajama shirt he wore.

Aran stumbled, nearly falling again as he tried to find the doorknob through touch. His vision was too blurred, too weak to be of use here.

The bathroom was opposite the bedroom, and he pulled open the door, tugging at the borrowed shirt as he slipped it off over his head. It lay in a discarded heap, the sweatpants following a moment later before he knelt in the bathtub, splashing water over his face and arms. It wouldn't be enough, would never be enough but for a few minutes, the water soothed the burning sensation traveling over his skin.

He closed his eyes, vision clearing as the migraine receded and shifted form, slipping into an echo of Tristan's favorite shape. The otter was the only mundane creature small enough to fit in the bathtub, everything else he was familiar with was land based and ill-suited to water or the cramped space between the tub, closet and toilet.

His otter shape was more silver than brown furred. More spirit than a flesh and blood creature. Aran let the water close over his head as he curled up in a tight ball beneath the surface of the water.

Ocean water or fresh would have been better but he'd take what he could get for now. And sleep as best he could beneath the water.

Neither Mariko or her husband would bother him, they understood his need for privacy while he tried to heal the damage he'd inflicted on himself. There was no power in bathtub still water dawn from a tap, but it eased the worst of the burns under his fur. It was the best he could hope for under the circumstances.

THREE
Tristan

Elizabeth Collins wasn't quite tapping her foot with impatience, but it was a near thing, judging from her sour expression. Tristan glanced over his shoulder towards the door, seeking help that wasn't going to come. Aran could have sorted the situation out or bribed her with one of the coins from his last souvenir dives, but he hadn't seen his brother since that morning.

"Sorry. Time... just got away from me and I had to make sure my brother was alright. I—it's family stuff and I haven't seen him since I was little. By the time I started school, he was already graduated and living on his own in Athens." Tristan said.

Tristan let his gaze drop to the tiled blue and white floor underneath his runners, trying for contrition he couldn't feel. "I had to stop at the drugstore for burn cream and gauze. Aran's kind of allergic to sunlight. I really need this job, for him and my parents."

Aran's health didn't depend on him, but it was as close an excuse as he could make without making up a wild story in its place. The part about the sun allergy was true.

Elizabeth folded her arms over a narrow chest, glaring at him before relenting with a sigh. "Fine. I'll buy it this time, but you'd better not be late again tomorrow for your next shift. That'll be the day I give you your last paycheck. Do you understand?"

"Yeah." Tristan said. "I get it."

He was too tired to fake innocence at her irritation or at her unpleasantly nasal voice. "I won't be late again, promise."

Elizabeth gave a dismissive little sniff, wrinkling her nose as though she smelled something foul beneath it. "I hope so, Gallagher. And do something about your hair, it's too long to be decent."

Tristan flushed, raking his hand through the shoulder length cut. It was a little on the shaggy side but that was nothing a trim couldn't fix, the next time he found a pair of scissors. It was the memories that stung more than the words. An elderly elementary teacher who had dragged him into the washroom, sat him on a toilet and cut his hair short while he cried in front of her. "I'll tie it out of the way but I'm not getting it cut because you think I should. It was traumatic enough the first time."

He couldn't help the biting smirk that formed, watching the outrage flicker across Elizabeth's face. If the only bit of revenge he could get today was petty, it was better than nothing. His boss had a firm idea of what was a respectable haircut and his refusal to cut it short was a persistent point of irritation to her. Long hair, in her eyes, was only suitable on women. "You should see my brother's haircut. Sure, he ties it back out of the way with whatever he can find but it's halfway down his back."

She opened her mouth, looked like she was about to say something and threw the dishrag she had tucked through her apron at him instead. "Just get into the kitchen where you belong, Tristan."

The day was shading to late afternoon by the time he got home and pushed the back door open. It screeched as it moved, the white enamel long since worn off the hinges as he walked into the kitchen with a load of groceries in his free hand. In socked feet, since the runners had been left on the back step, tucked under the sagging roof for protection against the coming rain. Shoes were for out of doors, not inside the house and sometimes not even then, given the number of times he'd gone barefoot as a child growing up. "Mom?"

She greeted him with a short-lived smile, dark hair loose over her shoulders. "You're off work early. If it's your brother you're looking for—he was here for a while this morning before he decided a bath was better for him than anything else. We had to use your old bedroom, I'm sorry."

"It's fine." He slumped at the kitchen table, accepting the small cup of tea she placed in his hands, brushing off her apology as unnecessary. "Just wish he'd called and said he was back for a little while. I would have blown the shift off; whatever Elizabeth thinks of me. How'd he manage to make it back?"

"Osprey." Mariko slipped a gentle hand over his shoulder, tucking a dark strand of hair behind his ear. "Barely. The bathwater helped a little, but he was struggling to breathe, and I made note of his heartbeat before giving him your bed. Ragged and too fast paced. Normal for you or I, I suppose but it was too fast for him."

Tristan snagged an apple from the basket in the middle of the table and bit into it, grimacing at the mealy taste. "I'll make a food bank run later. Was there anything I could have done to help? I—we... he was gone for most of my life before turning up again last year. Now..."

What could be said to that? Aran wasn't the easiest of people to understand, some kind of alien logic guiding him that only he could figure out. "He'll never be human, will he?"

Mariko wrapped her arm around his shoulders and let go a moment later. "There will always be things he won't tell you, Tristan. Give him a little space and he will come back when he's ready."

"Yeah." He looked down at the apple he held and tossed it into the compost bin. It was too brown and spotted to be worth finishing, except as plant food. "You aren't... mad at him, are you?"

His mother's mouth thinned. Her expression otherwise unreadable. "I'm angry, hurt by his leaving, yes. But I find myself once more playing peacemaker in our family. How I feel will be nothing compared to your father's feelings. The sooner Aran leaves this house, the safer we all will be."

"Where's Dad?" Tristan changed the subject, setting the cup with the remaining dregs of the tea down onto the table. Asking after his dad seemed a safer question to put into words anyway.

"In the garage, tinkering." Mariko cast a sour look towards the backyard and part of the detached garage visible through the screen door. "Blacksmiths and their toys. I believe it was a girl with a surfboard and a sticky engine this time."

"Good to know." Tristan put his hand on the kitchen doorframe, looking towards the stairs up to the second floor before skirting it for the back door and the detached garage space that his father used as a mechanic's shop.

As much as he wanted to check on his brother, it was wiser to give Aran some space until he felt like company. Trying to force himself on the older man wouldn't endear him to Aran. Fifteen years had made that clear enough.

The music in the small space was overpowering. Tristan winced, turning the volume and heavy beat down on the small radio perched on the tool crate. Little wonder his mother avoided the shop if this was what anyone had to endure for a few minutes inside the confined space. His father was only half visible beneath a secondhand car, almost inaudible swearing in Welsh at whatever he was contending with. Unsurprisingly there was no sign of the girl his mother had said was around. Only Steffon could have tolerated the raised to almost max volume of the music without flinching.

That by itself was a relief. Tristan sat gingerly in the ancient folding chair, waiting until his father rolled out from beneath the vehicle. "Hi... Mom said that you were here, and that Aran was back."

Any mention of his brother was a topic best approached cautiously. Aran wasn't the only one who had a temper in the family.

Fury briefly crossed his father's face before it cleared. Tristan hesitated, reaching behind his back and finding a pocketknife mixed into the mess of tools. He never planned to use it but the cool steel was reassuring in its own way, warming under his touch. Steffon wiped his hands on a graying rag before dropping it into a nearby bucket of soapy water. "He is, yes. You've come, seen and now what will you do?"

He hadn't actually seen his brother but there seemed to be no point in correcting his dad. Tristan looked down at his feet, the intended and biting remark dying unsaid. Steffon was as pleasant as always. "Nice to see you too, Dad."

The only good thing about his father's lack of hearing was his inability to discern tone in the words— even if he'd been brave enough for sarcasm under the mechanic's hard look. "Where-?"

The back of his neck prickled, and he turned to see the girl standing at the lighted space between daylight and the yellowish artificial light inside the garage. She was shifting from one foot to the other, anxiety on her face. Tristan looked away, expecting a strike to come from behind, delivered by his father. Relief washed over him when none came. "Oh."

Not the best greeting he could have given one of his father's clients but what else could he say? He reached over to the radio and turned it off, grateful that the device was no longer assaulting his hearing. "You're the one who had the sticky engine?"

"Yeah, a sticky engine and no interest in the shithole that seems to be the gas station washroom," She said.

Tristan made a face, remembering the state of that place for himself. Tile that was well past yellowing and heading into dirt floor territory, a broken mirror over a sink that only leaked rust colored water and a toilet that didn't look like it had been unplugged in a month or more. Once he'd found a cockroach hiding inside the disused paper towel dispenser. "No disagreement there. I've had to change clothes inside the men's place. You really don't want to take runners off inside it. Or put more than one foot down on that tile. C'mon. There's a bathroom upstairs you can use."

She relaxed marginally, touching the blue glass dolphin she wore on a leather cord around her neck. "Thanks."

Her accent was unfamiliar, as far from an American one as it could get. Tristan gave her a rueful look as he gestured towards the house. "You aren't from around here."

She snorted, dropping her hand from the base of her throat to her side as she left off playing with her necklace. "A white girl can't have a Jamaican accent?"

Tristan colored, feeling like he'd mis-stepped in his remark. "Uhm... sorry."

He toed his shoes off, leaving them by the door and held the screen door open for her. "I didn't think, I mean..."

It only felt like he was making the situation worse with each word and the fumbling apology as the back of his neck warmed with humiliation. "Shit."

She sighed, tugging at the elastic band she wore as a bracelet. "We can't all be English, can we? Those days with Port Royal and the plantations are over. There are whites there but we're a minority compared to everyone else. And I was just about to comment on you not looking much like your dad anyway."

Tristan sagged, sitting down in his place at the kitchen table. A moment or two longer couldn't hurt much, though his dad's client was looking antsy again. "I'm half Japanese so I got more from Mom than my dad. Doesn't matter, we're both oddballs in Seattle."

She almost smiled at that, though it was more of a twitch of the mouth before she looked away, desperation replacing the sarcasm. "Where's the goddamned bathroom?"

"Upstairs. I'll show you where." Tristan stood, scraping his chair against the linoleum floor. If only to buy his brother a few minutes to clear out of the bathroom if he could. If not, there was always the one connected to the master bedroom where his parents slept. The ensuite would have been the better choice but it lacked privacy, and only had a curtain strung across it for a 'door'. "C'mon."

He pulled the framed photograph from the wall, dropping it face down in a plant pot that had held something once, months ago—now it was a half dead stick partially buried in the dirt. She didn't need to know when or where it had been taken, or how old the black and white image was.

The bathroom was on the right-hand side of the short hallway, door slightly ajar. Tristan grimaced, knocking on it before clearing his throat and casting the girl a helpless look over his shoulder. "Just hang on a minute but there's always my parents' bathroom at the end of the hallway."

She nodded tightly and hastily made her departure into the master bedroom, slamming the door behind her. Tristan let out a sigh of relief of his own, kneeling next to his brother on the cool tile. The contents of the toilet bowl weren't exactly clean, but it couldn't be called vomit either, just bile. Aran's inability to keep solid food down was the only thing to be grateful for in this moment. There was nothing in his stomach that could come up. "Feeling better?"

Aran lifted his gaze, sweat dampening his hair to his forehead. *Marginally. Why?*

What could he say to that question? Tristan edged past him and sat down on the edge of the low bathtub, stirring a hand through the lukewarm water. "Because you weren't great this morning and we've got one of Dad's clients occupied in his bathroom. She really needed to pee."

Aran sat back, swiping hair behind one ear. *I know. I got her scent. She's human.*

"That's the problem." Tristan said. "None of us are and she can't find out. Irene was... bad enough, last year."

His brother snorted, expressing more in the sound than he could put into words as he signed. *So concerned with mortal life. Coyote or Sieh would call that perverse.*

Tristan sighed, changing the subject for the sake of his own comfort. "Doesn't matter. We need to get this cleaned up and you back to my room before she sees you and wonders how a Japanese lady and a Welsh blacksmith ended up with a blonde haired, blue eyed Irish son, twelve years too old to obviously be my brother."

Aran's mouth tightened in pain as he pushed himself away from the toilet bowl, flushing it. *It doesn't take a seer to know that the girl will end up wrapped into our family, one way or another, little brother. If she spends any time at all here, outside of being your father's client—she'll find out. Best get it over with.*

Tristan gave in, shoulders sagging at the logic presented in front of him. "Fine, whatever. But at least do something about your appearance, please. It'll be less confusing if you drop the Irish thing for the Greco-Japanese look you had back in the thirties. At least we'll look more like family."

Aran cast him a glance that was half bemused, half resigned. *If you wish, all right.*

Tristan slipped off his perch to lean against the closed door, watching with an envious look as the light shimmered and faded around his brother's body. Once, this had been as easy for him though he never would have tried changing how he looked to others. There was comfort in seeing the same face in the mirror every day.

Aran pulled the vanity drawer open, rummaging in the chaos of half used toothpaste containers and untouched burn cream before he came back with a hair elastic. He pulled his hair back into a ponytail, not speaking until he was finished. *Is it close to the photograph?*

"I'd say so." Tristan said. "Your memory's better than mine."

It was just a relief to see his brother as dark haired and Asian instead of the Greco-Irish look Aran had worn that morning.

Susannah was lingering outside the bathroom, turning the photograph over in her hands with a small frown on her face as she looked up from it to Tristan. Her gaze slipped past him to rest on Aran's face. Tristan felt his breath catch, a knot twisting in the pit of his stomach. "Hey—"

Aran's hand tightened on his wrist, cutting him off midsentence. Tristan swallowed, seeing the mix of curiosity and assessment before the older shapeshifter signed his words one handed.

Tristan flushed at the crude remark, pulling away. It was none of his brother's business about his lack of a sex life. "Shut up. Maybe you're willing to fuck a girl on the first night if she's interested in you enough. I'm not like you."

"Excuse me?" The girl looked outraged, the look directed towards him.

Tristan shook his head, cursing his brother silently. Even when Japanese, Aran was still a Greek warrior, with all that entailed. "Not me. Aran's just being an asshole who thinks he can get away with it because he can't speak."

"Ew." She regarded Aran with distaste, eyes narrowing with unhappiness. "I'm sure you're nice but it's going to take more than forty-five minutes before I sleep with someone after a first date."

Aran shrugged, holding his hands out in something like an apology before signing his name. Tristan gritted his teeth, translating for his brother. "Aran, meet...?"

"Susannah." The girl folded her arms over chest, looking unimpressed. "As... nice as this conversation is. I think I should get home. God knows how I'm going to explain that to my parents, and to be honest. I'm not as familiar with Seattle as I should be. Moved here about a month ago. Chinatown was an adventure last time."

"I'll drive." Tristan pulled a set of keys from his jeans pocket, tossing them into the air and catching them a moment later. "Lived around here my whole life. Aran can, and he's good at it but he's never bothered with a test or a license. C'mon, car's parked around the front of the house."

Aran could fend for himself; they didn't need to deal further with his brother.

Susannah didn't speak until they were standing in the patch of gravel that passed for the driveway. "My car will be ready soon, right?"

"Next day or two." Tristan said. "I'll drive it back to your place and scrape something together for taxi fare home."

It wasn't like he could have shifted form and run home in wolf or dog form, especially these days when he was stuck going between otter and human when the sun went down. He sighed, feeling a pang of loss for that time before.

"If you're sure..." Susannah trailed off.

"I'm sure." Tristan averted his gaze from her, unlocking the car with a beep. "I'm used to it."

He hung back watching as Susannah pulled her runners on and as she picked at the complicated knot that bound her shoelaces together. "Let me."

The pocketknife flashed in the sunlight and she froze, looking at him wide eyed before abandoning her attempt at picking the knot apart with her fingers. Tristan knelt at her feet and cut through the knot with a swift slash, leaving the raw ends loose and two or three inches shorter than they'd started out as. "Something Aran taught me before he graduated. Best way to undo Alexander's goddamned knot. Cutting through it. You might have to get new shoelaces though."

The only lesson, in truth but that wasn't something he could share with Susannah.

She made a face, stretching her foot out to examine the runner before putting it on the splintery back step. "Seems like you're close, all things considered."

Tristan shook his head, folding the little blade up and stuffing it into his jeans pocket.

Not that close to be honest. By the time I was starting school, he was already graduating it. He tends to complicate things without even trying."

"I'm sorry." Susannah said. "And thanks for the solution to the knot problem."

"You're welcome." Tristan stood, gaze flicking towards the overcast sky above their heads. "Looks like rain soon. Just tell me your address and I'll get you home."

FOUR

Susannah

Tristan turned the wheel at Susannah's instruction, following the map she had unfolded in front of her. "Nice street."

The boulevard was tree lined, older but the houses to either side had the benefit of looking like they belonged there, not just as bungalows due to be condemned in twenty years. Not like the rental house his parents had.

Susannah glanced out the passenger side window, a little frown on her face. "I guess. I still miss Kingston though. I mean, I've only been in the States for a month but..."

"You're homesick." Tristan said.

"Yeah." Susannah sighed, brushing a stray lock of hair behind one ear. "The culture shock's still the worst part about being here. Everyone's so white."

"You're white." Tristan glanced into the rearview mirror and pulled over to the curb, letting the engine idle.

She made a face, resting her head against the back of the seat. "I know. It's still weird seeing it for real though. Eighty percent of everyone living there is black. I was in the minority and happy with it. Used to be growing up, I wished I *was* black. All my friends were and I was the odd one who stood out. Goddamn American tourists always had to comment. I have to stop and think before asking the random black stranger for instructions because I don't know them. First instinct is to trust them over some Caucasian coffee boy or something."

Tristan cut the engine off, glancing away. "That's... hard."

"Yeah." Susannah rolled her window down, holding her hand out to catch the first drops of rain that fell outside the safety of the vehicle. "I mean, it wasn't like I was sheltered or anything—I know what the city is like and what parts to avoid at night, but I was happier roaming through some of the poorer neighborhoods than cooped up in Jack's Hill. If I had a choice, I'd take hurricane season over the cold here any day of the week."

She shook her head tiredly. "What about you?"

"Not much to say." Tristan looked down, sorting one handed through the console space between them. "Born and raised here. If you want to hear some real adventures, talk to my brother. He's got some stories to share."

He tapped his wrist against the curve of the steering wheel, a little frown furrowing between his eyes. "You're talkative for someone who just met me."

Susannah sighed, leaning back against her seat. "I'm lonely, and unlike Kingston—my parents keep me cooped up at home. The only time I manage to get a little space to myself—I have to lie, and I still think they see through it. They know I love going out on the water to ride the waves. Mom and Dad want me to commit to nursing school if I won't become a surgeon like they are."

"You're their little princess." Tristan said.

"Feels that way, yeah." Susannah rolled her window up as the rain started to fall a little harder outside the safety of the car. "I hate it."

She turned her head, resting the side of it against the headrest before drawing back in surprise, disquiet teasing its way into her thoughts. "Your... hands. I didn't notice earlier because you were signing for your brother and then you were driving but..."

A dull flush colored Tristan's cheeks as he looked down at his hand and stuffed it into his jacket pocket. "Yeah. I've got syndactyly. The doctors could have fixed it when I was born but Mom and Dad didn't have the money for it. Aran's got the same... defect. Think the story Mom told me growing up was that the doctor didn't know what to do about it. The bone structure's fine, healthy, I've just got the webbing between my fingers. Don't say another word about it."

Susannah let out an offended little huff, putting a hand on the door latch. "Wasn't really planning on it, you know. Thanks for the ride home."

"No problem." Tristan twisted the key in the ignition as Susannah climbed out of the car. "I'll bring yours back as soon as Dad's finished with it. Just do a little more research into vehicles before you buy. That year and model for Mazda is shit."

"Thanks, I guess I owe you. Exchange emails or phone numbers?" Susannah asked.

Tristan sighed and leaned over, rummaging in the space between the driver's seat and the passenger seat for a little notebook stolen from some diner named the Blue Cat. "Email. Nights are... bad for me. I keep my phone on silent most of the time, so I won't hear any calls from you around that time."

"Good to know." Susannah accepted the scrap of paper he offered her. "Again, thanks for the lift."

"You don't owe me anything but an engine repair bill—and that's mostly for my dad." Tristan's expression went flat, toneless. "No offense meant but I hope this is the last time we meet. You don't know what I am."

"Maybe not." Susannah said. "But I think you're just as lonely as I am here—you just don't want to admit it."

She stepped backwards to the safety of her lawn, folding her arms over her chest. "Call or bring the car back when it's fixed. I'll worry about what to tell my parents later."

Tristan snorted, hit the gas and executed a tight turn on the street, earning an irate honk from the slowly oncoming car before his taillights vanished out of sight around the nearby corner. Susannah cursed softly and dug for her housekey in her pocket, grateful it hadn't been attached to the same ring her car keys were on. "Thanks for nothing."

Tristan was less of a jerk than his brother but that wasn't a high bar to clear in her opinion.

No phones at the dinner table was an unwritten rule in her parents' house but Susannah couldn't focus on the meal in front of her. Takeaway was still takeaway even if it was really good Italian. She barely tasted it until her dad cleared his throat. "What?"

Brian set his knife and fork down on his plate, casting the phone a disapproving look. "Something important that you need to tell us?"

"Oh, no." Susannah reluctantly handed the device over to him. "Just checking for a... friend's text but he said he was away from it tonight. I'd just hoped he'd text me or email a bill over for the car."

Tristan definitely wasn't a friend, but the lie was easier than saying she'd accepted a ride from a stranger. Her father looked relieved, pushing the frame of his glasses back up to the bridge of his nose. "I know it's a change from Kingston but try to think of the advantages here, Susannah."

She bristled inwardly, trying not to show it as she took her dad's cleaned plate and set it on top of hers, putting both into the dishwasher. "It's cold, wet and you just want me to follow you into a medical profession."

Brian sighed, disappointment mixing with disapproval in his eyes. "Surfing is a hobby, not an occupation. Please listen to us."

Us. Susannah dropped the cutlery in after the dishes, not bothering to align them by type in the top rack. "You mean you. Mom's in surgery with someone's goddamned stomach or appendix or something."

Her dad's expression shaded more to disapproval than disappointment at her expletive. "Heather would say the same thing I would. This was an offer neither of us could refuse and if she was here, she wouldn't be happy about the swearing."

"I'll say whatever I want to." Susannah said bitterly. "I'm not eight anymore."

He sighed, dropping his face into his hands and scraped the chair back, screeching across the floor before he vanished into the nearby living room. Susannah slumped against the cream countertop as the sound of rummaging reached her. Brian came back a few minutes later with a small mahogany box in hand. "Maybe this'll help a little? The box is new, but the necklace has been in our family for a long time. My aunt wanted you to have it when you were ready."

As if a necklace was the solution to everything. Susannah opened her mouth and closed it before the protest could escape, as she opened the mahogany box as if it might bite. It was pretty, but nothing compared to the much smaller velvet box contained within it. The silver chain glittered in the light as she lifted it free, watching as the amethyst pendent swung in a small circle, dangling from her hand. "It's pretty but…"

Brian strode around to her side gently tugging it from her and doing the clasp up behind her neck. "For me, please? It's been gathering dust since she passed away. It belongs to you now."

Susannah bit down on her lower lip as the simple amethyst pendent rested next to her glass dolphin, wishing she was the kind of girl who could cry in front of others. She fumbled for the dolphin's cord and placed it in the box where the amethyst had rested. "Thanks."

Hope blossomed in Brian's face as he looked towards the kitchen table. "There's dessert if you want it."

Susannah shook her head, denying it and the temptation of the sweet treat he had in mind. "I've lost my appetite, thanks. If you don't mind. I've been procrastinating on a box or two in my room. Now's as good as any time to finally unpack it."

The hope in his eyes faded, once more disappointed as he sat down in his seat. "Of course. I'll save the leftovers for tomorrow if you want them."

That wasn't likely. Susannah touched the pendent at her throat, trying to pretend it was her dolphin before she strode from the breakfast nook and upstairs.

Her bedroom was larger than the one she'd had at home and the window was in the wrong place. The floor length curtains were a pale lavender her mother had chosen from a furnishing store rather than white. She squeezed her eyes shut tight, pulling a pillow and blanket over her body as she settled into the window seat instead of the bed. Like the curtains, the coverlet and bedding had been her mother's choice—rose pink flower print.

Sleep didn't come easily but when it came, it was dreamless.

FIVE

Aran

It was still daylight, but the sun was lower in the sky than it had been, half hidden behind the clouds. Too early for him to dare what he needed to do. Aran sat on the edge of the dock bordering the strait, legs swinging out in front of him before he gave up on the game. No one was paying any attention to him now but that would change if he were to undress and make a perfect swan dive off the edge of the dock into the deep water. True invisibility was impossible, what he was doing was making himself as forgettable as he could.

He let out a breath, resting his head against the support columns. "I did it to protect you, kit."

The words meant something to him, even if Tristan wasn't around to hear them or answer. He was speaking more to a memory than his brother. "You called, I answered. That was what I promised fifteen years ago."

A young woman's laugh sounded from behind and he turned to see the girl leaning against a post, dressed in a pink t-shirt and hole torn jeans. A leather jacket held slung over her shoulder. Aran glanced back at her and moved over, giving her room to sit on the dock next to him. *Lyra.*

She smirked, saluting him with two fingers in a quick outward flick. "*Da, eto ya.* Aran."

Aran rolled his eyes and scooted over half a foot, enough to allow Lyra space on the end of the dock next to him. *I thought you were in New York.*

Lyra hesitated, following the gestured words he used. "I was, for a while. There's only so much of high society I can take without deciding to pull one of my tricks on the bastard. Or bitch. I missed you. And that's assuming I read sign language right. Your version isn't the same as the traditional kind I learned, not ASL."

She sniffed, dismissive. "Fifteen years between us. I was fourteen when I had my first man. Some farmer looking for a roll in his own hay, he was fifty. Could have been my grandsire if I were human. I don't care that I'm nineteen and you're thirty-four. I was born in a barn in the middle of a Finnish winter, I never had the luxury of an endless summer like you, if that makes sense."

To anyone human, it might not have. It did to him, if only by the dint of a previous encounter with Lyra. Aran sighed, reaching out to cup the side of her face in one hand before dropping it back to his side. *You always were a Dane, Lyra.*

"And you were always Irish." Her answer was snippy. "You don't think I wouldn't be able to find you? Half Japanese with your hair halfway down your back. You're as easy to find as Sieh sometimes. Native American himself and Russian in his voice."

Aran dropped his hand back to his side, teasing the end of the cloth wrapped around his forearm. *He wasn't Native American when I fought him fifteen years ago.*

There was more to their conversation than his sign language and her banter, but the meaning was clear enough to him. *You went looking for me for a reason.*

Lyra shrugged, teasing the end of her plait between her fingers. "I can't have come just for fun? I haven't had a boyfriend since that time I dated Coyote's son. It wasn't the one you're thinking of either. He had his own boyfriend, last I checked."

She quieted, picking at a stray thread in her t-shirt sleeve. "You can't count on my word; I know that but I'm telling the truth for once. You scare me but I love that sometimes. It's worth the risk of being with you."

I wouldn't hurt you... Aran said.

"On purpose? Hell, no." Lyra glanced at him, eyes flickering a cat like green gold for a moment before their natural blue returned. "But I've heard the stories about you. Least, what I think I've heard anyway. Shapeshifters are liars, I know that better than most people. You tell me if I'm right. You could drag me under and drown me if I ever took you for a ride without precautions in place. I've only got the one life. How many times have you died and brought yourself back after a time in your own little Valhalla?"

More times than he could count, truth be told. Aran grimaced, pulling a hand through the dark hair he'd left loose around his face. *Fair point, Highsmith.*

She was a kit by the standards of their kind, a child but there was no one else he would have trusted to ask what he was thinking of. Or dared to trust, truth be told. *I need your help.*

Lyra nearly laughed, resting her head against his shoulder until she saw the burned, discolored skin on his forearm. "Oh."

Yeah. Aran looked away, wishing that the cool breeze off the ocean was doing more than it could to ease the little flickers of pain he felt as he moved. They were all tiny signs of internal breakdown on him and a night or two of swimming wouldn't be enough to reverse the damage. *I know enough of you from folklore, what they managed to get right anyway. You're a trickster and supposedly very good with illusions.*

It had never been a part of Norse folklore but there were the occasional tales of her cousin stepping into an elevator shaft and falling—not realizing that the elevator hadn't been there in the first place. *The lift was your work?*

Lyra smirked, a fond look crossing her face at the memory. "It was. The wild chicken part was the best bit of that trick. My grandfather laughed when he heard it from me."

She gave him a sly look, tilting her head slightly as she glanced at him. "Next question?"

Can you do something about this? Aran gestured around them, taking in the busy activities of the dockworkers and the tourists disembarking form a nearby cruise liner. If he jumped now, it would only attract unwanted attention from outsiders. More so if he stripped jeans and t-shirt off first.

Lyra followed his hand, shaking her head. "Too big a space. I don't have that kind of power, but I can do up to the start of the dock behind us."

She smirked, delivering a light punch to his shoulder. "What makes you think I'm actually a girl right now, and that this isn't one of my little tricks?"

The air around her wavered, bearing an effect like a summer heatwave before the illusion fell around them. Aran rolled his eyes, putting a hand between the ears of the white furred panther sitting next to him. *And they accuse me of showing off. Fine—you can create illusions good enough to trick even me. I believed you, Lyra. What do the humans really see when they look this way?*

She purred under his touch and the shimmery heatwave effect restored her human form. "Just a couple stray cats sitting on the end of a dock, hoping for fish that probably won't come. You could have sex with me right here in full view of everyone and all they'd see was those cats humping each other. You're safe to do whatever you want to right now."

Thank you. Words couldn't express how grateful he was for that as he pulled his t-shirt off with a small hiss of pain as the cotton rubbed against the blistered skin. The jeans were easier, kicked off and folded into a neat pile next to it.

It was a small thing taken for granted by outsiders, but he liked the little ritual of the act. There was some comfort in it as the battered runners followed.

Lyra watched him, intrigued appraisal in her eyes as she traced the line of his body. "Mm... yummy. You shouldn't have to cover up the scarring. It's something to be honored, not hidden."

The few old lines on his shoulders and arms, maybe but not what was written across his back. Aran twisted awkwardly, tracing the one line he could feel, diagonally across his spine. *It's more truth than I care to admit to. Tristan's my brother and seen my back but I've deflected every question he's asked about the man responsible for the beating. There was no honor in that, just his idea of discipline.*

Even after so long, he could still remember each sting of the lash against his back. The scarring was something he chose to keep as a memory of that and his own promise never to submit to another in the way he had to his former master.

Lyra looked down at her feet, sly humor fading from her eyes. "I'm sorry."

She took a step back, collecting her jacket. "I'll hold the illusion as long as you need but if you need to go, best make it now."

Aran hesitated, looking over his shoulder towards the pavement bordering the dock. *Look after Tristan for me, please. He's our kind but he's still a kit.*

"Got it." Lyra managed a weak smile at that. "I know his scent and even if I didn't, we've met briefly before. I know where to find him."

She shaded her eyes with one hand, voice and tone lightening with her next words. "I knotted his girlfriend's shoelaces together."

That was as good as a promise from the little trickster. Aran pulled her close against his body, not caring about his state of undress against Lyra's jeans and t-shirt. If he didn't care, neither did she—she rested her head against his chest before taking a step back away from him. "Go on then."

Aran turned away, looking into the water below them and let himself fall, turning it into a dive that barely made a ripple on the surface. The salt water soothed his burns, and he closed his eyes. This was more home than any place on land would ever be. Even smelling of oil and human waste, there was still some power in the water.

It swirled around him, healing the burns faster than he could have done on his own. Aran breathed a sigh of relief at that. All that he had feared, the loss of control and the... fading were no longer at the front of his thoughts.

He knelt on the sandy floor, sorting through the cache he'd buried and marked with a scrap of bleached cloth. The linen wouldn't last much longer, exposed as it was to salt water and age but for now, it was enough to tell him where he'd left a small pouch of antique gold coins and a few precious bits of jewelry. The pieces would make a small supplement to his parents' meagre income, more than what Tristan was able to make washing dishes at the diner on a good day.

Aran pulled the leather pouch from where it lay and emptied it into his hand. Every piece was there for later. He'd retrieve it when the need came for it. Right now, clothing was what mattered. He stood as the current swirled around him, answering his call as much as it—she wanted to see him clothed in the familiar undyed tunic of a soldier.

Habit but a comforting one despite his adoptive parents' dismay.

The water tugged at him, more insistent than she had been before. No longer teasing now as much as pleading with him to forget the mortal world above and surrender to her. It wasn't in his nature to submit but she was a kinder mistress than Poseidon had been. All she wanted of him was to have his own free will and choice.

Whatever he chose, she would respect his decision though deciding it would leave him with a pang of loss, if he refused her.

She tugged at his tunic again, a play of light on water resolving into a fair skinned, silvery haired young girl. Unlike him, she was unclothed, the light of the world above shimmering through her body.

If he wasn't certain his brother was capable of taking care of himself, he might have refused the little ocean spirit, but his own needs mattered more than Tristan did right now. He pulled her close, pressing his mouth against hers in an attempt to shove thoughts of his brother out of mind. They weren't what he needed when he needed to focus on healing and his own recovery.

Memory, here, now was an inconvenience, not something to be thankful for.

She pulled on his arm again, insistent and showing a hand that was webbed from knuckle to fingertip. It was plain what she wanted even if she was incapable of the speech to express her words. Aran shifted form, letting go of the clumsy human mask in favor of his natural shape.

The spirit burbled something beyond his skill to understand, petting him along the dark mane and scrambling onto his back. Her hands resting between his shoulders, not tugging on the mane. She was his rider, but he had the choice of where they were to go.

It was nothing exciting from a human point of view but there was a small sea cave he knew where he could rest and finally get the sleep he needed to heal from the last lingering burns on his skin.

Light shimmered around them and faded as the little cave came into focus. Aran pillowed his head on his arm as she hummed something softly, touch gentle as she brushed her hands across his body. Healing him as much as she sang him to sleep.

The shadows drifting across his vision were gentle, welcomed—not the painful, forced attempts at rest when he walked on dry land.

SIX
Martin

The bookstore smelled of dust and warm leather from the stacks arranged in the front window. Martin let out a sigh closing the photo album on his daughter's sheepish expression. The Gallagher boy was at fault for drowning her, but it was harder to hold onto anger after a year—easier to try and move on than cling to fury at the death. Nothing was going to bring her back as much as he wanted otherwise. Shapeshifters were dangerous but some of them were like any wild animal. Best if left alone.

He toyed with the phone cord, twisting it around his fingers before dropping it. The parents weren't responsible for what the pups did and Tristan had very little power of his own. He was less a threat than his brother. The curse had been justified a year ago, now he was tempted to find the boy and remove it. He'd intended it for Aran, binding the older shapeshifter to human form but his effort had been deflected, rebounding on the boy instead.

The bell over the door tinkled and he looked away from the spreadsheet visible on the computer screen. Inventory and taxes would have to wait until closing to be done—he didn't run one of the last remaining independent bookstores in Seattle to abandon a loyal customer base when they came through the door. "Is there anything in particular that you're looking for?"

She gave him a brittle smile for her answer and held a sheet of notebook paper out for him to read. "Greek mythology. I heard you had a bit of a collection here."

"From who?" Martin gave her a long look and switched from spoken word to sign language. The skill had been hard to learn but worth it years ago. "I'm sorry, but I know most of my regulars here. You aren't one of them."

She didn't seem to take offense at the words, straightening the strap of her tank top as she looked away. "Let's just say I'm in town for a few days, trying to track someone down."

"I see." Martin said delicately. "I file my taxes on time and properly, Miss..."

The pattern picked out on the girl's shirt was a peacock with its fan-like tail spread out in shades of gray and silver. She blinked, looking thrown off track by the remark, signing in a flurry of gestures. "I'm not with the IRS or police. I'm not here about that. And it's Echo."

"Echo. Pretty." Martin stepped around the counter and flipped the sign in the window to closed. "Named for the nymph, yes?"

She nodded reluctantly, looking away. "Yeah. Can you help? I've spent years trying to find this guy and I heard you did a little sideline outside of bookstore owner."

Martin hesitated at Echo's words. What she'd heard or uncovered through rumor wasn't supposed to be common knowledge. "Sometimes, for a few more... unusual clients but—"

"They say you're a witch." Echo said. "That's more use than a gods damned psychic, I've heard."

"It isn't something I advertise much." Martin pushed his glasses back up to the bridge of his nose. "Just because I'm unlikely to burned at the stake, doesn't make what I can do, any less dangerous. Or liable to be shot for it if anyone's sufficiently frightened of what they see I can do. Why, if I may ask."

Echo hoisted herself up uninvited onto the counter, swinging her legs back and forth against it. "Because it was over at the forum I host, little tidbits of news and folklore mixed together."

Martin sighed, reevaluating his opinion of Echo downwards a notch or two. "Then I'd say you need to find yourself a new hobby, Echo. Conspiracy theories rarely do anyone good. I'll admit to being the witch you think I am but stay off the internet for a while, please."

She scowled, looking offended. "It's truth, and you well know it. If only you could remember what it was. Amyntas was yours once. You made him to be your pet, long before you were imprisoned."

Humoring the girl seemed like the only safe or logical course of action right now. Martin grimaced, seeing the disappointed look of another customer outside his door. "Echo, please. Now isn't the time or the place while I have a business to run. And if I ever knew anyone by that name, it was a long time ago."

She cast him a look of loathing as she slipped from her perch, striding for the door. "You ought to remember, Carpenter, since he killed the woman who would have done anything for you. Even betray her own family for your love."

Echo held the door open, standing in the hopeful customer's way. "Hope you remember the truth eventually. He was Amyntas when you knew him. I'm pretty sure you know him again by Aran or something."

"I see." Martin said. "That seems... unlikely but I'll take your theory under very careful consideration. And I hope you find better help than I'm able to provide."

Echo paused long enough to hit the signal button at the corner of the street and then flip him the bird a second later. Martin watched her departure with a mix of relief and disquiet. If anyone needed serious help, it was her. Echo had spun him a story without giving him any details as to how or why she believed what she did but that was every conspiracy theorist's line of thought. The Greek mythological angle was new though. Until he knew more about her, he couldn't trust her to behave rationally. Someone was going to have to be watched for a while in case her claims turned into violent action. He'd already lost a daughter; he wasn't going to lose a wife or his business as well. "Good luck, Echo. I hope you find who you're looking for."

SEVEN

Susannah

Breakfast was prepped and eaten on her own. Susannah crumpled her father's note and tossed it over her shoulder without looking as her phone beeped with an incoming text message from Tristan's number. She replied without reading the message, stuffing it into a fleece hoodie pocket. An hour or two wasn't that long of a wait and judging from the angle of the weak sunlight through the kitchen window, it was already past lunchtime. She'd slept late, undisturbed for once by her parents. The least she could do in exchange was the laundry while she waited for the car to show up again.

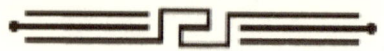

Tristan tossed her the keys and she caught them in her left hand, getting to her feet. "Favor for a favor? Your dad fixed the engine or whatever was wrong with it the other day. I should take you home instead of relying on a taxi. Seems fair, anyway."

"Home problems?" Tristan asked.

He was perceptive. Susannah grimaced, touching the unfamiliar pendent at the base of her throat. "If you count an unwanted family gift and no idea how to get around Seattle a home problem. Sure. You don't *have* to play tour guide though."

"You surf. I figured I'd show you a good place for it." Tristan turned away from her. "There's Alki beach and then another spot three hours outside of Seattle that I go to—for privacy. Thought you might be interested."

The thought was tempting. Susannah hesitated, torn between refusing and watching tv on her computer or getting out for some fresh air. Fresh air won out in the end. "Your brother isn't going to be there, is he?"

"Not this time." Tristan toed his shoe across the unbroken pavement of the driveway. "He either does his own thing or he's... getting treatment for his health. It's complicated."

"Cancer?" Susannah asked, going to the first thought that occurred to her.

Tristan lifted his gaze, glancing at her. "Something else. It's his business, not ours. He did try to apologize for the other day and insisted on packing a little picnic for us. I had to humor him and accept it so don't blame me for the peanut butter and honey sandwiches or the cheap chocolate bar he put in a cooler bag. He's not much of a cook."

Peanut butter and honey didn't sound like the worst late lunch she'd ever had. Susannah forced a smile at the prospect. "He's trying to get us together, isn't he?"

"Kind of, yeah." Tristan strode around to the front passenger side of the car. "You drive, I'll navigate. Don't know about you but I'd like this done before nightfall comes. Got some stuff of my own I'll need to deal with then."

"Fair." Susannah said. "Let's go."

She followed Tristan's directions, hitting the highway as soon as he told her to and peeling off onto to the first turn he spotted, three hours later. The gravel parking lot was nearly empty when she cut the engine, pulling the keys from the ignition. Tristan's little trail between two trees led down to a scrap of rocky beach. Susannah let her shoulders drop, the salty smell of the ocean easing the tension she felt. This wasn't the warmth of Jamaica's summers or the same look but Tristan's presence made it feel a little less lonely, a little more like a home. She sighed, accepting the half of whole wheat bread and peanut butter sandwich he offered her. "Thanks."

Maybe this would all be worth it in the end. "Should have brought a wetsuit or something. For swimming."

She couldn't imagine anyone braving the water in just a t-shirt and swim shorts. "Tristan?"

He looked up distracted from his phone as he tucked a strand of dark hair behind one ear. "Sorry, texting Aran. Trying to persuade him to join us. If—if that's alright with you."

Why wouldn't it be alright with her? It wasn't like this was a date, Aran's interference aside. "Is he coming?"

Susannah drew her legs up to her chest, watching the waves lap against the shore as Tristan finished his text message and set the phone aside. He was still a stranger to her, but she was willing to be patient in spite of her curiosity. "Tristan?"

His gaze strayed to the sky before he dragged it way from the horizon. "He's coming, yeah."

"Tell me about him?" Susannah smoothed a hand over the blue and tan tartan blanket beneath them, worrying at a hole in the woolly cloth. "It's only fair since I nearly blurted out my whole life story the other day. Is he always an as—like he is or did he learn it?"

That earned her a short lived, dry smile. Tristan found a rock at random and tossed it into the water, skipping it once, twice and a third time before it sank out of sight. "My parents would know more. They knew him longer than I have. With twelve years between us, there wasn't much interaction for very long. Like I said, he was graduating by the time I was starting school."

"No other siblings?" Susannah asked tentatively.

"No, at least none I know of." Tristan's mouth thinned with unhappiness. "Mom and Dad are married but that doesn't mean they haven't consented to separate lives outside of the marriage. It's just me."

"That must have been lonely." Susannah said.

"I managed." Tristan found a sharper edged rock and pocketed it with a sigh. "We should start thinking about heading back to the city now if we want to make it home before nightfall. And it gets cold here—I don't think you want to experience that."

She didn't but that didn't mean she wanted to leave quite yet either. Susannah watched as the sun dipped a little lower in the horizon. It was still bright day out, more or less but the color of the light hinted at the hour. "I don't suppose there's a bathroom around here?"

She wasn't a city girl by a long stretch but using a tree was closer to the bottom of her list. It just wasn't done in Jamaica. Too dangerous or too humiliating depending on the locale. Tristan shook his head, looking apologetic. "Sorry. I like this little spot because there's no outhouse or amenities. It's... peaceful."

Maybe it was, but not when she was half worried about poison ivy or venomous wildlife. Susannah let out a resigned sigh, looking back up the trail. "Not even toilet paper and a stick?"

"I'll remember that for next time." Tristan shifted position, getting onto his knees as he packed up the last of their improvised picnic. "Or I'll remind Aran to. He doesn't always think about these things."

"So I noticed." Susannah said. She walked off, praying that nothing would bite her while she had her jeans down around her runners when she went into the brush. No one told her off for using a tree as a bathroom as she re-emerged from the 'shelter' the woods had given her, much to her relief.

Voices, well, a voice sounded, distracting her from her admiration and she switched on the small penlight hanging from her keychain. "Tristan?"

He, she recognized, but not the older guy in a white, nearly knee length t-shirt. Susannah kicked her shoes off and stuffed the socks into them before picking her way across the stony ground. "Tristan? Why are you...?"

That was his name twice but what else was she supposed to say? Tristan's 'friend' had his hands on Tristan's bare shoulders. Susannah shivered dipping a hand into the water and flinging it away from her. The Pacific was freezing. How Tristan was bearing the temperature without flinching was beyond her. "Hey—"

Tristan pulled free of the stranger's grasp, a look of shock on his face at the sight of her before the other guy forced him to his knees. And beneath the water. Susannah swore, hopping awkwardly to avoid the worst of the rocks and slimy weeds coating them before she dove into the water.

It was deeper than she expected, five or six feet in depth but nothing she hadn't encountered before. She'd been diving to fifteen feet comfortably since her ninth birthday. This was nothing to her, all things considered. Susannah bit down hard on her lower lip, trying to ignore the cold as she pulled at the newcomer's wrist.

His grip only tightened on Tristan's shoulder as she gave him an ineffective whack against the stranger's arm, trying to separate the two by clawing at the newcomer's wrist. Susannah surfaced, hair plastered against her scalp and dove again, inhaling water as something seized her plait from behind. She kicked out at whatever it was and found nothing until she came eye to eye with a pale haired and fair skinned... girl. Superficially it looked like a girl, but her heart and organs were visible through the skin and her fingers were webbed from base to tip.

Susannah choked, backpedaling wildly away from whatever it was as her eyes burned from salt exposure. There was no sign of Tristan now, or the guy responsible for the attempted drowning.

Her own survival mattered more, as the creature hissed, and lunged at her. Susannah stood, trying to retreat towards the safety of the beach as the water current pulled at her body, pulling her off her feet and under the water again. She shrieked and only produced bubbles as the naked girl thing seized her ankle in a hard grip. It looked translucent and light, but its weight crushed the last of the air from her lungs. Susannah thrashed as dark spots swam in front of her vision.

Darkness overwhelmed her until a low urgent voice penetrated the shadows. Susannah gasped, back arching as she spat up salt water over the orange blanket around her shoulders. Someone pressed a mug of coffee into her hands before her vision cleared enough to make them out. "You—Arden, right?"

She couldn't make out his answer, but the resigned look he gave her told her enough to correct the name she'd used. "Aran. Sorry."

Aran made a face, glancing towards the ocean and held a pad of paper out for her to read. "What were you thinking, trying to go for a swim in an ocean you don't know anything about?"

In retrospect, it was a valid question. If she'd thought instead of reacting, things could have been different. "I wasn't, but someone was doing a damned good job of trying to drown your brother. And then... there was the sea monster thingy."

Susannah shuddered at the too clear memory. Panic and thrashing around trying to escape should have blurred what she'd seen, not sharpened it. "She was almost see-through. Heart and that shit. She—she didn't even have lungs."

Aran's mouth tightened in unhappiness, but not surprise. Susannah swallowed, rubbing at her aching throat. "What the hell was that thing?"

He sighed, raking a still damp strand of dark hair behind one ear before he wrote an answer on his notebook. "Scientifically, nothing anyone would recognize. Folkloric, she—it was a siren."

"Some fucking mermaid." Susannah muttered. "She had legs, I think I saw that much."

Aran gave her a rueful look, sitting on a spare blanket with his legs underneath his body. "The species aren't deep sea divers; they prefer coastal areas away from people. You must have invaded her territory by accident."

"You know a lot about it but thanks for the convenient rescue." Susannah winced, rubbing her ankle before pulling the too long jeans up her leg. "Ow..."

Her leg was bleeding sluggishly, shallowly lacerated from the creature's sharp nails. Aran rummaged through a backpack, wrapping the cloth bandage around her foot and leg. Susannah let out a sigh of relief. "You didn't say how you knew about these... uhm, sirens."

Aran paused, hesitating in his written words. "They're like any animal. Leave them alone and they'll leave you alone. I do know that they'll lure sailors to their deaths, the lucky ones drown. The unlucky ones have five minutes of fun before they're eaten."

Susannah gagged, retching onto the beach at the thought. "Fun?"

"Sex." Aran scrawled a set of lines underneath the word for emphasis. "Apparently they're close enough to human that they can carry half human babies. They're also a single gender species."

"Lovely." Susannah wiped her mouth, bundling the blanket closer around her shoulders. "Just wanted what I needed to know at—at..."

The sun glittered off the water, blinding her before she looked away. "It's dawn? It was closer to night when I tried to rescue Tristan."

Tried and failed to act as lifeguard. She quieted, tasting salt in her mouth. Whether it was from her own tears, or just salt water didn't matter. "We need to go to the police station and report his... his body as missing. And find his murderer."

If murderer could apply to the siren thing Aran had described. Susannah bit down on her lower lip, tasting blood and salt in her mouth. "Can they reproduce with humans? What do the babies look like?"

Aran gave her a long look, writing in his notebook again. "They can, yes. But pity the sailor who does. The babies look like she did and won't survive long on land."

He followed up with a question of his own, somehow putting a sarcastic edge in the written words. "This is about revenge?"

Susannah took a sip of the coffee in the thermos, wincing at the thick, tarry flavor of it. If Aran had made this, his coffee skills were shit. "There has to be a report filed. We can't sit here waiting until his body washes up on shore."

Aran's mouth thinned before he looked down at his notebook. "He's not dead. I won't tell you how or why I know this but he's safe. Tristan will show up again when he wants to."

"But... I saw him drown." Susannah said. "Someone was holding him under."

"You thought you saw him." Aran's written words were gentle. "The police aren't going to believe your report when it turns out you were the one who dove into the water fully clothed and unprepared for the current. Susannah, you were the one who almost drowned last night. If I hadn't been in the area long enough to drag you out of the water, you would have."

Susannah opened her mouth and shut it again, smoothing unfamiliar denim under her hands. "Damn it."

Damn Aran if he wasn't right. The too big jeans and t-shirt weren't hers and hadn't had been what she'd worn last night. "Fine, alright. But I'm not going to let some siren or mermaid or whatever stop me from going out on the water again. I was swimming before I could walk. I'm not going to give that up."

She cast a bland look towards Aran's hands, noting the syndactyly Tristan had mentioned. "I thought that was supposed to be rare. One in a certain number of people or something."

A shadow crossed Aran's expression before he stood, drying his hair with a fluffy white towel. He didn't sign his words this time or write them down but the gesture to the car was clear enough. As were the keys he idly tossed into the air and caught again.

EIGHT

Aran

He didn't need a driver's license to be familiar with the task. It was almost impossible to get around Seattle without a car and the focus required was an effective distraction for his thoughts. Susannah's necklace had been a blue glass dolphin a few days before—now it was the unpleasantly familiar amethyst teardrop in its place. With luck, she would remain ignorant of its history, or its origin but that didn't make it any less bitter of a memory. His adoptive father had crafted the thing as a leash for him, intent on nothing more than control.

Aran felt the wheels shift beneath him before he wrenched hard on the steering wheel, dragging it back into the proper lane with a frightened squeak from Susannah. Distraction would only get them killed here. He'd survive it. The human girl wouldn't. He winced, cursing the metal box and the beginnings of another migraine behind his eyes. The pain always started this way for him, and drugs intended to work for mortals wouldn't do a thing for him.

"Aran?" Susannah's voice wobbled as she spoke up. "There's a turn off and a dive diner nearby from the looks of it. Pull off before you get us both killed. Tristan says you're a good driver but right now it looks like you're about to puke."

There was no argument there. Aran slowed the car down and fumbled the turn, taking it haphazardly before parking across too stalls in the lot. He went to his knees in the grassy median, retching up bile until her arm slipped over his shoulders in an attempt at comfort. He brushed her off, shaking his head. She meant well but the only touch he'd tolerate was his little brother's.

The poorly planned swim had erased the scent of vanilla clinging to her skin but the scent of cooking oil, grease and artificial cheese product on a grill was nauseating. Aran gritted his teeth, steadying himself on the door for a moment before finding an open booth in the far corner of the diner. Susannah followed behind him and sat first, glancing over the menu tucked behind the hot sauce and ketchup. "Just toast and better coffee, I hope than what you made me drink earlier."

Aran forced a short-lived smile, pulling out the notebook again. "Probably. I'm not much of a cook. Most of my food comes from the Cat."

None at all, truth be told but there was no way he could reveal his inability to keep food down to an unknowing, mortal girl. As for the siren Susannah had seen, that was more real than she realized. The creature had been attempting to protect him from the young woman, repaying him for the ride he had given her several days earlier. She hadn't realized that she was killing the girl until he'd interfered, separating them. Susannah had been nearly unconscious by that point, until he'd dragged her onto shore.

Susannah took a swallow of the coffee the waitress set down in front of her, wrinkling her nose at the flavor. "Day old and burned on top of it. God, this is a shithole."

"I wouldn't know." Aran passed her his note, glancing wryly around the diner. "You chose this place, not me."

"Point." Susannah swirled the grayish liquid around her mug, watching white flecks surface and sink again. Milk that was just as poor as the coffee itself. "Can I ask about the siren, mermaid thing again? I saw it—her but I'm not sure she's real, exactly. I mean, I could have swallowed salt water. Is there any chance she was a figment of my imagination, or something?"

"What do you think?" Aran tore the used sheet of paper from his notebook and crumpled it into a ball.

Susannah was quiet for a moment, looking unenthusiastically at the charred toast that the waitress set before her. "That I regret coming here if the food is greasy and burned. The mermaid thing was... real but I don't know how her species escaped biologists' attention. Or tourists with their bloody cameras. They aren't supposed to be real."

She played with the tail end of her plait, brushing it against her palm. "And how do you know so much about them, anyway? I hear you, but I want to know."

Aran sighed, writing beneath his earlier message. "People know more about the moon and space than they do about the ocean. I had a friend once, when I was living in Greece, taken by a siren. She lured him from the boat, and it wasn't until a month later when people found what was left of his body. We never did find her. And that part of the mythology seems accurate—at least about their song."

Susannah tugged the coil bound notebook from him, lingering over the battered and salt damaged cover before she looked up at him. "I'm still not saying this is possible, I barely believe in them but is there any way to protect myself from her?"

Aran pulled a wad of paper napkins from the dispenser and held a hand out for the stolen pen. "Have a better voice? I'm teasing a bit, but women don't seem to be as affected by the song."

He hesitated, weighing Susannah's skepticism against the other things that called the shallow water home. Her disbelief was a safe thing for him but letting her go unprepared any longer was just as dangerous. "Sirens are dangerous only when you're on the water and you invade their territory. I'd watch out more for the gods damned kelpie. Similar behavior but worse, it's a shapeshifter."

Dangerously close to home, especially for him but she needed to know, even if she kept the cynical edge in mind. "It won't just take unlucky fishermen; it'll take anyone, and it can look like anything it wants to."

Susannah gulped, grip unconsciously tightening on the knife in her hand before she relaxed. "Thanks for the warning. Sirens can be defended against, sort of. The other things can't be?"

"I've never found an easy way of dealing with it, except through a leash." Aran touched the base of his throat, wishing for the words that would never come again. Paper and pencil or sign language left something to be desired, nuance wise.

Susannah shuddered, wrapping her hands around the coffee mug. Its taste might be something to be desired but at least it smelled warm. Aran looked away in distaste, finishing their current conversation with a final note. "Is there anything else?"

"From the creepy, almost supernatural shit? No." Susannah said. "Breakfast? Anything you want?"

Aran grimaced, denying the question. If the diner considered this 'quality' food, it was wiser not to chance it himself. The lack of an appetite was the least of his worries as the diner spun before him.

"You should." Susannah's voice and expression were concerned. "Don't know what you had for supper last night but I kind of know the look of a migraine when I see one. My parents are doctors. Food will help, a little."

Maybe it would, maybe it wouldn't. It wasn't a matter of hunger, just that he couldn't keep much beyond honey and his adoptive mother's tea down without throwing up again. Aran sighed, taking a burned slice from Susannah's plate, and buttering it before he took a cautious bite of the toast.

His stomach rebelled the moment he swallowed the mouthful. Aran lurched to his feet, darting for the men's washroom just in time to retch into the toilet. Little came up, except for the partially chewed mouthful of blackened bread and bile.

The door handle to the men's washroom rattled before Susannah sounded on the other side.

Better than he was now that he'd rid himself of the toast. Aran sat back on the balls of his feet, wiping sweat from his forehead. Trying to eat had been a mistake but at least it distracted Susannah from the discussion about sirens and kelpies.

He twisted the sink tap on, splashing water into his face before turning away from the mirror. Even tepid water was better than nothing.

"Fine." He signed the word without thinking, barely noting the blank look that slipped over the girl's face. His attention was elsewhere, briefly on his stomach and then deeper, further back on the small hum in the back of his thoughts. It wasn't a call as such, but its meaning would have to be investigated. "Payphone in the back. Your parents should be able to find the diner."

That was no answer at all, judging from Susannah's irked expression at the note he passed her. Answering the call mattered more than her annoyance. She would never understand how different he was from her, or what compelled him to obedience. Tristan had an inkling of what drove him but like the human girl, couldn't understand either.

80

Witches were dangerous but he needed to speak with one of them, and the only one he knew in Seattle ran a used bookstore in a small corner of the downtown. Aran sneezed, catching a scent of dust, flowery perfume used to scent the air and cat. Alone, none of the three were appealing. All three together were nearly overpowering to his sense of smell.

Whether the man would be willing to speak with him remained to be seen but the attempt would be worth something for his brother's sake.

The woman behind the counter glared at him, folding her arms over her chest. "You can turn around and get out of my husband's bookshop. Hide all you want but that will never change what you did, Gallagher."

Aran snarled softly, warning her off and she shrank back, deflating as she averted her gaze from his. All defiance wiped away by the little growl. It would be less effective with Eva's husband, but the reminder was enough for the time being. There were levels to things and even the youngest shapeshifter kit had more power than a human did. He slapped the notebook on the counter, open to his answer. "Maybe it doesn't but I made a promise to protect my brother when he needed help. Irene interfered when she shouldn't have."

"You think that was help?" Eva's husband's voice was cool, tight with anger as he stepped out of the back stockroom. The man signed his words with a contemptuous snort. "What you did?"

Aran drew back, leaning against the cashier counter. Martin Carpenter wasn't much of a threat to him, not dressed in brown shirt and slacks with a pair of glasses perched on his nose. The best that could have been said of the owner was that he was brown all over.

"Someone's going to hear this and think you're accusing a Japanese guy of something. And then what? I've heard that one bad review from a customer is enough to tank a business sometimes."

A customer walked inside the small bookshop, got a glimpse of them and hastily retreated to the furthest bookshelves she could find. It was wise of her, he was in no mood for company, even if half of the conversation—Martin's answers could be overheard. The bookseller scowled, eyes narrowing in outrage. "What's one review to me? And you can't speak to save your life."

Aran shrugged, ignoring the attempted insult. The witch wasn't so reckless to throw fire or whatever else he was capable of doing, in a bookshop. There was too much paper around to risk it. There was a time for pen and paper, there was a time for sign language and Martin was familiar enough with it. *For once, I need your help, not your accusation, Martin. I'll never consent to having my power bound or stripped from me, but I need to fake being human a little better than I'm capable of.*

Martin scowled, hands dropping back to his sides. "And what makes you think I'm able to help you? Or that I want to? The curse on your brother was meant for you, but you threw it off as if it was nothing."

That answered one question and only left another in its place but that was a line of inquiry for another day. Aran leaned against the nearby bookshelf. *Because my brother has a human girlfriend now.*

It was only half a lie, Susannah was starting to trust Tristan but whether they'd start labeling themselves a couple was on them, not up to his manipulation. *I thought of everything that happened lately, you'd want to see her protected from me, witch. I'm the kelpie I warned her about in a truck stop diner.*

Martin bristled, still clinging to his look of loathing. "What makes you—"

Aran turned away, ignoring the bookseller's glare as he flipped through a secondhand hardcover pulled from the shelf behind him. *Because I want to see my little brother happier than he has been in a long time. And you're the only witch I know who has a bit of genuine power, not the psychic gift belonging to LaLaurie or Marigny.*

The binding weakened in his hands as the pages turned sodden and gray, going brown as the paper the words were printed on decayed, rotting as though it had been sitting abandoned in the rain for a week.

Martin blanched, the color draining from his face as the remnants of the book fell onto the hardwood floor. He didn't wet himself, much to his credit, but there was a definite fear scent in the air where he'd been sure before. Or he just cared about his books, it was hard to say. Aran stepped on the ruined pages, tearing them underfoot. *There's my brother and his family, no trouble for a witch to deal with, I'm sure but then you've got those above them.*

Aran held his hand out, roughly at doorknob level. *Tristan's abilities once he gets a century or two behind him.*

He lifted it several inches higher, giving Martin a dry look. *Mortal but still beyond what my family is capable of doing. Fenris, Helen Takala and Sigyn. Loki.*

Martin's color had gone from white to more grayish now, with the sharper scent of piss in the air. Aran wrinkled his nose in disgust, half tempted to finish his measurement but only if the witch didn't wet himself in the process. *Even if power was taken out of the equation, my kind are still apex predators to yours. You live here because Coyote permits it, not because you have the strength to take his territory away from him.*

A heavy thud told him all he needed to know as he strode over to the door and put his hand on it. Eva had fainted clean away on him. A few minutes and they'd recover. He'd done what he'd come to do and there was little point on dwelling on them beyond that if Martin was unwilling or incapable of doing what he'd asked of the man. There were others, Clotho and her sisters, Coyote or somewhat further down the list, Hades himself.

The hard words spoken to his back were in Greek. Aran turned at the sound and went to his knees on the floor, hand pressed against his chest. It did nothing for the vise around his chest as he stared up at Martin's scowling face. It was the last he knew before darkness settled over his vision.

He woke beneath water, flat out on his back amid broken tile and shattered columns. Aran groaned, rolling onto his side and sat up, burying his face in his hands. The witch had suffocated him until death. Not a difficult thing to do, even to a human but Martin's attack had come too quickly, too unexpected for him to counter it. Only one man could have done that and he had been imprisoned for centuries.

A ball rolled out of nowhere, stopping at his feet. Aran glanced at the black and white sphere before the sixteen-year-old young woman stepped out from behind one of the pillars. Aran grimaced and tossed the ball back to her. The blonde hair and dark eyes marked her as the youngest of the three fates. "Clotho."

He coughed, pressing a hand to his throat in disbelief. "How...?"

Echo had taken his voice, he shouldn't have been able to form a verbal question.

She dropped to her knees beside him, cradling her ball in her lap. "Only because you called to me before you left the bookstore. Using my name was enough to get my attention. Do you remember this place?"

Aran swallowed, sweeping his gaze around the ruined hall. The stables had been a quarter mile from here, the meadow just beyond it. This had been his home and his prison once. "Poseidon's domain. Why here?"

"Why now?" Clotho countered his question with her own. "Martin did more than kill your body, he banished you from Seattle. That's not something a mortal witch can do to someone with your power. Not unwillingly."

Aran sighed, raking a hand through shoulder length hair that hadn't been blond for over a year. The fair coloring was distracting. He grimaced, letting the slight warmth of the change flow over his body. As much as he hated to admit it, he'd gotten used to the half Japanese, half Welsh shape over the Greco-Irish look he'd worn so briefly. "How long has it been?"

85

A shadow crossed Clotho's face as she stood, resting the ball against her hip. Her other hand reached for his, helping him to his feet. "Two weeks. I was able to find you, Lachesis healed your wounds, but it took that long before you were able to wake."

Two weeks so close to death that he may as well have been mortal. Aran closed his eyes, pained. "Oh, hell. I need to go back. My brother..."

"Tristan isn't your—" Clotho caught herself and corrected her words. "He isn't your brother by blood. You don't owe him or his parents' loyalty."

Aran paused, lifting his gaze to look at her. "If I hadn't sworn on the Styx, I would agree with you, but I did, seventeen years ago."

Clotho bristled and subsided, still scowling like the teenager she appeared to be. "You're a fool then but if you think you can live through this, so be it."

Her free hand closed on his forearm, squeezing for a moment. "Hades won't answer any prayer of yours, you have no need of what he can offer but if you need advice, seek out James. I believe he still owes you a debt."

The English soldier was a dead man. Aran turned away, tracing the cracked line that marred the nearest mosaic decorating the wall. "He doesn't owe me anything. And his word was worthless."

"Because he was mortal?" Clotho kept pace with him, unperturbed by the harsh tone.

"Because his word can't be enforced by an oath." Aran said. "Not on the Styx or any other river."

Clotho stopped him short, folding her arms across her chest. "One would think that was an advantage, not a flaw of being a shade. And I think I should disagree.

He can be bound, just not by his word. He *can* help but only if you call upon him."

She looked up at him, seriousness in her eyes. "All it takes is spilling your own blood to summon him. You need no other rite."

"I'll think about it." Aran said. It was all he was willing to promise to the youngest of the three women.

He went to his knees, letting the light shimmer around once more around his body until the black horse stood where he had stood on two feet moments before. Clotho snickered and scrambled onto his back, tangling her hands through the mane. She nudged his sides, encouraging him into a trot and then a canter before Aran moved into a full out run. The girl wouldn't stay long on his back—she had her own business to attend to, but he could give her a ride to remember. No mortal would see or remember her unless she chose it in the land above.

NINE
Tristan

Midafternoon again and one of the few days his boss was willing to let him trade his shift with someone else. Tristan flipped through the paperback in his hands before dog earring the corner. Try as he might, he couldn't enjoy the story held in its pages, not when Aran had left him once again for parts unknown. It might be a month or two, it might be years before his brother decided to show up again. "Damn him."

Susannah's scent filled his nose, and he gritted his teeth, turning to see her standing behind him with a surfboard cradled in one arm. Her hair was plaited out of the way, and she was clad in a wetsuit unlike the time before when she'd dove after him in a mistaken attempt at rescuing him from his brother. She had filled him in about the late afternoon in question, giving as much as she could tell him from her limited perspective. She'd seen a victim 'drowned' and lost to the Pacific. The truth was more complicated than that.

"I didn't think anyone knew how to find this place, on their own at least." Tristan said.

His territory wasn't as big as Coyote's or Aran's strip of the Pacific Ocean bordering Washington, but this was his space. No one should have come here except for him or Aran. He only put up with his brother because he didn't have the strength to challenge the older shapeshifter in a fight.

Susannah let the board lie faceup on the ground, sliding her hand around his before releasing it. "Then you shouldn't have shown it to me, Aran's little game aside. He wants us together, however else we feel about it. The first time was on him, this time—I actually brought a map. And no one told me you would be here tonight. Well, this afternoon. I told him that I wasn't going to let some siren critter keep me out of the water, you better believe it."

Tristan opened his mouth and closed it, skeptical. "You sure that's what you saw? I mean, no offense to my brother but he's a liar."

Susannah snorted, flipping the tail end of her French plait over her shoulder. "He seemed sure enough to warn me about it. And I don't think anyone would forget seeing a girl so pale that her organs were visible."

She shuddered, biting down on her lower lip. "She didn't have a heart. Don't ask me to explain that one,

I can't. So, if I'm here to catch a wave or two, what are you doing here? Brooding?"

Tristan placed the book into a plastic bag, dropping the sealed contents into his knapsack. "Is that really what it looks like?'

"Just a bit." Susannah inspected the sleeve of her wetsuit and glanced towards the water wistfully. "Really, what's the deal with you and Aran? The age thing makes things complicated, but it isn't hard to see the tension between you two. There's lonely and pissed off, and then there's... this."

She was perceptive and he wasn't sure how he felt about that. Tristan closed his hand around a promising looking rock and tossed it into the air, catching it once and then twice before drawing back and throwing it into the shallow water's edge. "You were the last person to see him before he took off. I'm not jealous that you were but it's the lack of notice he gave when he did it."

The second rock was in his hand and sailing through the air to land short of its target in the water. Tristan sighed, running his hand through his hair. "I should be used to this, but it still hurts. It was here, help —dealing with some crap of mine and then boom, he's gone again. Didn't even say goodbye."

"That doesn't make it right." Susannah followed his gaze, teasing the end of her braid between her fingers. "At the very least, he should have said something."

Maybe Aran could have said something, but it was a place he'd never be able to follow his brother to. Wherever Aran was, it wasn't a place for him. "Mom said he needed to treat himself for his photodermatitis and the best way to do that... wasn't here in Seattle. But it doesn't feel like I can trust her any more than him these days."

A flicker out of the corner of his eye had him sitting up straighter, frowning as he tried to get a better look at it.

"Tristan?" Susannah was frowning, uncertain. "What is it?"

With luck, just a flash of light off of metal. If not, that was better not dwelt on. He stood, ignoring her as the black horse picked its way through the shallow water, coat still dripping with moisture. Its eyes were pale, not brown. "Shit."

This wasn't an ordinary horse, and he was cursing Susannah's stupidity as much as his brother's. Neither were idiots by any definition of the word, but the timing was about as poor as it could get. And she wasn't supposed to be here. "Why now?"

"Why now what?" Susannah was giving him a bewildered look. "Tristan?"

"It's complicated." He snagged her wrist in one hand, trying to pull her up the narrow dirt trail. "But that horse isn't exactly... safe. C'mon."

She pulled free, crossing her arms over her chest. "Not a chance. I don't know what kind of game you're trying to protect me from but you're as bad as Aran if you're trying to gaslight me into believing that thing is just a horse. He kind of warned me about the kelpie the same day he told me about the siren. I've done my own research since then. Irish fucking waterhorse that likes to drown people and eat them. Sometimes lures them into getting onto its back for kicks."

Tristan bit back on the soft snarl that threatened and balled his fist instead. "Wonder if he's told you too much here. And for why."

He took a breath, trying to shove his temper back into the little box it belonged to. "Look, horse or kelpie or whatever—that thing is my brother's and it only answers to him. I only ever rode it once and that was when I was five. With a friend of his holding onto me. She was the only one who could get on its back without being thrown."

Susannah gave him an arch look, looking from him to the horse and back again. "It's a long bit of justification but it almost sounds like you're trying to protect it, more than me. Aran called kelpies shapeshifters. What's really going on?"

She glared at him, taking a step away. "We've known each other for about six weeks now. Maybe in books that isn't enough time for a boyfriend, girlfriend thing to start but I'd hoped for friends, at least. Or trust."

Tristan opened his mouth and closed it again, forcing himself to relax and take a steadying breath. There was nothing in Susannah's questions that meant he had to tell about his own shapeshifting problems—but Aran had started this when he'd mentioned the kelpie thing to begin with. And maybe a little warning would help. "I—fine. I'll say as much I can but don't count on much. Aran talks but he never actually says anything. Not even to me. He's... he's not exactly human."

He sat down on the driftwood tree, watching the horse like creature warily. "I don't know how my parents did it but apart from the fifteen years he wasn't around, he's been their adoptive son. And that... kelpie in the water. He's the shapeshifter he warned you against."

Susannah's eyes narrowed but she stepped carefully over the rocks, taking a seat next to him on the bleached log. "Kind of explains what I saw in the diner after trying to rescue you. Not much of an appetite. Did he, uhm, hunt before?"

"He doesn't eat at all." Tristan looked down, folding his hands in his lap. "So no, I don't think folklore got that part right. But he does drown his victims, occasionally. It isn't a habit, I hope."

"You hope." Susannah gave him an askance look. "Tristan..."

He sighed, watching as the horse finally turned away and slipped beneath the water. "There was a girl last year but that was just to protect me, I swear. Doesn't make it right and I tried to do the same thing you did for me—save her but she still died because of him. She had a gun, I wasn't exactly in a place I could defend myself and he dragged her under before I could stop him."

Distaste flickered across Susannah's face as she drew her legs up to her chest, folding her arms around them. "At least you're honest about something now. It doesn't mean I like it but at least it's the truth."

Some, if not all of it. Tristan rummaged through his backpack and came back with a small, slightly overripe apple. "I only know a bit about him. The kelpie thing and what he says is true about his past but shit, if I can trust it now. Shapeshifter equals liar and he's done enough by not sticking around to make me wonder about that sometimes."

"Tell me." Susannah snagged the apple from him and took a bite of it before cradling the fruit in her hands.

Tristan kicked at the ground, sending sand and smaller pebbles skittering away from them. "Over six thousand years old, for a start. Apparently had a wife and kids of his own, long before Mom and Dad were even born. I bought it when he told me, but I was only five then. Don't know if he was telling the truth or just trying to entertain me with something. He used to have the Belfast accent in his words, so I know a bit of that's true—he's Irish, or he was but before that."

He shrugged helplessly, taking back Susannah's apple, and polishing it off to core and stem. "He's nearly immortal, or at least he claims that. There's also some crap about the Greek river or something but I don't know how much that's true. The only thing I really feel like I know for sure is that some point between leaving when I was little and coming back last summer, he got his throat cut or permanently wrecked his larynx. Won't say how and it didn't occur to me to ask until now."

Susannah cast the ocean a look of regret and bent down, retrieving her board as she changed the subject. "I guess the time out on the water can wait. Why don't we head back to your place? Mine sucks, at the moment and I want to get out of house arrest tonight. My parents are watching me like hawks, thinking I'll run off and try drowning myself again. I could do without a little adult supervision for a few hours."

So could he, in truth. Tristan stretched, climbing to his feet with a last check of the sky for the time. His phone would have been more accurate, but the red and silver cellphone had been thrown at the nearest brick wall a week ago, shattering the screen and making it a paperweight instead. "Jamaican? And then there's something I want to show you at home."

Susannah blinked, looking at him in surprise. "Are you actually asking me out on a date? Of your own free will, not because Aran tried to get us together?"

Tristan blushed, looking down at his runners. "I guess, yeah. You don't mind?"

It was past the time when he waited for Aran to tell him what to do anyway. He wasn't the five year old kit anymore, even if he'd never reach the age his brother claimed to be. Who could tell if that was even the truth or just another story that he'd been fed to distract him.

TEN

Susannah

Tristan's idea of Jamaican sucked. Susannah looked down at her curry and shoved it away from her, only half touched. He could have credit for the attempt but that was about all she was going to give him. The American version of a familiar dish was a disappointment and she put a couple bills onto the table next to her plate. Food waste was something she objected to but this was a dish only stray dogs would find appetizing. Or her only friend.

There didn't seem like there was anything wrong with his metabolism, in stark contrast to his older brother's.

Susannah shifted in her seat, grateful when the bill came. Paying for the meal meant freedom and a chance to officially meet Tristan's family. The first time, over two and a half weeks before didn't count as meeting the parents.

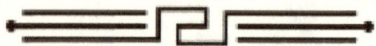

Her stomach knotted as she looked up at the front of the house. "Will your parents like me?"

"They will." Tristan sounded more confident than she felt, cutting the Honda's engine off.

Susannah swallowed, hearing the lie but grateful for it anyway. If Steffon and Mariko were barely enamored with their adopted son, there was no telling how they'd see her. Hopefully it was a good impression, she'd changed from the wetsuit to a light gray t-shirt and jeans before their early dinner at the Jamaican restaurant. "Thanks."

What she was wearing would barely have passed muster if she was in Tristan's place and meeting her parents for the first time. They expected a certain degree of class, which wasn't to say Tristan's family lacked it, but he wasn't the kind of guy they would have wanted her dating. Too bad for them, this was her choice, not theirs. "Wish me luck..."

It was almost a prayer to whatever was out there watching, whether it was god or something else.

Tristan's hand closed over hers and she gulped, noting the thin set of his mouth as she glanced at him. From the looks of things, he was just as nervous as she was about this. "Wish us luck then."

One way or another, she was about to leave an impression on Tristan's parents. Hopefully it would be a good one by the end of the evening. One look at Tristan had her quailing, nearly dropping his hand before the moment of truth. The doorbell rang, echoing somewhere in the house before Mariko answered the front door.

Susannah hesitated, drawing a blank at what Tristan's mother thought was good manners. "Uhm."

Mariko's laugh was gentle as she offered her hand to Susannah. "We are neither diplomats or in Tokyo, Susannah. I think we can dispense with formality for now. My son's mentioned a little of you in the past few weeks. You're the Jamaican surfer, yes?"

"Yeah." Susannah fumbled for her answer and settled for keeping her gaze fixed on the thin, ancient carpet underneath her socked feet. "I've heard more about you from Aran than Tristan, honestly."

Mariko's brief short lived smile slipped for a second before she brushed a hand through silver touched dark hair. "Kaito has always been... unpredictable."

Susannah exchanged a look with Tristan and only got an unreadable answer to her question. "Erm, Kaito?"

"Aran." Mariko lifted one shoulder slightly and turned away, gesturing to the living room. "He rarely uses it lately, but the name is his."

"Oh." Susannah deflated, hearing the cool note in Tristan's mother's voice. The earlier warmth had vanished and she didn't know how to fix that. "Good to know."

She sat down on the couch, trying to relax and failing to, even when Mariko brought a small tray with a teapot and cups into the living room. Less than fifteen minutes as a guest and she was already feeling like she had misstepped somehow. "Did—have I said something wrong?"

Mariko took a careful sip of her tea and set it down on a coaster. "Tristan has never brought anyone home before. It is nothing on you but my husband, more than I was, was expecting the girl to be Japanese."

Susannah felt her shoulders drop, hurt by the remark. Steffon wasn't in the living room but that didn't make the opinion sting any less. "Steffon's Welsh. Why should he care?"

Mariko's mouth thinned, echoing what Susannah had seen in Tristan's before. "Because he is Welsh. He's stubborn, child. You shouldn't take it personally."

Susannah dashed a hand across her eyes and got to her feet, leaving her teacup abandoned behind her as she made a beeline for the front door. She left it slightly ajar, sitting on the porch step. "Fuck... and I thought my family was bad. At least they didn't object when I brought old boyfriends' home and they turned out to be black. There wasn't a lot of other choice in who I dated in Kingston. The minute you bring your white girlfriend home, it turns out to be the Welsh dad who complains. And he isn't even Asian."

"Sorry." Tristan was a step or two behind her, shame in his eyes. "I thought he would be in a good mood tonight but all that stuff about Aran..."

"Is he ever in a good mood?" Susannah dashed wetness away from her eyes. "Or is he the bigot acting in defense of a minority?"

"Honestly, no." Tristan said tiredly. "Wish I could say otherwise but he's always been grumpy. Aran doesn't help things much either, I don't think."

That was an understatement if she'd ever heard one. Susannah quieted, blowing her nose into a crumpled Kleenex she found in her jacket pocket. "Because you're human, trying to raise a kelpie, is that it?"

"Yeah." Tristan looked away; unhappiness clear in his expression. "Something like that. Can I make this up by showing you a little place up in Rainier Park? It's away from Seattle and I think you might like it. I mean, it's not surfing but it's still out in nature and you might like the hike there. I'll see if I can convince Aran to come as well. He'll be on his best behavior if we can find him. Right now, I've got something I need to do."

"Your weird nightfall thing." Susannah said. "Some point, you're going to have to explain that to me, whatever it is. I haven't asked until now because I've wanted to be polite but it's getting inconvenient for both of us."

"I know." Tristan said. "I will, I just need time to figure it out, that's all there is to it."

"I hope so." Susannah glanced down at her tissue and tossed it into the plant pot that contained some unidentifiable and dying twig denuded of its leaves. "When?"

"Soon. As soon as I figure out the details, I'll text and pick you up." Tristan flipped his phone open and closed it again, looking at the black screen before he pocketed it. "Well, after I get a new phone anyway."

"You better." Susannah bent down, retying the shoelace that had come loose. "I'll hold you to that."

Tristan's answering laugh was weak as he looked towards the sky once more. The shadows were longer than they were even if it wasn't quite dark yet. "Sure. I thought we were working on trusting each other here."

ELEVEN
Aran

The only food in Aran's refrigerator was a bit of cheese and moldy bread. Tristan sighed, closing the door on it and leaned against the counter. "I won't ask about whatever you're planning with me and Susannah, but I know when you're trying to change the subject. You aren't telling me something here. And you weren't exactly open with me before, about your age or your past. We're both shapeshifters but I don't know how much I can trust your word these days."

You suggested bringing her to the family cabin, not me. Aran signed a distracted answer, expression distant and elsewhere. *I only gave you a nudge out of that door. The implication being what… exactly?*

"Shouldn't you know?" Tristan said. "She's human, we aren't. I'm cursed. I need you there for moral support."

I see. Aran's mouth thinned in distaste. *How is that going to work, given my particular needs? I've never been more than two days inland and I have to be sure to follow the river.*

"We'll figure it out." Tristan skimmed an unused takeout menu at random, trying to decide what he was more in mind for and if it was within his limited budget. "We have to. Susannah—"

Aran sat on the bare kitchen countertop, resting the back of his head against the nearby cupboard, one leg drawn up to his chest as he cut Tristan off midsentence with his own words. *She's nice and she doesn't have anyone around here. I'm doing it more for her than you, kit. But if you want to know what your part in this is, I'm hoping this will push you into finding a way to break your curse, without my help. I won't steal your identity just to cover for you at night.*

Tristan shook his head, trying to keep his voice even as he reconsidered his choice of words. "Not even if I ask you to swear on that river you like so much? I can't do this without you, not if I want to keep our family safe."

Aran contemplated the glass of water in his hands before setting it aside without addressing the problem or lack of it of the Styx. *Susannah's been over to the house three or four times in the past couple weeks according to Mariko, at least from what I heard after the fact. Unless her car is on the edge of completely breaking down beyond your father's skills at repairing it, she wants to get to know you a little better. And you're holding out on her. Sleep with the girl, take her on a few dates. I'm not telling you to mention we aren't human, but it might make the... discovery a little easier later on.*

That was assuming Susannah even decided to stick around if she learned his secret. Tristan shoved his hands into his pockets, tasting discomfort in his mouth. "Our father, not just mine. I like her but why can't it just be as friends? What makes you think she... wants more than that?"

Aran meant well, probably but he didn't have a lot of experience with ordinary women. Tristan glanced away, wincing as he bit down on the inside of his cheek and tasted blood in his mouth. "Why does everything come down to sex with you?"

He wanted to ask more than that, but he knew the warning look flickering across his brother's face and the way Aran's hand tightened slightly on the glass. "Forget it. Let's just get the old cot into the car and ready for tomorrow morning."

Changing the subject was probably the wiser course of action right now. He turned away, pulling the hall closet door open. The old army cot had to be somewhere in the tangle made of a vacuum cleaner, a wet mop and assorted odds and ends related to housework. "Aran?"

His brother's hand was gentle on his shoulder, squeezing for a moment. *About eight thousand years to answer your previous question. A life like ours can be lonely. That's why I do the sex thing. Everything else is boring after a while. Your parents married and love each other but they aren't what you could call entirely devoted to each other either.*

105

Tristan glanced back over his shoulder at Aran, disquieted by the reference to his brother's true, apparent age. "They don't, do they?"

Aran's smile was short lived, wry. *Not all of their adventures in Chinatown involve protecting its residents from the cops or worse, no. Sometimes they just need a break from each other for a night or two. You know how tense things are at home—even before you introduced a white girl into the family.*

That was a little on the too much information side of things for his tastes, but it was too late to erase what his brother had said. Tristan pulled half-heartedly on a promising looking box and froze, shielding his head from a strike that never came from above. Aran catching it before it could fall more than a few inches from the shelf.

His brother was faster, stronger than he looked but it wasn't often that he put his full reflexes on display like he had right now. Tristan gulped, edging out of the way and standing. "Thanks."

Even his little trick with the soapy plate a couple weeks ago, much to his boss's wide-eyed disbelief had been a pale shadow of what Aran had shown off right now. "Is there anywhere else I could look for the cot? It isn't in that mess."

Depends. Aran pushed the box onto the shelf overhead and leaned against the closet door. *I donated it to goodwill six months ago. Looks like you and Susannah are sharing the bed for the time we're there.*

He liked Aran but it was difficult not to resent him either. Tristan let out an unhappy little snarl at the answer. "She's right about you, you really are a jerk sometimes. Fine, I'll play your game but don't expect me to be happy about it. And just as a side note for later, it took me a while to figure this out when all the guys at school were noticing the girls. I was happier with my corner of the library and a book."

If the cot was out of the question, they could at least go to the local sports store and pick up a few things that couldn't be hunted down for food. Susannah was the outdoorsy type, but she'd probably draw the line at skinning and cooking rabbit over the fire. "Don't go anywhere."

Wasn't planning on it. Aran said.

That was all well and good, but he knew how much Aran's word was worth when the Styx wasn't involved. If the older shapeshifter wanted to go off and do his own thing, very little would keep him from doing it. Tristan sighed, leaving all but his wallet and driver's license in a clear spot of graying carpet. "Sure, you weren't. Seventeen years absent and you haven't changed as much as you think you have. You're still going to take off on me and leave someone brokenhearted on the beach, waiting for you to come back."

Tristan took a breath, steeling himself before his resolve could waver. "You left me there with nothing, but a note and a pillow made from your old jeans. I was five, damn it. I'd ask if you considered that, but I know you didn't. You never do, near as I can tell. That's the part that fucking hurts the most."

He swallowed, gaze drawn to and trying to look away from Aran's closed expression. His brother was always hard to read but this time he couldn't look away from the edge in the older shapeshifter's eyes. Nothing human looked like that, nothing human could. "I don't want to reference a stupid Disney movie, but I had more sympathy for *Captain* Jones when his girlfriend never bothered to show up despite a promise to. He was creepy, yeah but he got one thing right, having family walk off or never show up when they said they would, hurts. I waited for you; you know. Seventeen fucking years."

It would have been wiser to stop there, to watch the slight narrowing of Aran's eyes as the color flickered from dark brown to wolf amber but he couldn't keep the next words from escaping from his lips. "I don't care if it's your nature or whatever, sometimes I wish you were a little more human. Maybe you'd goddamned get it sometimes. People don't just walk away from kids and leave them stranded on a beach in otter form."

The heavy plate came from nowhere and narrowly missed his head to shatter against the wall next to him. Tristan went still, breathing hard before he turned on one foot and slammed the apartment door behind him, slumping against the corridor wall opposite the front door. "Fuck!"

He crossed the thinly carpeted floor and drew back, driving his foot against the wall outside the apartment and cursed the pain that seared through it. If it had been anyone else, anyone human—they would have made an attempt at following him out of the apartment. It wasn't in Aran to do the same, as much as he wanted his brother to. "Damn it!"

The only person he could talk to right now was Susannah, despite the risks in getting her further involved with his family. "Fine, you wanted this for me. I'll talk with Susannah in the morning, but I'll handle the changing on my own, thanks."

He was old enough to do that by himself despite the risks involved. Aran didn't need to get tangled up in something that wasn't his problem. Talking to himself wasn't the sanest of ideas but it helped settle his breathing enough to focus on the phone in his hands. Susannah's number wasn't in his contacts list yet but after this, it would be. That much was certain. From now until dusk was only a waiting game, and then dawn would give him back his human shape.

It was too late to make it to Alki beach or the one he'd claimed as his own, and he wouldn't have even dared if he'd been in any mood for a nighttime swim. Curling up otter shaped in a corner of Aran's unused bed was the best he was going to get tonight. Just because his body wasn't human, didn't mean the emotions weren't and he woke to sunlight streaming through the window, the pale gray coverlet tucked up over a bare shoulder.

His mouth felt dry, coated with something before he forced himself to sit up in Aran's bed, reaching for the glass of ice-cold water on the nightstand. "Thanks."

Aran wasn't around but that was no guarantee of his brother's absence, luck willing. Tristan rubbed a hand across his eyes and located yesterday's jeans and t-shirt at the foot of the bed. It only took a moment for him to find the phone as well. Small and black, plugged into a portable charger. Susannah's text visible on the screen. "Shit!"

He'd overslept and now she was in the apartment lobby, waiting impatiently. Tristan cursed again, pulling a shirt on at random. Blue gray this time, and a size too big. One of his brother's from the lingering scent on it. "Damn it."

Blaming Aran for this could wait. Right now, it was pull a hairbrush through his rat's nest and try to tidy it before sweeping a small glass bottle and capped syringe off the bathroom vanity. Its contents and the syringe were nothing he needed. His brother might. At least it paid to be cautious where Aran's health was concerned. The unlabeled bottle could help.

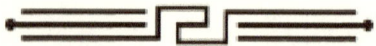

Susannah and Aran were both waiting for him by the time he found them in the lobby, one impassive and unreadable. The other, bouncing impatiently from one foot to the other. Tristan swore again, quieter this time and pressed the little kit into Aran's hands. "I hope you know what you're doing with this shit."

Aran's mouth thinned as he pocketed it, glancing sideways at the faintly outraged look on Susannah's face. *She doesn't know, gods hope it stays that way, but it isn't heroin or something else.*

"Doesn't make it less of a poison." Tristan said flatly. "And you owe me for this, mixing a sedative into the goddamn milkshake I had last night. Things were too... nice after the fight and you know it."

What do you want? Aran said.

Tristan forced himself to relax, seeing the alarm replace Susannah's look of impatience as she took a half step away from them. "You know what I want tonight. Or the night after. I don't think I need to say."

Especially in front of Susannah. She knew about Aran; she didn't know about him. Yet. He took a steadying breath, counting to five before letting go. "Whatever, it's a long hike and we'll never make it if we argue in the lobby. Let's go."

TWELVE

Susannah

Breakfast was a quick affair, just a granola bar chased down by a fast-food restaurant's pathetic excuse for orange juice. Tristan sat in the front passenger seat, hair still damp from the sudden and brief rainstorm that had struck just as they crossed the guest parking lot to where his car sat, waiting for them.

Susannah fidgeted with her phone, checking the reception as the little bars vanished one by one until the crossed-out circle showed in their place. Tension between Tristan and Aran was one thing, uncomfortable and sullen silences were another. "So... where's the cabin you mentioned yesterday?"

Tristan twisted around in his seat, pointedly ignoring his brother as he looked at her. "Somewhere in Rainier Park. It's quiet there and away from the city which counts more than it seems like. I used to come here a few times with Aran before—before he left me. After that, I made the hike as often as I could on my own."

"You hiked from Seattle to the park?" Susannah couldn't help the skeptical note in her voice at that. "That's... a long walk."

Tristan shrugged, folding up the map he held in his lap. "I knew the way and I'm used to it. Besides, I had time. I used to spend a month or two up there before coming back home. Someone had to make sure it was in good condition for the following year. No one else was taking care of the place."

A hint of bitterness slipped into his words. "It sure wasn't Aran."

Susannah opened her mouth and closed it again, at a loss for what to add to that conversation. Sympathy or a simple "I know", felt out of place and unwanted. "Right, I guess. Once we get to the park, how long will the hike take?"

"About six, eight hours ish." Tristan had the grace to give her an apologetic look. "Hope you don't mind sleeping rough in the backcountry."

"After time in Jamaica?" Susannah forced a weak laugh after Tristan finished the translation. "One of my best friends had a little place out in the interior. Mom always insisted I take one of my other friends with me just in case—but if you're worried about me being a city girl. I'm not. I can handle a few mosquitos and I doubt we're likely to stumble across a crocodile while hiking. The cabin doors were always locked, and we had a guard dog just in case. So Seattle is almost boring in comparison."

"Boring?" A flicker of hurt crossed Tristan's face. "Really? I'd..."

Susannah winced, wishing she'd chosen better words than the ones she'd used. "I didn't move here because I wanted to. My parents got job offers they decided not to refuse. Sure, the money's better in America but they never asked me whether I wanted to leave Kingston for Seattle."

"Got it." Tristan looked away and pulled the map from the glove compartment in front of him.

Susannah sighed, resigning herself to an uncomfortable silence in the vehicle and entertaining herself by watching for interesting cloud creatures in the sky. "Great. You're pissed off at your brother, and me now. This is going to be a fun few days."

It was a relief when they were able to climb out of the car and stretch their legs before the long hike to the cabin. She had the lighter of the two loads, Tristan had the other pack and Aran had the compass looped on a cord around his neck.

The first hour or two were tolerable, the third wasn't as she sat down on a fallen log, rubbing ruefully at the blister forming on the back of her foot. "Ow."

Her sores weren't bleeding yet, but they felt raw and itchy despite the socks Susannah wore. Tristan doubled back on the barely visible trail, concern on his face when he saw her seated on the log. "Feeling all right?"

Susannah slipped her boot back on. "I'm fine, biggest issue is the blisters, but I'm used to them. Used to run around barefoot in runners nearly all year round. Or sandals. Another hour or two of this and maybe I'll be asking for bandages, right now they aren't so bad."

She looked back along the deer path, catching sight of his brother. "Aran seems like he's struggling though."

Aran was supporting his weight against a nearby tree, shoulders slumped in exhaustion. Tristan's gaze followed hers as a dark look crossed his face. "Let him. He's done enough since last night. And since I was five."

At least he was talking to her now. The tension between the two guys, on the other hand, could have been cut with a knife. "Okay. What happened? You guys alternate between treating each other like family to, well, not. What's the deal?"

"He threw a plate at my head for one thing." Tristan said sourly. "Guy's got one hell of a arm on him when he wants to. I could live with that; it's leaving when I was five and not looking back for over fifteen years."

This was going to be a long camping trip if she was going to be stuck between two unhappy siblings. Susannah sighed, brushing a hand through sandy blonde hair. "Maybe this trip will be good for something. The two of you can work out whatever issues you have between you."

Tristan snorted, looking unconvinced. "Sure. But if it makes you feel better, help him. I'll see you up the trail a bit."

Susannah bristled at it and bit back on her words. Now wasn't the time for ruining what was going to be a tense trip if those two didn't resolve their issues first. She stood, making her way back to where Aran was steadying himself on the tree trunk. "You alright?"

Aran nodded, looking past her to Tristan's retreating back as he tore a scrap of paper from a notebook and wrote his answer on a piece of paper in the same elegant hand he'd displayed the other day. *Better now, I think.*

Susannah pinched the bridge of her nose between two fingers. "You aren't alright, you're tired and looking like you're about to collapse on us. Hasn't anyone told you about taking water with you?"

They did—do. He held the empty bottle for her to see. *Finished it half an hour ago. I know I should have rationed it better but some of it went to rubbing across my neck.*

His hair *did* look a little damp. Susannah glanced away, trying to find inspiration in the leaves fluttering in the light breeze. "It's not Arizona or Florida here."

Truth be told, she was finding it a little chilly, wrapping her sweater closer around her body. As dry as either state was for her, Washington was just... cold but Aran looked like he'd been out in the sun for hours with minimal protection, a flush clinging to what she could see of bare skin. "Let me?"

She offered her hand, asking silently for his wrist. He laid it in her palm as she looked down at the combat worn skin there. The webbing that joined his fingers to the first joint was dry, flaking a little. Susannah made a face, tearing her eyes away from the sight as she laid two fingers across the inside of his wrist and counted inside her head. "Normal heartbeat?"

Forty. Aran closed his eyes, sucking in a breath as he pressed his free hand to his side. *I'm a swimmer.*

Susannah gave him a long look and released his hand. "I counted it at thirty. I don't *think* you're suffering from heart disease but I'm not a doctor and if you're a swimmer, you probably don't have anything like that."

She brushed a loose strand of hair from her eyes, cursing herself as much as Aran in the moment. "Look, I'm not supposed to make a diagnosis or anything, I'm going to nursing school, not medical but this sounds like bradycardia. It's stable, near as I can tell but this trip just got a little more dangerous than I'd like it to be. If your heartrate drops lower than thirty, we're in trouble."

How much? Aran wrote his question out on the margins of the paper.

Susannah turned the notebook to read the message, grimacing. "Shouldn't you know? Aran, this could be serious. And I doubt your brother carries atropine in that backpack of his."

Aran had the grace to look briefly ashamed, crumpling the paper in his hand before he wrote on a clean sheet of paper. *He doesn't, normally, no. I kept a bottle, just in case. Jeans pocket. Just draw it up to halfway and make sure the bubbles are gone.*

Susannah grimaced, handling the small glass bottle gingerly. "Its 'prescription' is a handwritten note taped to the side. I could get into trouble for this, you know. Atropine's a nightshade derivative. If I get this wrong, it could kill you."

She sat back on the balls of her feet, looking at him. "I guess that's why Tristan called it a poison. Good to know he's got some bloody medical knowledge after all."

Aran's laugh was a thin rasp before the spasm had him tightening his hand on hers. Susannah winced, rubbing at her hand. Even exhausted, Tristan's brother was stronger than he looked. "That wasn't funny."

Aran shook his head, bracing the pad of paper against his leg as he wrote again. *I know, but it's a choice between a poison and a surer death in the woods. And at the least, this'll help my heartrate a little. I trust you.*

"It's still dangerous." Susannah said. "There's trust, and then stupidity. I think you're slipping over that line."

Please? Aran held his notebook out for her to read.

Susannah sighed, swiping hair out of her eyes. "Fine, but your parents better not sue mine. Or charge me with manslaughter or whatever gets attached to accidental atropine poisoning. If you need this, why the hell did you agree to coming out with me and Tristan?"

I promised him. Aran's written words were wobbly, the answer straying down the page from where it should have been neatly handwritten. *And I try to keep my word.*

"There is such a thing as being free to refuse, you know." Susannah looked down at the bottle and syringe in her hands as her mouth went dry. "He would have understood. Family usually does."

Not really family. Aran said. *And he feels like he—he was abandoned fifteen years ago. Mariko, Steffon, my brother aren't the sort to easily forgive when hurt. Grudges tend to last.*

"Explains why you called him spoiled, I guess." Susannah swallowed, squinting at the little numbers printed on the syringe's side and drew the drug up to the halfway mark. "I hope you know what you're doing when you ask me to do this for you. It's kind of dubious at best, breaking some medical law into pieces at worst if it goes wrong. I'll never be able to work as a nurse if it comes up."

Aran shrugged, offering her his right arm. Susannah gulped, placing the needle's tip at the right angle and slipped it into the crease at his elbow. She closed her eyes and pressed down on the plunger, trying not to think about what she was doing to him.

His hand covered hers, steadying it as he pulled the syringe from his arm and discarded it beneath a small pile of brown leaves. Susannah bit down on her lower lip, fighting the hard lump in the pit of her stomach. "Let's... not do that again, okay."

A bit of color had come back into Aran's cheeks but for how long the drug would last, she didn't know, watching him.

Susannah stood, shifting the weight of the backpack so that it sat more comfortably on her shoulders. "Is this a shapeshifter thing or just yours personally? Tristan told me a little, you told me more but I'm still not clear on the whole supernatural thing, exactly."

Aran made a face, exaggerating his shrug slightly. Susannah sighed, looking away. "Can't type and text out here, figured. At some point you're going to have to teach me sign language so we can have a real conversation without Tristan translating for you."

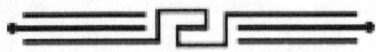

The only evidence of Tristan's presence was a strip of bright red cotton tied to a tree branch. Susannah flipped at it, swearing inwardly as she looked back over her shoulder. Aran was kneeling on the deer path, bracing himself with one hand. "Well, we have a trail and a compass to follow but how are you holding up?"

Aran shook his head, breathing labored as he closed his eyes.

Susannah answered for him, dropping to a knee next to his side. "That good, huh."

She quieted, slipping a hand over his forearm. "I'm not going to dose you with atropine again. I can't. We started late and Tristan said it was a day's hike to the cabin. We're losing the light here."

Dusk was falling, turning the emerald of the leaves to black around them. Aran had the strength to look at her and sit, pulling his notebook out. *Stay the night then and continue come dawn. I can walk you through setting up a campfire and shelter.*

"Not a city girl." Susannah rubbed at her shoulders, relieved that she'd have a break from carrying her backpack. "And I did a few years in the Jamaican Girl Guides. I know how to set a camp up and start a fire with a flint and steel if need be. Can't hunt but we're only staying one night, and you won't eat anyway."

She rummaged through her backpack, coming up with a flashlight before she found the flint and steel she wanted. "Take it in shifts as much as we can?"

There was no water so they'd have to be careful with their campfire but a source of light and warmth would be a better start to their evening than not.

Susannah knelt, tongue in the corner of her mouth as she struck sparks onto the small pile of twigs and leaves between them, breathing a sigh of relief when the sparks caught and turned into small flames before she dropped bigger pieces of wood into its heart. "Whew…"

Good to know all of her skills hadn't faded there. Aran tugged on her arm, holding his notebook up for her to read. Susannah warmed her hands in front of the fire, reading the message written on the page. "What? Oh, yeah."

She pulled her boot off, wincing as the sock went with it and took the scab forming over the blister with it. "Ow, fuck it."

Aran frowned and made a vague gesture she interpreted as a "Let me see". Susannah glanced away and gingerly extended her foot out to him. "What's this going to do? I was prepared for camping the night, but I'd hoped we'd actually make it there before dark."

The light breeze and the unfamiliar owl cries in the distance were making her nervous despite her earlier confidence. Aran gave her a disillusioned look and shifted position with a barely hidden groan as he placed one hand on the ground, still cupping her foot with the other. Water bubbled up to the surface, pooling in a small dip of ground before he lowered her foot into it. Susannah hesitated, uncertain at the good this was going to do. "How…?"

Aran sighed, giving her a look that silenced her before he glanced down at Susannah's blistered foot. The water flowed, soothing around the abrasions and she

120

flinched, nearly pulling away in disbelief. Somehow Tristan's brother was doing this, playing the part of healer as she watched.

Susannah swallowed, using the orange glow of the fire to study her foot. Whatever Aran had done, he'd taken care of the blistering, as if she'd never suffered it in the first place. "Thanks, but...?"

It was just another layer and mystery to him. Susannah pulled sock and boot back on, retying the too long laces around her ankle. "Serves me right for not breaking them in before, I guess. Where'd you learn the water trick?"

Aran crumpled the used sheet of paper up and cast it into the fire, pulling pen and notebook out from the knapsack. *Never learned it. I always... knew. Healed Tristan the same way, before we met. Left him bruised before we met, had to keep questions from coming up and he asked me to. I'm not good but I try to be.*

Susannah tossed a stray stick of her own into the flames, watching as it charred in the heart of the fire. "I never really believed it until now. Guess I was just trying to hold onto normal life, but I can't, can I? Not around you."

She tucked a strand of hair behind one ear, sitting cross legged on the blanket that would serve as their only sleeping bag until they could leave the improvised campsite in the morning. "The healer thing kills my vampire theory, doesn't it?"

Aran managed a soft rasp that might have been a laugh for anyone else as he took pen and paper up again. *Because I don't eat and I'm allergic to sunlight? Or is it the living in Seattle thing?*

At least he had a dry sense of humor in his written words. Susannah blushed, spearing a marshmallow on a sharpened stick. "Kinda, yeah."

Aran snorted, rolling his eyes. *It's a theory, but no. I'd rather die than be damned. They don't do daylight any more than I can, and they don't look like pop culture pictures. They're more like slugs with a taste for human livers, not blood. They bleed acid as well.*

"Really?" Susannah asked.

The ones here do. Aran gave her a rueful look as he handed his notebook back to her. *Don't go into the old smugglers' tunnel unsupervised. Can't speak for the ones who like Russia or eastern Europe though. More human in appearance but they're vicious when they want to be.*

Susannah shivered, drawing her jacket closer around her body. "I'll keep that in mind. Avoid the goddamn Pacific northwest version of sandworms of Dune, or whatever. You know, you're less of an asshole than Tristan thinks you are."

At least she was enjoying Aran's company more than she had when they'd first met.

He chuckled for a moment, pressing his hand against the base of his throat as the color drained from his face. Susannah let her marshmallow stick fall into the fire, not caring about the sweet treat as she knelt next to him. "You alright?"

Whether Aran liked it or not, he was her patient tonight, even if their surroundings were less than ideal. She stood, draping the blanket over his shoulders. "I don't know what's wrong with you but resting will help. Like I said, I don't mind taking the first couple hours watch."

They didn't have a choice in who would take the first watch and keeping their fire alive. Aran was in no condition to and touching him felt like reaching into the heart of the flames, burning up with a fever that hadn't been there an hour or two ago.

Aran managed a wan smile, settling down with a plastic wrapped camping pillow on the bare ground by the fire pit. Susannah swallowed, biting down on her lower lip at the sight of his written words. Far less tidy than she remembered them being. "Just try to get some rest, okay."

Of all the times, not to have a radio or cell coverage right now and all she could do was sacrifice her sleep to make sure Aran was as comfortable as he could be.

THIRTEEN

Aran

The fever had broken with first light, but it hadn't put an end to the raw, peeling skin on his arms and shoulders. He could feel it, little signs of internal breakdown as he used a sapling to stand. Aran stirred a stick through the ashes of their fire, making sure it was well and truly dead before limping a step or two away from their campsite.

Susannah's concerned gaze burned as much as the pain in his joints before she moved up beside him, wrapping his arm around her shoulders. "I thought I told you to get some sleep last night."

He'd intended to feign rest but there was no way to tell a human he didn't need such a mortal little habit as sleep. Aran closed his eyes, trying to keep as much of his weight on his own feet rather than burdening Susannah with his body and her backpack. He ignored her words and pulled away, looking towards the narrow path that led to the cabin. Two miles was barely a spin around a city block for him, under ordinary circumstances.

It was also more than he could bear as he went to his knees in the dead leaf matter, his vision swimming in front of him. Aran rasped, trying to draw in enough air to breathe. His parents and brother would be alternatively furious and disappointed but there was no hope but to trust a human with his secrets. Theirs could remain quiet for a bit longer. He didn't have the strength to write his words now as he put a hand on Susannah's arm, signing awkwardly with his free hand. *Stop. I need to sit for a moment.*

The fallen tree trunk alongside the trail was as good as anywhere to sit. Aran sank down on it, breathing as shallowly as he could as his heart skipped a beat or two. Pain squeezed at his chest like a vise. *I never wanted you to find out this way, let you live a mortal life in relative peace, but...*

He sagged, dark hair falling into his face. *I'm past being able to keep my own secrets. My family might disagree but I've no blood with them. I don't owe them anything.*

Susannah looked uncertain, fear flickering across her expression before she hid it. "That's been said before, Tristan and your family have mentioned you were adopted. What else is there that you haven't shared since last night? Beyond the shapeshifting healer thing, I mean."

Aran lifted a trembling hand, shielding his eyes from the morning sunlight, steeling himself for the story he was about to tell the human girl. Telling his brother had been one thing, years ago. Tristan had grown up in their world. Susannah hadn't. *I've only given you pieces of the story, not all of it. I left parts out to spare you from the dark.*

He took a breath and choked, throat closing before he forced himself to focus past the pain as he put pen to paper. *I'm not mortal.*

Disbelief crossed Susannah's face at his written words before she fidgeted with an amethyst pendant on a silver chain. "I want to say you're crazy but I've never... err, met anyone who sounded so serious about this."

Aran hesitated, choosing his words carefully now. Too much and he'd only drive Susannah away, too little and she wouldn't believe the story he was telling her. *I'm —I was Greek long before I was Japanese. It... usually means blonde. I only chose half Japanese because Tristan was worried about appearances—we don't look like brothers.*

"I'm not sure it would have mattered to me." Susannah said. "People adopt."

Less common in 1938. Aran missed a curve in an S and winced, cursing the tremor in his hand. *Ask Tristan, he can show you the photograph after you get back to Seattle. I'm telling you now because you deserve the truth. All of it, not what I edited.*

The memories were sour; he pushed them away roughly and pulled his legs underneath his body, sitting up with a small groan. His wife and the children had no part to play in the story, they deserved to stay in the past where they belonged. Not dragged into the light of day. Aran closed his eyes, trying to find what little comfort in the cool breeze that teased his hair against his forehead. It was harder to look at Susannah than it had been, lit by sunlight instead of the previous night's fire. *There weren't many who could match me for power in those days and only one who could command me. I answered only to Poseidon then. It was a named word, not one I used for myself but you—you would picture it as…demigod, if your mythology was any good.*

Susannah dropped to a knee next to him, uncertainty fighting with resolve. "I'll stick with shapeshifter, thanks. Less superiority in the name. So you're nearly a god. How does someth—someone like you end up tied to Tristan's family. And couldn't you just heal the damage if you're so powerful?"

She was frank. Aran managed a weak attempt at a smile, trying to breathe as little as possible through the pain in his chest. *You're blunt, my brother will like that. If he ever gets around to asking you out on a second date. I could, if I wasn't bound to the ocean but there are limits, checks on shapeshifters with my kind of power. I don't know if it's self-imposed or if we were forced to it, but I can't be on land for long without suffering the consequences of it. Mostly the dry skin and difficulty breathing but if I'm unlucky, it—it could end with my death.*

He pressed a hand to his chest, wincing as he felt his heart stutter. *Not enough to kill me for good, I'm too powerful for that but the… results are unpleasant in the meantime.*

Aran saw the question in her eyes before she asked it. *Out here? No, there's no one to call even if there was cell reception. Just keep heading north, you'll see the cabin soon enough. Or Tristan will meet you halfway. I can't go any further.*

Susannah wavered, glancing around the trees. "I shouldn't, you know. The right thing to do would be turning back and finding a cell tower somewhere, not leaving you alone in the woods while you're sick."

Aran managed a thin chuckle, shaking his head. *That would raise more questions than answers, I'm sorry to say. Shapeshifter blood isn't like human. And this body is dying. I'll give you as much of the story later if I can but for now let's just say I'm more—more spirit than flesh and blood critter.*

He lifted the necklace Susannah wore, letting the amethyst pendant hang for a moment before letting it settle against the base of her throat. *I've seen this piece before. The chain isn't what I remember when it was made but Steffon made it to leash me. I gave it to an English soldier. He must have given it to his own kin— it's too delicate to be a man's bauble.*

There was still a little power in the necklace so it was safer in her hands than anyone else's. She couldn't use it and likely never would. The longer it was kept out of the hands of someone who could, the better.

Susannah covered it with one hand, looking sickened as she read the wobbling message on the notepaper. "I'm not going to pretend to understand all of this but your own... dad made this to—what, control you? What would that do?"

Aran pushed off from the tree trunk, kneeling on the ground instead. *I imagine he meant it as protection, in his own way but it just meant trading one master for another.*

"You were a slave." Susannah's voice went flat as she reached behind her neck for the little clasp. "I've read enough history to figure that out without needing to make the connection Americans do. Does Tristan know about this?"

He might. He didn't have the strength to stand, even if he'd wanted to. *He was five when I told him*.

Susannah let the necklace pool in her hand, revulsion in her eyes. "I'll take that as a no then. Damn it, we're going to find a way to free you from your dad, and Poseidon—if he's real. Don't think I didn't notice how you used his name like he was an actual person earlier."

She squeezed his hand, folding his fingers around the pendant. "Honestly, I never wanted a two hundred and fifty year-old family 'gift'. Dad gave it to me because he thought it would make a good consolation prize for moving here."

Susannah stood, hefting her backpack onto her shoulders. "I don't like the idea of leaving you here when the cabin really would be safer, but the Gallagher kids seem to have a stubborn streak. And I really want some answers from Tristan about the shit he hasn't told me yet."

She turned back to look at him. "If I assume he isn't any more human than you are..."

Aran gave her a slight tilt of his head in acknowledgement as he held his notebook out. *Mortal, not human, no*.

Susannah snorted, scuffing at the ground with one hiking boot. "Figures. You know, a god— godsdamned war wasn't how I wanted to spend the rest of my summer."

She strode off between a pair of birch trees, muttering to herself until she was lost around a bend in the trail.

He had enough strength left to fold jeans and t-shirt into a waterproof bag, marking the place with a scrap of bright red ribbon before his knees gave out beneath his weight. A woman's gentle hand brushed over the curve of his shoulder, and he forced his eyes open to see her. *Thana?*

Mythology had given her the wrong gender and demeanor. She was death but she wasn't as cruel or spiteful as the stories said she was. She offered him a sad smile and sat back on the balls of her feet, left hand extended for him to take. "It was always Thanatos in the tale, what little they told of me, but I preferred your version better. Still do."

She quieted, helping him sit against a nearby tree. "You're taking more chances with your life in the past few weeks than you did in the last two thousand. The ocean is your element, not earth. You shouldn't be here. I worry about you when I'm able to watch."

Her hand covered his for a moment before pulling away. "Do you deliberately seek death or is that just a trait of being nearly immortal? Everything ends, Amyntas. Even the gods can."

Aran managed a weak chuckle at the chiding tone as much as his 'birth' name. *Haven't heard that one for a while. I promised my brother I would stay until he was safe. That means until Tristan's curse is broken.*

Thana sighed, mussing with her brown hair. "You always were too loyal for your own good. I assume you know who placed it on your brother a year ago, and why."

He did but there was no point in retelling something Thana had already witnessed. *I know, yes.*

131

"He's still hunting you." Thana picked up a handful of grass and let it fall back to earth once more. "Despises Tristan but hates you more for Irene's death. And... you should know your former master is missing from Tartarus."

She made a face, pulling at the zipper of her gray hoodie. "Fates know how he escaped but he's been absent for twenty years. It is... irritating being a guard without a prisoner."

She *would* find it irritating. As one with experience on the other side, it was more understandable. Aran choked, spitting up a little blood as the vise squeezed around his chest. *You don't answer to anyone. And you weren't... Poseidon's pet.*

"Just humanity's." Thana said dryly. "I'll admit it doesn't come with the same suffering he put on you but... the wars I've seen, the conflicts and the plagues."

She subsided, resting her head against his shoulder. "I have to see all of that. Anyone else would be spiraling into nihilism by now but... I've got my daughter to remind me about the good parts."

She sniffed, casting Aran a bemused look. "Hope, if you can believe it. I don't need to see her to know she's around. I'm grateful Pandora opened that jar ages ago. Cute child for a perpetual three-year-old."

Thana stood, helping him to his feet and away from the tree. "Let's bring you home for as long as you need to heal. I think I can get my brother to release you from your promise though Lachesis won't be best pleased. I'll speak with her later."

It was a relief just to let go of a failing body and let someone else lead for a while. Thana could be trusted as a skilled healer.

FOURTEEN

Martin

Memory shouldn't have hurt as much as it did, nor should it have come in the form of a delicately carved cedar box. Martin let it fall from his hands to the thin carpeted floor at his feet as he went to his knees in front of Echo. She looked on, a bitter twist to her lips as she put a hand on top of his head.

Bile rose in his throat as he choked, pulling free of her touch as he fell onto his side on the carpet. The black hole of childhood memory gone, filled in with a past he'd never known as forgotten. There was ringing in his ears that threatened to overwhelm him as he retched onto the carpet. "What..."

Echo was more than the bitter student of mythology that she'd claimed to be at their first meeting. And... he was more than the witch he'd thought he was. Imprisoned in a human shape, without knowledge of his true identity. That was more of a curse than the one he'd put on the Japanese boy.

The pain receded by inches, fading to leave his head clear. "Why didn't you tell me before?"

I tried. Echo signed her answer, kneeling next to him. *You weren't ready to listen but you're free for the first time in twenty years. Now we can help each other. I want Aran's head on a plate for killing my lover, you want him as well for murdering your daughter. It is fair.*

"So it is." Martin straightened up, brushing dust from the crumpled shirt. "I owe you more than I thought I would."

More than he cared to acknowledge, truth be told. Echo's little revenge quest meant nothing to him. She was just another toy to play with and leave behind when finished with. Her life and purpose meant little to him. There were greater powers out there.

What will you do? Echo gave him a long look, staying on her knees out of respect as Martin got to his feet.

He teased a bit of her hair between his fingers, pensive before tucking the strand behind her ear. "Be patient for now, there's so much I need to think about for myself. But I will deal with the wretched warrior after I see what's left of home."

After so long, it was doubtful anything would be left standing. Time, and his absence had taken care of that.

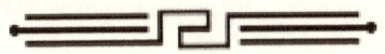

He stepped over a fallen chunk of stone, lingering in front of a largely intact tile mural. A charioteer and four dark horses before the chariot. The beasts' genders couldn't be told from a mere picture, but he knew them all the same. Dame, sire and two daughters. One slain in combat, one lost and beyond his reach, the male in the group fled to parts unknown. Parts that wouldn't remain unknown for long if he had his way.

His daughter had been mortal, but she had been beloved until her death a year ago. At the hands of a shapeshifter. A lot had been forgotten in those years spent captive in mortal flesh and blood, but his fury was as sharp as ever. The curse he'd intended for the warrior had rebounded on the Japanese boy. Ill intentioned, maybe but still worth it for the pain the act caused the boy's family.

He turned away from the mural, sorting through a pile of rubble until he found the handle and the leather strips fixed to it. The handle was still in good condition, the leather was brittle, crumbling as soon as he lifted it from the ground.

The back of his neck prickled, and he turned, seeing the platinum blonde haired woman sitting on a stump of what had been a column once. "Echo."

She smirked, greeting him with a lazy gesture of acknowledgement. He snorted and folded his arms across his chest. A lack of a voice did not mean she was incapable of speech in this time. Signed words were as easily understood as a naturally spoken language. "What do you want?"

His head on a plate, as the saying goes. Echo tilted her head to the side, casting him a pensive look. *She may have been his daughter, but she was my lover and Amyntas killed her. You should remember that. You were there eight thousand years ago.*

"So I've been told." He glanced around the hall with a look of distaste. "But I've been imprisoned in mortal guise for too long. My memory isn't what it should have been."

Fuck Mnemosyne. Echo's words held a blunt edge in the gestured answer. *She's willing to bed shades in service to your brother. Why wouldn't she give you your memories back for the same night of entertainment. And a god may be more fun than the mortal dead.*

"A god." Martin said slowly.

Echo gave him a look that was somewhere between disillusioned and askance, signing rapidly. *Eight thousand years imprisoned in Tartarus. The only way you escaped was assuming a human shape and beginning a life in that city twenty years ago. Never thought you would settle down with a wife.*

Her emphasis on the last word was sarcastic. *The life of a bookstore owner doesn't suit a man who used to command the seas herself.*

"How could I know anything else, if it was only in my dreams?" Martin asked dryly.

He silenced Echo with a hard look. "And I'm not entirely without power in this lifetime. It may be more witchcraft than what I once had but it was enough. For now. The boy's cursed. His brother is obligated to stay, watching over him."

I see. Echo looked unconvinced but unwilling to press the issue further. *Amyntas is still a problem either way. You must deal with the wretched shapeshifter. He killed my lover.*

Ah. There it was. Martin glanced away, pensive. Echo was still motivated by revenge rather than despair. Narcissus hadn't been her lover as much as Amyntas's long dead daughter. "That hasn't been his name for a long time. You know this, you took his voice."

Echo scowled, gesturing something rude in response. *What is a name? He could call himself Flower and it wouldn't be his. You created and named him. In that, at least, he's more your son than not.*

Martin growled under his breath, resenting the implication in the signed words. "I created the kelpie but don't call him my son. Amyntas's isn't any blood of mine."

So be it. Echo leaned back on a fallen pillar, bracing herself as she signed lazily. *But I hope you have a plan if your brother or his pets interfere. And there is the girl...*

"What girl?" Martin demanded.

Echo snorted, teasing hair around her finger before she released it to drift in an unseen current. *The Gray one who has a lot of love for water. She'd spend every minute she could on it. Blasted woman is half siren, seems like. But she shouldn't be difficult to deal with if she's separated from Amyntas and his adopted brother...*

She gave him a guarded look. *But she is for you to deal with, not I. I wouldn't presume to challenge you or your decisions.*

FIFTEEN

Susannah

The clearing was beautiful when she stepped into it, more of a small meadow with a few wildflowers dotting the long grass and a natural spring deep enough to bathe in, if she wanted to. Susannah paused, itching for charcoal and a sketchbook before she glanced towards the cabin at her right hand. Rough cut logs, cedar shingled. Blue and white lace curtains in the windows. Someone had intended for this to be a home, more than the rental property was in Seattle.

"It was Mom's job. The curtains, I mean. Dad did most of the work in building the place."

Susannah startled with an expletive, turning to see Tristan behind her. His step had been so silent, she hadn't heard him approach. "Shit! She does good work, I guess. Chose a good location even if..."

She hesitated over the words. "They're... uhm..."

"Loitering in the park?" Tristan gave her a wry look before it faded into caution. "Where's Aran?"

She flushed, scuffing a foot across the ground. "I swear I didn't to leave him, but he insisted. I hope he managed to make his way back to Seattle."

That was the hope anyway, the pain in his eyes had said otherwise. "He did..."

Susannah made a face, looking at Tristan's closed expression. "We're going to have to have a talk about a few things. Aran told me about your curse. I know you're a shapeshifter now. I didn't before he confessed everything."

Tristan sighed, shoving his hands into his jacket pockets. "You weren't supposed to find out. I thought you would freak out."

"Not about that." Susannah said. "Not anymore but I'm not happy with you either."

It was an effort to keep her voice from shaking with anger as she folded her arms over her chest. "It's the lying I hate. Aran was more honest than you were, and he had more reason to keep things to himself."

Tristan looked away, taking a seat on a bench under the cabin's overhang. "Is there anything I can do to fix this?"

"No." Susannah shook her head. "You aren't getting off that easy. I'll think about it but I'm not going to forgive you right off the bat."

She strode closer to the cabin door, tugging on the handle before leaning against the rough wooden exterior. "The only thing he didn't tell me was much about your curse. I think he was trying to respect your privacy there."

Tristan nudged her out of the way and pulled the key from a hidden spot in the little overhang with another sigh. "Damn him. He's my brother but he thinks he's above the rules Dad set."

She let her backpack go, setting it on the floor as her gaze traveled around the interior of the cabin. It was small, a larger kitchen space and a bedroom beyond it. The bed visible through the door, took up much of the space with a smaller trundle bed beneath it. "Tristan?"

His shoulders were stiff, set before he put a tin can of sauce into an open cupboard. "What did he tell you exactly?"

"Everything." Susannah took a seat at the kitchen table. "At least as far as I could tell, anyway. He said he was closer to an animal spirit than human. I know your dad was the one who put a leash on him as well. He didn't say when, but the implication seemed to be a long time ago."

Tristan dropped his gaze, flipping a box of spaghetti onto its side. "Dad never told me that part, neither did Aran. And he isn't an animal spirit. He's a literal force of nature, near as I can tell."

He sat down in one of the other chairs, running his hands through his hair. "He's told you more about himself than he ever told me. Look, the power he has scares the shit out of me. Aran—he's not your average shapeshifter. He—he's nearly a god and I don't know why the fuck he's still around. He could go anywhere he wanted to but stays in Washington instead."

"Maybe it's for you." Susannah said.

"I wish I could believe that." Tristan tightened his grip on the pocketknife in his hand so that his knuckles went white. "It didn't stop him when I was five. It won't now. The only thing that seems to work is swearing on the Styx and that's just a river in mythology. It isn't real."

He cut himself off abruptly, scraping the chair back against the wooden floor. "None of this matters, okay. All we need to know is that he isn't human, and his priorities aren't something we'll ever understand."

"If he's so dangerous, why do you still call him your brother?" Susannah asked.

Tristan opened his mouth and shut it again with a quiet snap, half turning away before the pocketknife buried itself into the nearby window frame. Susannah gave him an askance look and pulled the knife from the place it had been thrown into. "Good aim. Even better throw."

Tristan forced a wan smile at the compliment. "Thanks. I taught myself after Aran... left. I'm good, he's better. Just watch him throw a good ceramic plate at someone's head."

Susannah tapped the blunt edge of the knife against her wrist and set it down safely in an unused flowerpot in the window. "We should still go back for him. It's not safe out there alone and sick. It's the right thing to do."

Resignation crossed Tristan's face before he nodded. "All right. But I don't think what we're going to find is going to be pretty. I know enough about his ki— people to know he'll either go to insubstantial mist critter or worse, if he dies on us."

What could be worse than the mist critter Tristan had mentioned? Susannah glanced at Tristan's bleak expression and decided not to ask.

She pushed a tree branch out of the way, following a step or two behind Tristan as he shaded his eyes with one hand and traced week-old slash marks in the bark of a nearby tree. For someone who had grown up in the city, he was a decent trail guide. "What are you looking for? Aran's sick, he couldn't have gone far—"

Her foot dislodged something from the earth, and she blanched, tracing the curve of it with her eyes. "Tristan...?"

Her stomach twisted in discomfort, and she backed away from it. "It—those are..."

Tristan gave her a bleak look and dropped to one knee, handling the radius and ulna gingerly before he shook his head. The smaller bones were already crumbling into dust at his touch, but the larger ones were tougher. "Aran broke his arm once, a long time ago. Three or four places and he mentioned it in case he needed to be—be identified."

Susannah tasted bile in her mouth, trying not to look to closely at the round curve of the skull Tristan excavated from the dirt. "But to go from sick to... dead in the woods, the only thing that could have killed him was an animal or exposure. I'll buy that, maybe. But not seeing human remains, and not bones. It takes longer than that for decay to occur."

Tristan's mouth was a thin line of unhappiness as he set the skull down into the hollow he dug out with his hands. "One, Aran's not human. Decomposition doesn't apply to him in the same way it would for us, and his body was already breaking down."

He sat back on the balls of his feet, brushing a dark strand of shoulder length hair out of his eyes. Resolve showed in his eyes even as his shoulders sagged in defeat. "Did he tell you anything before?"

Susannah shuddered, kicking a loose lump of dirt onto the shallow grave. "Just that he was pretty powerful for a shapeshifter and that he couldn't be on land for long without suffering for it. I didn't take him literally when he said it."

"He's not one for metaphor," Tristan stood, brushing more dirt from his jeans. "Most days anyway. "Anyway, just because we found his bones, and fuck if that doesn't sound as creepy to me as it does you—doesn't mean he's permanently dead."

"He said that too," Susannah said weakly. "More spirit than flesh and blood critter. So I take it this isn't the end for him?"

"Not if I know him as well as I think I do," Tristan said. "Which until he told you more about himself than I was aware, I thought I did."

Susannah swallowed, feeling the chill run down her spine at that. "Fun, right now I just want a shower and some bleach so I can wash this picture out of my head. Human—err, shapeshifter remains weren't how I wanted to spend a few days at your parents' cabin."

Tristan looked away, rueful. "No running water but if you leave an offering by the spring, whatever lives there, might be happy to let you have a bath without drowning you for intruding."

She wasn't a believer any more than he seemed to be, but it seemed wiser to humor Tristan's request, if only for the sake of whatever his brother was. "Sure, and... thanks."

Maybe the soak would settle her stomach after their disturbing discovery. It couldn't hurt in any case.

Try as she might to get some sleep, she couldn't. The memory of the remains still echoed in her thoughts, haunted her dreams when she tried to banish them. The curve of the skull, the bone white flash of teeth. Susannah shuddered, sitting up and buried her face in her hands before she lit the candle with the matchbox in the bedside nightstand. "Fuck..."

The curve of the pelvic bone and the smaller bones of the arms already crumbling into powder as Tristan tried to lift them from the dirt. It had been an anatomy lesson she hadn't wanted to learn. One made more stark by the bones being his brother's remains.

Electricity would have been nice but there was none to be found in the cabin. Tristan's family lived simply when they lived here at all. Less than they had once upon a time. The only one who maintained the cabin much these days was Tristan.

She shivered, as much from the nightmare as much as the cold and pulled a spare quilt around her shoulders as she edged towards the kitchen table, stepping carefully to avoid the pair of backpacks piled in the middle of the floor. No one had seen fit to put them into a carved box beneath the larger window since their arrival the other day. They'd had other things on their minds since their grisly discovery.

Rain struck the rooftop in a way that was almost comforting if it wasn't miles from Kingston and everything she'd loved about Jamaica. The storms here were too cold for her liking, lacking the humidity and heat she'd grown up with. "How much longer?"

It was impossible to tell where the sun was going to rise, hidden behind a tree canopy but the chirping of birds seemed to hint at soon. Susannah grimaced, blowing out the candle and setting it down on the kitchen table before she dressed quickly, pulling on jeans and a t-shirt. The jacket followed a moment later. "Where are you?"

Susannah stepped out onto the little slate step and into the drizzle, searching the area in front of the cabin. The half wild garden behind the home was just as empty and she turned away, frustrated. Aran's fate was clear enough. Tristan's was less so. He changed each night whether he wanted it or not. That didn't mean dead.

Sooner or later, someone was going to have to make a move but where and how—when they didn't even know how to break the curse on him, she didn't know. The original witch, according to Tristan. Martin Carpenter, but whether he would was anyone's guess. It didn't feel likely to her.

The spring burbled, glittering in the morning light as she circled around it, sitting on a flat rock that jutted out over the water. More of a pond than a spring, really but who was she to argue with Tristan's definition. Or his brother's power. Whatever it had been before, the clarity of the water looked like Aran's work. She let out a breath, dipping a hand into the water and letting the droplets fall back into it. "I'm probably just talking to empty space right now but if there's anything out there willing to listen, you need to know I'm not sure how much of this to believe. Demigods, witches—they were just mythology or superstition before I moved here. They weren't real. Now I'm tangled up in someone's stupid little blood feud and I don't even know whose."

Was it Aran's, someone else's or just a case of several people needing to be sat down in neutral territory where they could talk through whatever issue they had with each other. Susannah sighed, bracing herself on one arm. "I'm not religious but I could sure as hell use a sign here. Something to tell me what to do."

A crow called, flapping overhead before it landed on a nearby tree branch, watching her with a look of curiosity in its eyes. Susannah sat back on her rock, drawing one leg up to her chest. "Please don't tell me you're my sign."

The bird croaked, almost sounding like it was laughing at her before it took off again, flying right at her. Susannah ducked, shielding her head from it as its claws scraped over her shoulder. "Damn it! This isn't what I meant, and you know it, bird!"

Something purple glittered at her feet and she swore again, dangling the amethyst pendent in front of her eyes. "Some fucking sign. I gave this back to Aran and I don't think he had time to go anywhere in his condition."

"Susannah?"

She turned, pocketing the necklace as Tristan's voice sounded. "You're back."

"Yeah." Tristan draped yesterday's shirt over one arm. "Not something I wanted to tell you, honestly. The curse, I mean."

"I know now, it doesn't matter." Susannah pulled the necklace from her pocket, showing the amethyst in her cupped hand. "I still don't know what the deal is between you and your brother but if I'm going to be dragged into some kind of supernatural war or something and still be your girlfriend—everyone needs to be sat down at the table for a real talk. Starting with the necklace. I swear I got rid of the bloody thing."

If there was going to be a war, nothing was going to be accomplished by hiding out in the woods and praying it would pass them by. "We need to go back to Seattle, and we need your bother, if he's anything like he says he is. He's the only one who understands how this shit started."

Action was better than reaction and she wanted a strong enough cell phone coverage to start browsing for a therapist. Finding human remains in the woods still haunted her even if there was nothing anyone could do about them now. The rapid decomposition rate probably meant dust more than bone anyway. "Please?"

If she was still dreaming about it, it was just as clear in her boyfriend's expression. "It'll be good to talk to someone, if we can."

In broad strokes, if nothing else. Very few people were going to believe the truth if she came out with all of it.

Hesitation flickered across Tristan's face before resolve followed it. "Not sure we can talk to anyone but maybe you're right about heading back to Seattle."

As much as she regretted cutting their little vacation short, this was for the best. Rainier Park was beautiful. "Maybe we'll get another chance later."

Hope always counted for something, right?

SIXTEEN

Susannah

Her sense of smell wasn't as strong as Tristan's but even she could catch the scent of rain on the air as they stepped out into the parking lot that bordered the edge of the park. Susannah shrugged her pack off in relief, tossing it into the trunk of the car. The hiking trip had been a bit of a disappointment, but she was better for going. And it reframed her feelings towards Tristan and his brother. They'd given her the honesty she'd asked for, even if it had cost Aran his life to do it.

She bowed her head, scrolling through the voicemail and texts on her phone. "Nothing from anyone but my parents. Fun."

Was there any chance Tristan would be able to persuade his family to let her stay a while? Anything was better than the confrontation she was dreading over the dinner table. "I have my own life, but they still want to tell me how to live it."

A few raindrops splattered against the concrete as the sky darkened overhead. Susannah wiped the screen dry, pocketing her phone. "What's the plan exactly? We never really discussed what to do while we were at the cabin."

"Breaking the curse and that means going to the guy who put it on me." Tristan said.

That was it, but it left a question of where to find the man and how to persuade him to lift it. Susannah moved around the side of the car, slipping inside the Honda's warmth. "Do you think he will?"

"Hope so." Tristan twisted the key in the ignition, letting the car idle as he leaned his head back against the headrest. "It's not like he's any friend of Aran's m—ex-employer, right? He's just a witch."

Who was trying to reassure who here? Susannah tapped her wrist against the car door, staring out the window. "You grew up in this world, I thought you'd be comfortable with some of the stuff in it."

Tristan put the car into drive, navigating the parking lot up to the gravel road that led onto the highway back to Seattle. "Shapeshifting doesn't always mean faithful if that makes sense. Aran's the pagan one in the family. I'm... nothing. The gods were just stories to me. Stuff Mom told me to get me to sleep growing up."

"We still need answers." Susannah said. "Martin's the best one to give them to us. I'm willing to take that chance if you are."

"Yeah, but he isn't very happy with me after what happened to Irene." Tristan checked over his shoulder, giving way to the heavier logging truck as it passed by them on the road.

Susannah made a face, glancing at the small mirror in the sun visor. "Seems like it's just something Aran needs to work out with Martin. You were innocent in that mess. He started it, Martin took things into his own hands and here we are. Halfway to a war no one wants."

She flipped the visor up, pulling a map of Seattle from the glove compartment. "You know the city better than I do. Where does this guy work?"

"It's a bookstore." Tristan swung the car onto the off ramp, frowning a little in the rearview mirror. "Don't know the name off the top of my head but I think Aran's been there to browse a couple times. Never actually came home with anything that I've seen though."

Susanna scribbled notes onto the empty margins of the map, rereading the cramped scrawl. "Just out of curiosity, what's down in the old tunnels? Aran mentioned them before, you know."

"Pioneer Square?" Tristan pulled the car over to the shoulder of the road, putting the flashers on. "A couple ghost tours, that's about it. Mom made me promise never to explore them."

"And you listened to her?" Susannah gave him a wry look. "I thought the shapeshifting would make it easier to escape from danger or fight it."

Her curiosity was piqued more than dissuaded now. "We might as well learn what's there, just in case. Knowing might be useful."

She'd always had an interest in forgotten history. If they could combine the two, all the better for them. "Please? I can't think of a better date, or distraction from what's waiting for me at home after having my phone turned off for a few days."

"If there's time, but it's technically trespassing if we leave the tour guided parts. We'll need chalk and a flashlight." Tristan said.

"We've got both in our backpacks." Susannah leaned back against her seat, folding the map into its original brochure form. "The more I know about Seattle, the better."

Tristan was wavering, she could see it in his eyes. He nodded after a moment, swearing in Welsh before he put the car into drive again. "Alright. But we're only doing this because I want to get rid of seeing Ar—someone's decomposing body in my head."

That made two of them. Susannah shuddered at the flash of memory. Bone shouldn't have been as frightening as it was but she preferred them to be unidentifiable and anonymous. "Good enough for me. How are we going to explain this to your parents, ignoring the whole nearly immortal shapeshifter thing Aran does."

"With luck, we won't have to. Phone." Tristan took one hand off the wheel to toss the small cellphone into her lap. "That's Mom's number, Aran's text."

Susannah looked down gingerly at the short message visible on the display. "Yeah, that doesn't make it sound any less creepy. People don't come back from death, usually. He's saying he's at the Waterfront, waiting for us."

She sighed, pushing a strand of stray blonde hair behind one ear. "Delay the Pioneer Square trip for another day? Three hours to Seattle, dealing with the Martin guy and then I guess I'm going to have to face my parents for walking away without a note or warning in advance I was hanging out with a guy. Plus, your thing. You literally can't do nights."

"Yeah." Tristan's mouth tightened in unhappiness as he looked out the windshield towards the faint smudge that was Seattle's skyline. "We'll figure out the order later but there's just enough time to reconnect with Aran and confront the book guy. After that, I'll be cutting it too close for comfort."

That raised one more question for her. Susannah chewed on her lower lip, wincing at the small taste of blood in her mouth. "I wonder, the curse—can't Aran break it for you? If he's got so much power..."

"He's tried." Tristan said flatly. "Martin's not your average witch. Never met one outside of him but I've heard they mostly do nasty stuff to the human body or manipulate people's feelings for kicks. This is... different. Aran can't touch whatever it is. Martin's the one who put it on me, as far as I can tell, he's the only one who can take it off."

He lapsed into silence, refocusing his attention on the drive back to the city. Susannah shrugged it off, reluctantly playing with the amethyst pendant. Silent rides were fine with her when she was preoccupied with her own thoughts.

They detoured, taking a less familiar route from suburban Seattle to the waterfront, parking half an hour later. Susannah was out of the car first, already searching for Aran and not seeing any sign of the older Japanese guy on the dock. A knot of tourists wandered past, chattering in German and briefly interrupted her search. Susannah cursed, standing on tiptoe before catching sight of a blonde-haired guy in a too big t-shirt and jeans, cloth wrapping both forearms. "Is that...?"

Tristan followed her gaze, nostrils flaring with whatever he was scenting. "Yeah, it's him. Different shape but I think I'd know my own brother when I saw him. He's got a few tells, doesn't matter what shape he uses. Used to be the Irish accent, now it's his haircut and the Greek tunic. The bandaging around his forearms too, sometimes. At least I've never seen him without wrapping his arms."

"And the scent as well, I'm guessing." Susannah said dryly.

"That too." Tristan didn't blush as he glanced back at her, hopping the heavy chain that marked the edge of the parking lot and the Waterfront's boardwalk instead.

Susannah hung back, watching the interaction between the siblings with a knot of discomfort in the pit of her stomach. Just when she was starting to get used to Tristan's more uncanny senses, he occasionally showed off without thinking. He was better at pretending to be human than his brother but there were brief flashes of how different he was from an ordinary guy. Little things he seemed unaware of and took for granted.

She scrambled over the chain, joining them in time to see Aran's signed answer, whatever it was. "Hey, nice to see you back from, well, you know."

Aran laughed though the thin, raspy sound had her wincing and drawing back a step. That was something she was never going to get used to. The ragged, breathless attempt wasn't natural or comfortable. Susannah looked down at her boots, toeing it against the worn boardwalk. "Sorry."

It didn't take an expert to see how the attempt hurt him, or the way he put a hand to his own throat with a small wince before signing something a moment later.

"He said there's no reason for you to apologize." Tristan looked from his brother to her, leaning against a concrete post. "He's lived with this since Echo cut his throat."

He frowned, casting a look over his shoulder at his brother. "Though I'm not sure if you mean Echo, a girl, or echo like the other thing."

A look of impatience crossed Aran's face before he signed again and struck Tristan lightly across the shoulder. Tristan flinched, rubbing at his upper arm. "Ow. Echo, the girl, sure. Anyway, now that we're all caught up, we have errands to run before night comes. Susannah was thinking we go over to Martin's bookshop for a talk. Since he's the one who put the curse on me. Then I was going to give her a ride back to her house."

Aran bared his teeth and snarled softly, one hand tightening at his side. The other squeezed Tristan's shoulder before Tristan pulled away, a look of discomfort at the gesture. "We're in public. I don't need sign language to see how much that pisses you off but Martin's our best and only choice we've got. If you can't and Coyote won't. We have to talk to him."

"Coyote?" Susannah interrupted the conversation with a slightly trembling raised hand. "He was an option all along?"

"He wasn't." Tristan translated for his brother again. "Territorial thing, maybe. It's complicated. Shapeshifters are kind of apex predators."

"Great." Susannah slumped on a nearby park bench, dropping her head into her hands. "Just when I was getting used to your... uhm, species? People? It turns out you think you're on top of the goddamned food chain."

"I never thought that." Tristan glanced away, eyeing his brother narrowly. "It's just what he said. It'd explain a lot but I'm nowhere near that kind of power. Or attitude."

"Still fucked." Susannah flipped her plait over her shoulder, standing. "Anyway, maybe he can answer my questions as much as yours. If Martin's as connected as its implied, he might have answers about the two hundred and fifty-year-old necklace Dad gave me. We've spent long enough muddling through shit. Let's get down to the real work."

If they were never going to be capable of an ordinary girlfriend, boyfriend relationship, she might as well throw the towel in and accept things as they were. Whatever they were, risk of a supernatural war included.

SEVENTEEN

Tristan

The bookstore looked unimposing from the outside but that was nothing to what it held in it. Tristan glanced at the red and white awning that covered the front window and door. They were counting on a lot and that, without Aran to keep things civil.

He made no move to turn the engine off as he stared at the red brick exterior. The curse had only been a year but it was a year he was never going to get back. It had been hated but the nightly change was familiar, if not comforting now.

"Tristan?" Susannah asked.

He pushed the thoughts away, pinching the bridge of his nose. "I shouldn't be as used to it as I am but..."

"People adjust, they get used to things and they learn to live with them." Susannah let the seatbelt slide back into its place. "They'd go crazy if they didn't. Not knowing what to do without it is normal."

Her short-lived smile wobbled. "It just makes you human, more or less. That's a good thing. Might not be comforting to Aran, but for us, it should be. You made it a part of yourself, now you want to change it. That's a big change, even if you hate what it means, meant for you. It's going to take time, but we'll never know if we try."

Tristan looked down, steeling himself and pulled the keys from the ignition. "Martin's only a witch. Everything will be fine."

Susannah's confidence was something to envy but she'd never seen the man a year ago. Didn't really know what he was like. Even with the confidence boost she'd attempted to give him; his mouth was still dry as he pushed the bookshop door open. Martin's wife was at the cashier counter, glaring as the little bell tinkled overhead. Tristan swallowed, looking down at the book list he'd written down at random. They were titles he already owned but that was just an excuse to talk to the witch. She wouldn't know what was on his shelf or not. "I was looking for a Welsh copy of Last Kingdom."

Martin's wife gave him a passing look, nose wrinkling as though she smelled something sour underneath it but she typed the search into her computer. "Are you sure there is one for a book that's only been out five years?"

"I was hoping Martin could track it down." Tristan crumpled his booklist in his hand, stuffing it into his jeans pocket. "I think my brother mentioned it in passing a few weeks ago and if anyone knows about that, your husband might."

She sighed, straightening her glasses and looked towards the stairs leading up to the second floor of the premises. "I don't like you, Gallagher. Whether or not you actually did it, you were there the night my daughter died. I can't forgive that. I'll tell you this, not because I think you deserve to know, just because Martin's become... different lately, ever since the that girl started working here part time."

"Which girl?" Tristan asked.

She made a face, barely hiding the scowl that twisted at her mouth. "Calls herself Echo. Never says a word to anyone but she signs just like your brother does. I never would have hired her, personally but I'm not in charge of that. My husband is."

"Where is he?" Tristan hastily derailed her before the conversation could turn into ranting about employees.

"Oh." Eva's expression darkened as she gestured towards the stairs. "Probably shelving history books or in his office. If he isn't occupied with *her*."

Susannah pulled Tristan away, grimacing a little as she tugged on his arm. "She's no help at all and you said you wanted something quick to eat before meeting your brother."

Susannah's superficial fib could be appreciated for what it was, as part of their plan but he wasn't going to back away now because of Eva's hostility. Tristan shook his head, taking a step away from her. "If she can't help, he can. It's just a book, it won't take long."

She sighed, dropping her hand back to her side. "Alright but call me in twenty minutes. I saw an interesting little café nearby. I want to get a snack."

"Bring a brownie back?" Tristan asked.

"Sure." Susannah pulled a paperback at random from a nearby shelf and set it on the counter, placing a twenty on top of it. "Just this one, thanks."

Eva bristled but rang it through, placing it into a paper bag. "Enjoy your book."

Her words and tone couldn't be more at odds than they were. Tristan gave Eva a worried look and climbed the stairs to the second floor. "Martin?"

The bookshelves to either side of him were devoted to nonfiction, history and political science. Nothing he'd find interesting. Tristan flipped through a hardcover about world war two and put it back in its place. "Martin?"

Martin stepped around the corner, an opened cardboard box of books resting against one hip. "I don't believe—you're the younger Gallagher boy. The shapeshifter."

"Yeah." Tristan slipped a hand into his jacket pocket, trying to find a little comfort in the cool metal of his pocketknife. "You knew that a year ago. It's your curse on me."

"I see." Martin gave him an appraising look. "Are you going to tell me about it or am I going to have to make a guess?"

The back of his neck prickled. Tristan swallowed, trying to ignore the sliver of ice that trickled down his spine. There was a hint of something in Martin's voice that was colder, different than the frightened, furious man a year ago. "I just want you to break it for me. Please?"

Martin laughed, setting his box down on the bare floor at his feet. "Amyntas never would have begged me. I thought his brother would have been raised the same way."

"I'm not my brother." Tristan said.

"No, you aren't." Martin looked down pensively at the collection contained within the box. "You're weak, a pup. I won't tell you how to break my curse or do it myself. You didn't drown my daughter, no. But you were there when she died. You're guilty by association, I think."

Martin took a step closer, forcing Tristan back the same distance as the older man placed a hand on the dusty bookshelf. "I could give you a taste of your brother's frailty instead."

"Pass." Tristan took another step back, looking over his shoulder for the first step down the stairs. Breaking his neck was the last thing he wanted to suffer today. The vise squeezed around his chest, and he went to all fours, retching up salt water between his hands. "Fu—fuck."

Black spots danced in front of his vision as he forced himself into a standing position, bracing himself on the varnished railing. He felt for the next step below him and missed it, reflexively tucking into a ball as he went down. Nearly, anyway. The back of his head struck the edge of the staircase, sending sparks and pain through it. Tristan groaned, reaching up to touch the warm stickiness matting his hair to his skull. "Ow."

Martin's footsteps echoed nearby, pausing at the bottom of the steps. Tristan opened his eyes against the light, seeing polished dress shoes and the slacks as he managed to sit up. "Don't touch me."

Martin chuckled, tangling his hand in Tristan's t-shirt collar as he dropped into a crouch next to him. "No. I think it's time you knew who you're dealing with, boy. I may consider breaking your curse if you bring me your brother. Tell him his former master is looking for him."

Tristan shrank back, breaking Martin's grip on his shirt. "If I refuse?"

"Then you'll remain cursed, and I'll never stop hunting him." Martin released his grip on the t-shirt. "Run, little otter."

Tristan blanched, seeing Eva's white-faced expression from where she stood frozen behind the counter. He scrambled to his feet, fighting the nausea that came with the sudden motion and the pounding ache in his head before he pushed the bookstore door open. He didn't stop until he was outside the café, hands braced on his legs, panting until his breath steadied.

Susannah emerged with a coffee and a small bag clutched in her other hand. "Got what you wanted?"

"No." Tristan straightened, still shaking. "He pushed or tripped me off the top step. Said... if I didn't bring him Aran, he wouldn't break the curse. He—he said that my brother's m-master was looking for him."

"Oh." Susannah's color went from pink to a sickly green. "Did Martin say anything else?"

"Before I fell? No." Tristan swallowed. "We need to talk to Aran. This matters to all of us but I can't drive in this condition. I think I hit my head hard enough to end up with a concussion."

At least that was the only way to explain the pain and nausea he felt. "We didn't ask for this, but I think we're heading towards the war you mentioned."

EIGHTEEN
Aran

Lyra's sense of timing was at best uncanny. She was waiting for him on the pier, leaning against one of the wooden pilings. She'd cut her hair since they'd last met, leaving it short and framing her face. Aran glanced out across the water, not caring that the tourists disembarking from a nearby liner were staring at him. A cotton tunic, sandals and the bandaging wrapping his arms wasn't a common sight in Seattle.

He didn't intend to change his clothes.

Lyra followed his gaze out across the Pacific, frowning a little before she slipped her arm into his. "I'm not one of those shit-ass psychic empaths you find in New Orleans or Jamaica and you're nearly impossible to read but you aren't exactly hiding your feelings right now. What's wrong?"

Aran cuffed her lightly across the shoulder and sighed, pulling his eyes away from the expanse of water. *I let my brother and his girlfriend go to meet Martin alone. I don't know if that was the right choice, since you returned my leash to the girl. It's safer with her than not, but still... you remember what it looked like.*

"I didn't, not until you described it. Again." Lyra said. "If I saw it before, it was a long time ago. A little amethyst without a setting? I'm the kind of girl who would be more likely to pawn it than analyze it for value. I was a whore and pickpocket during the Revolution, not a jeweler or fence interested in that stuff."

Your memory is better than you think it is, that was it, yes. Aran said. *I thought it was lost or destroyed but I found the gods cursed thing, around the neck of my brother's girlfriend.* Aran said.

Lyra made a face. "Gray isn't exactly uncommon, you know that. She could be anyone."

She isn't, Aran tightened his hand on the rope barrier between them and the water down below them. *And the girl is the image of her late aunt. To say nothing of having been given the woman's name.*

"Oh," Lyra toed a runner across the salt worn planks, looking down at them. "That sounds like a story."

One I'm not privy to, even were I interested. Aran released his grip on the rope as the fibers weakened and frayed. *I've had... dealings with Steffon in the past, not solely as his adopted son during the war.*

"I'm almost afraid to ask," Lyra's words had a tremor in them as she picked at a hole in her blouse hem.

"Considering my own father was on the Viking side of things over a thousand years ago. He told... stories of the Irish captive who sank part of the fleet. That was you? And what the hell did Steffon Gallagher have to do in it? He's Welsh, not Northman."

Aran touched the base of his throat, feeling the weight of a leash he hadn't worn for years. *He doesn't trust me, that's all that matters. And he knows I haven't forgiven him for binding me in the first place.*

Lyra swallowed, the scent of fear clinging to her skin. "No mercy, huh."

No, Aran glanced out to sea once more. *It isn't in my nature to be forgiving. If he finds out his son's girlfriend has my leash, he's going to find out how pissed I can get.*

"Lovely," Lyra stuffed a shaking hand into her jacket pocket. "Shift it a few thousand miles north and across the continent and you've got a Pacific Northwest version of those pirate movies. Tristan isn't going to be very happy if you kill his dad but let's save the dragon versus kelpie war for the bigger issue right now."

She sighed, pinching the bridge of her nose between two fingers. "I was a rat sitting in front of the bookstore your brother went into. Didn't see everything but Tristan took a nice little tumble down the stairs. Slipped in and out quick enough to get a bit of paper they forgot to clean up. Wasn't much written on it except for Poseidon's name. Dunno if that means anything to you."

Aran gave her a brief look, concealing his disquiet from her with nonchalance. *And if it did, what would you think?*

Lyra trailed a hand over the fraying rope, unhappiness in her eyes. "I'd wonder about your wisdom when you weren't around to hear me. Two—three times captive by humans?"

He managed a thin rasp of a chuckle and cupped the side of her face in one hand. *Just unlucky. And as strong as I am, Poseidon was stronger. Thank the fates, he's been long imprisoned now.*

Some of this would have to be investigated but only after he gave himself a much-needed distraction.

I tend to let my brother handle his own affairs. Aran said. *He's old enough to look after himself. He doesn't need me hovering over him.*

"So..." Lyra lifted her gaze up to his, trailing off suggestively.

Aran rolled his eyes, ruffling her hair with his hand before gesturing away from the Waterfront. *I'd ask if it was just you but I want this as much as you do.*

Aran pressed his mouth against Loki's, tangling one hand through her hair as he straddled her on the bed. She let a soft sigh out, lips parting slightly as she pulled him close. The flannel bedsheets were rumpled underneath them, the coverlet more off than on the bed. All she wore for basic modesty was a sports bra—the lingerie had been tossed aside to hang limply from the half-opened nightstand drawer.

She almost purred, arching her back as he nipped her lightly on the side of the throat. A thread of dark blood trickled across her skin, staining the white pillowcase underneath her head.

166

Someone knocked on the apartment's front door and paused, repeating it with more urgency. Aran caught Loki's hand before she could trace the line of old scarring across one shoulder, signing awkwardly with one hand. *Don't*.

She feigned a pout and shoved halfheartedly at his weight, rolling onto her side as she propped her head on a closed fist. "You should get that."

Aran glanced towards the ajar bedroom door and snorted, shaking his head. It wasn't important and if it was, his brother had a key. Tristan could let himself in. He pulled Loki closer to his body, cupping the side of her face with his hand. *It isn't important*.

"It's your brother," Lyra sniffed, nostrils flaring as she caught Tristan's scent despite the distance and the closed front door. "We should—"

Her words were silenced by the kiss Aran pressed to her mouth. She muttered something unflattering in Finnish and slipped her hand across the curve of his shoulder, gingerly avoiding the flushed, peeling skin there. "Mhm..."

The front door latch rattled before the lock turned in the door and it opened. Tristan stepping inside, Susannah a step or two behind him. "Ar—Shit!"

Aran snarled, baring his teeth at the unwelcomed distraction. Lyra looked no happier though her hiss of displeasure was softer, more cat like than his own. They were busy, his little brother's interruption wasn't welcomed. *Leave. Now*.

"I'd love to, but I had a little accident down a flight of stairs, and I could use a bit of reassurance about a potential concussion." Tristan's gaze was drifting anywhere but around the messy bed. "And you said I could walk in here as if it was my own place, six months ago. No one mentioned the only use you have for an apartment was sex."

Aran growled under his breath and swept a discarded towel around his waist. He seized a heavy ceramic plate from the small island in the kitchen nook and held it frisbee style. *Get out, kit. I don't miss unless I want to.*

Tristan blanched, gaze falling towards Aran's waist before he mumbled something in Welsh and retreated, tugging Susannah behind him. The human girl was as pink as Tristan was pale with embarrassment.

Lyra padded out of the bedroom after Aran, wrapped only in the turquoise coverlet. "I guess our day is ruined anyway. Are you going to go after him to check on the concussion? It *was* a bad fall."

I don't have a choice. Aran glanced away, setting the plate into the kitchen sink with a tired sigh. *Like it or not, I'm a healer. The plan was to talk to Martin, not get Tristan thrown down a set of stairs. And there was the note you stole from him.*

"Yeah." Lyra located her t-shirt from where it had been discarded over the back of a chair. She pulled the pink cotton over her head, showing the silver outline of a panther stalking its prey on the front. "I'm tempted to get the hell out of Seattle but there's no telling whether or not you need me, so I'm sticking around. Anything I need to do in Louisiana can wait. Besides, I don't need my brother as much as he thinks I do. Just because he's Aleksander of Kyiv and I'm not a warrior..."

She sniffed, pulling her hair into a sloppy pair of short pigtails. "I'll keep watch over the kits like I promised you. Have since I took Susannah's necklace from your bones and returned it to her."

That gave him pause, glancing at her with a small frown.

Lyra admired her reflection in the side of the unused toaster sitting on the counter and took a step away, turning to lean against the fake marble. "I was the gods damned crow that flew over her head if you must know. My grandfather had a laugh about that, I'm sure. I hate bird forms."

She gave him a slight push, glancing pointedly towards the apartment's front door. "I'll hang out here for a couple hours, stress clean up a bit while you check Tristan for his head injury and get answers about the little mission he assigned himself."

Aran gave her a fond smile and pulled a wash abused gray t-shirt out from under the bed, tugging it over his head. The silvery green light of Lyra's gate shimmered out of the corner of his eye before fading.

Regret wasn't something he was called to often, but his brother did deserve an apology for the lack of warning.

NINETEEN

Tristan

"So... that happened," Susannah glanced down at her phone, tossing it from one hand to the other. "Tell me we didn't just walk in on your brother having sex with some girl here."

Tristan winced, wishing there was bleach nearby to erase the mental image of Aran's choice of midday entertainment. "He's Greek. They either do things differently there or..."

He trailed off, unhappily. "Either way, he's a warrior. I don't think stark naked has the same meaning for him that it does for us. He can't use a phone and he doesn't like to text. I should have been more careful, sorry."

Susannah forced a weak smile. "Nothing for you to be sorry about. Aran should remember the old sock on the door though. As a courtesy."

"Should but won't." Tristan brushed a bit of dark hair from his eyes. "It's like him to not pay attention when he's... preoccupied. Wouldn't be the first time I've gotten a good look at everything of his. Probably won't be the last either."

Talking about this wasn't pleasant but it was preferable to the weight of his last paycheck in his jacket pocket. "Besides, someone would say it was my fault for not giving him a little advance notice we were coming over. I'm too used to walking in there like I own it. Pretty sure the landlord assumes I share the lease even though I never put my name down. The man's that disinterested in his tenants."

Cassandra had handed him the slip of paper with a shake of her head and gesture towards the front door of the Blue Cat. Her niece had looked almost overjoyed by the humiliation of receiving severance pay in full view of the lunchtime rush.

He looked down at his phone screen, wishing the tight itchy ache beginning to make itself known would just fade. They'd left Rainier Park around midmorning, camping the night before on the trail and it had taken three hours to get back to Seattle. The errands with his former boss and Martin hadn't taken nearly as long but they had been halfway across the city from each other. And they still had a tentative dinner at Susannah's house —with her parents. "If we go now, can we make an excuse for why I have to leave early?"

Susannah blinked and then awareness crossed her face as her expression fell. "Oh, yeah. We can. It's the curse, isn't it?"

"Yeah." Tristan rubbed at his arms, looking away. "Forget the concussion. The change will fix that for me, but I'd rather not freak anyone out or expose my family to danger. No one's supposed to believe in shapeshifters. We'll make it to Pioneer square tomorrow."

He caught sight of Aran out of the corner of his eye, seeing his older brother standing by the apartment door, thankfully in jeans and a t-shirt now though Aran hadn't bothered with socks. "Unless you're willing to help. I'll owe you for this, and accidently walking in on you in the... sex thing."

His cheeks burned at the memory permanently burned into his mind. "Please?"

Aran snorted, signing his answer. *Only because of that. And pray Susannah's been silent on dating you. Borrowing your identity is one thing, You know I'll never be able to mimic your personality, kit. You're so reserved, it's almost cold. I'm not.*

"Noted." Tristan trailed a hand across the corridor wall. "And that's unfair, I'm not cold. Am I?"

"What's he saying?" Susannah was looking between them, wariness in her eyes.

Tristan grimaced, trying to ignore the persistent discomfort across his skin. "He's calling me so shy I push everyone away from me. It's not like that but he can't see it. There's... sex, and then there's not sex, like it's a choice. I'm ace."

"Oh." Realization dawned in Susannah's expression before she scowled, directing it towards Aran. "Not everyone has to enjoy sex. Shit, I thought that was

173

something you'd know after six thou—six years exploring every corner of Europe. It isn't binary."

She backtracked, cutting herself short as an elderly woman passed by them with a wheeled walker and a middle-aged man that could have been the woman's son. "How do you sign for bastard in Greek?"

Aran cast her a faintly bemused look and shrugged. Tristan shifted from one foot to the other, resisting the urge to scratch at the itch. It would feel like fire later, if he resisted the change but for now it was bearable, just. "There isn't one, or he doesn't know Greek sign language very well. We—I can go longer with your mom if I let Aran borrow my identity for the night."

Susannah made a face, eyeing Aran narrowly for a moment. "A few weeks ago, I would have said a flat out no to that idea. Now, Christ, what's happening to me to make me consider that a good suggestion?"

She swore under her breath, striding for the elevator. "Better make this worth it then. This is just a little meet the parents evening before we throw ourselves into hell again."

You chose her. Aran signed, barely keeping the bemusement from his expression.

Tristan gritted his teeth, half tempted to flip his brother the bird as he jogged a step or two after Susannah. "Wait."

"Yeah?" Susannah paused, one hand on the elevator button before she dropped it back to her side. "It's agreed, isn't it? Aran's going to take your place as my boyfriend for the night."

"Is that really what you want?" Tristan stepped aside as the elevator doors opened and a mother with a wailing child and a phone in her other hand staggered out, her expression harried.

"Honestly, no." Susannah scuffed a runner across the thin carpet in front of the open elevator door, toeing at a particularly worn patch as she looked down. "No one said how he's going to keep food down and my parents are going to expect him to eat something without throwing up. That's not even taking into account the bit where he's mute. There's no conversation he can have without you translating for him. My parents don't know sign language."

She sighed, twisting a leather bracelet around her wrist. "Maybe if I didn't know who you were—I could pretend a little better. Now... I know too much to lie convincingly. And Aran's kind of... uhm, indiscrete. My parents know a little about you but the picture I gave them was the exact opposite of your brother."

Subtlety had never been Aran's strong point, Tristan stepped into the elevator, touching the button to hold the door for Susannah. "We could skip, maybe? Nights are going to be a problem for me, but you could blow the evening off."

She sighed and sneezed, wiping her nose on her jacket sleeve. "Wish I could. It'd be nice not to do what they expected of me for once but..."

Susannah trailed off. "It feels like I'm just as trapped by family as Aran is, sometimes. That's why I wanted to see the Pioneer Square tunnels so badly. They're underground but the exploring will be a nice distraction from family shit, for a little while."

It wasn't a long ride down to the apartment lobby. Tristan watched the numbers descend from three to main before stepping out of the elevator. "I still can't go. An otter at night isn't going to be much use to you as a boyfriend or guide around them."

"Unless it was daylight and we slipped away from the ghost tour." Susannah said.

It was a possibility but an unlikely one. Tristan shoved his hands into his jacket pockets wincing at the little flare of pain that came from the action. "Maybe. I'd feel happier if it was after hours and if Aran went with you though."

"Never venture into cenotes alone, never wander into unknown tunnels without a buddy." Susannah said dryly. "Fine, that's the first lesson I learned from diving Port Royal's ruins. I'll ask him later if we're planning the trek for tonight."

She put a cautious hand on his arm, dropping it when Tristan flinched away. "Maybe we'll find an answer to both our questions down there. How to break your curse if Martin won't do it. And a few improbable genealogical answers for me."

"Why improbable?" Tristan asked.

Susannah snorted, flipping her hair over her shoulder. "Because as far as I know, my family's been Jamaican for a while. British before that. No one ever lived in Washington state until now."

"And you think you'll find them in Pioneer Square?" Tristan gave her an askance look, folding his arms over his chest.

"Hell, no. The trip down there is just an excuse to ask mythological questions to Aran." Susannah said.

She quieted, a flicker of worry crossing her face as Tristan shifted from one foot to the other. "And you really need to go."

He had to. Did he want to? Not really. Tristan forced an attempt at a smile, wishing for anything but this right now. "Bad things happen if I try to fight changing. It hurts to resist it."

"Oh." Susannah bit down on her lower lip and looked away from him. "We'll solve this, figure out my family stuff and whatever deal Aran has with that bookstore owner. I promise."

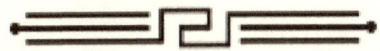

Her promise echoed in his thoughts, made more special by being meant honestly. Aran couldn't have said the same if whatever he claimed about the Styx was more than a story. She hadn't been forced to promise him anything, not like his brother.

Tristan hesitated at the water's edge, looking back at her standing a few feet beyond him. Susannah looked anxious, hands twisting in the hem of her shirt as she watched. He pulled the t-shirt off, discarding it with less care than he would have otherwise and waded out deeper into the water.

He went to his knees with a gasp, taking as much of a breath as he could before diving beneath the water. Only when he was beneath it, not caught between land and ocean did the tight, itchy feeling crawling over his skin recede. When he resurfaced again, dinner clutched between his paws, it was in otter form once more.

TWENTY

Susannah

Susannah dashed wetness away from her cheeks and gathered Tristan's abandoned t-shirt and jeans into a tidy package. The wind picked up, teasing a few loose strands of hair around her face as she turned away from the water lapping at the edge of the beach. Hearing about Tristan's curse was one thing, seeing it was another. He'd barely been able to stand by the end, sinking to his knees in the Pacific Ocean.

This time she'd forced herself not to dive after him. The water off of Alki beach was too shallow for diving, this close to land for her. For an otter on the other hand, it was deep enough. Susannah swallowed, sitting down on the sand with her legs drawn up to her chest as

Tristan surfaced again. Long, slender built and as unlike his human form as it could get.

She started, blinking rapidly as the hand rested on her shoulder and pulled away. "Wha—oh, hi. Where'd you come from?"

Aran sighed, taking a seat next to her on the red and white checked blanket a tourist had forgotten. He held his notebook out for her to read. *I was already here, just taking a moment to keep my strength up.*

Susannah accepted the coil bound book, reluctantly tracing the inked lines of Aran's words. "I still don't know how that works. What *are* you, exactly?"

Aran made a face, brushing a hand across the base of his throat as he looked towards the water as his brother surfaced with a fish clutched belly side up in his mouth before the otter floated contentedly in the water. Susannah handed the notebook back, watching Aran write on the page below his previous answer.

He capped the pen, tapping it against the inside of his wrist. *If you're looking for something more than demigod, I don't have an answer to your question. A spirit tied to the water, maybe? All I know of myself is that I can't go far from it without suffering for the attempt.*

"Sorry." Susannah kicked a runner off and retrieved it, picking at the knot tied in the shoelace.

Don't be. Aran wrote his answer on a fresh sheet of paper, half his attention still on the water. *I would show you but there is some… danger in it. Lyra stole a notebook from Martin, and she's been watching over you and Tristan for several weeks now.*

He tucked a strand of dark hair behind one ear, looking older and wearier than he appeared to be. *Martin… is my old master. I should have seen it sooner, but I was so concerned with you two that I didn't. Only Pos—he could have put that kind of curse on my brother. A mortal witch doesn't have that power. They're only psychics.*

Susannah opened her mouth and closed it, torn between outrage and gratitude for having someone spying on her. She changed the subject with a shudder, seeing the bleak look in Aran's eyes. "Explains the thought about this turning into a war. How the fuck are we supposed to fight a god?"

You can't. The tip of Aran's pen dug deep, nearly tearing the paper as he wrote.

Susannah stilled his hand, fear souring in her mouth. "Neither can you if you were Poseidon's slave. What can he make you do if that's a thing he's capable of?"

Aran shook his head, glancing away.

Silence for a few minutes was fine with her. Susannah scraped a handful of sand into a small pile in front of her and kicked at it, scattering the grains. "It's not that important but I chose to blow off a meet the parents date to sit on the beach tonight. Tristan said he was kind of willing to show me around Pioneer Square but only during the day. He thought it would be safer if you went with me."

Now? Aran's brow furrowed as he looked down his notebook. *You're certain?*

She had been but that had been before dusk had fallen and she'd seen Tristan's change from her boyfriend to an otter. "Honestly, I don't know but I can't go back home. My parents are trying to force me into their idea of a good daughter. Nursing school is their plan, not mine. They only dropped to something they think is lower because I fought them on medical school. I haven't been able to make my own decisions for years, feels like."

All right. Aran doodled a head and the front legs of a horse in the margins of the book, mouth thinning before he scribbled the little creature out. *Don't move. I'll be back soon.*

She had nowhere to go. Susannah drew back, watching as Aran climbed to his feet and shifted form. Unlike Tristan's change, his brother's was smoother, more controlled. The light was similar, but it didn't wash over Aran's body and obscure him as much as wash through him, fading the older shapeshifter around his edges until the owl was left in his place.

He took off on silent wings as she watched until he was out of sight. Tristan emerged a few moments from the water a few minutes later, chittering something incomprehensible. Susannah managed a weak snicker at that, offering her hand to him to sniff. "Can't imagine that's very fun. Your brother's an owl. You aren't. You stayed away because you didn't want to end up his lunch."

Tristan sneezed, resting a small head on her hip and curled up in a ball beneath the abandoned picnic blanket. Susannah rolled her eyes in exasperation and watched as the clouds drifted across the nearly full moon overhead. Whatever Aran's plans were, she hoped he would be quick about it.

The owl returned before dropping something onto the blanket next to her. Susannah reached for the sheath, pulling the sword out to reveal an inch or two of steel before she drew away from it. "You own a katana?"

Aran landed on the quilt, shifting back to human shape moments before he slid the weapon safely out of sight again.

182

"I'll take that as a yes." Susannah said awkwardly. "It—she's pretty?"

Why they'd need a sword just to wander around Pioneer Square's hidden tunnels was a bit beyond her. The worst they'd encounter was a few piles of rubble or rats. Unpleasant, maybe but nothing that needed a weapon to deal with. Susannah sighed, reluctantly encouraging Tristan out from beneath the red and white checked blanket. He nipped at her fingers, barely drawing blood and stood on his haunches, impatiently climbing her shirt sleeve to settle over her shoulder.

Susannah groaned, trying not to jostle her boyfriend too much as Aran managed a choked, thin snicker at Tristan's decision to lay over her collarbone. "I'll give you one for persistence. And apparently understanding every word I say. You aren't going to let me do this alone, are you?"

Tristan's little chirp as he braced himself there, paws digging into the black cotton of her shirt seemed to mean yes. Susannah let out an exasperated sigh and gave him a brief pet over the head. "Fine. Just don't fall off. I'd hate to explain to your parents I lost you below ground."

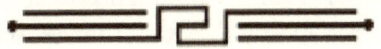

She was regretting it forty-five minutes later. Tristan might weigh a lot less in otter form but he was still a burden against her shoulders and neck, perched awkwardly across them. A small knapsack would have made his weight easier to bear. Susannah slowed, bracing herself on the nearby brick wall, squinting into the darkness of the tunnel. "Aran. Aran?"

Her voice echoed oddly against the dusty stone, and she swallowed, wishing that she could see the sky overhead instead of enclosed brick. Whatever else the place had been before it was sealed off, it didn't feel like a place for the living right now.

Tristan chirped anxiously, nearly slipping from his perch before he seized a lock of hair in his mouth and *tugged*. Susannah stilled him and set her boyfriend on the ground in front of her. "You and me both, to be honest."

She could barely see five feet in front of her, everything beyond that, lost into the darkness. "Aran!"

There was nothing wrong with his hearing, just his voice. If she called for him, he had to answer, unless he was too far away to hear her. "C'mon, where are you?"

Susannah's call echoed faintly in the distance, bouncing off century old brick and stone. Aran snarled softly, grip tightening on the sword he wore at his waist.

Seattle's mostly forgotten tunnels weren't places meant for humans, at least not the routes unmapped by local tour guides. Aran glanced away, letting his eyes adjust to the near blackness of the tunnel. This wasn't his world and it had more in common with Agesander's realm than his former master's but the similarity between a tunnel and the underworld would be enough to satisfy a shade.

He trailed a hand over the rough brickwork, finding the thread or two of moisture dripping down the wall before he dropped the hand back to his side. That bit of water was too thin, too weak for him to use and it was poor form to try drowning a dead man. James Gray's shade wouldn't appreciate the attempt, even if it could have brought him to his knees. Fire or sunlight was another story but that power beyond his ability. Water was his element, not its opposite.

Aran gritted his teeth, closing his hand around the blade's edge hard enough to draw blood from his palm. The slash ached, feeling like fire as he let blood splatter against the hardpacked dirt floor of the tunnel. Black against black was impossible even for him to see but that wasn't the point of the sacrifice. *I don't know the words. My... master never needed them, but I know the rite to call a shade. I need your advice.*

The language didn't matter as much as the intent here. He could have written his words out and burned them, to get a similar effect. Signing his plea was as good as spoken for what he wanted.

"Blood will be enough." James stepped through the narrow gap of a branching path, appearing from nowhere like the shadow he was. "Bread and sausage would have been preferred but I doubt such would have occurred to you. I'm told you don't need sustenance in the way a mortal does."

It hadn't. Aran made a face, sheathing the katana. *I don't. I do need your advice, Captain.*

Signing his words was easier when he didn't have a weapon in his hands. *My brother's friend shares your name, and your... appearance. You could be brother and sister...*

185

The shade had the same sandy blond hair and something in the set of his mouth or his eyes had been echoed in his descendent.

James gave him a brief, troubled look. "My sister died over two hundred years ago, she's at peace. I guided her to the ferryman myself. She cannot be the same woman."

See for yourself tonight. Aran said dryly. *The girl even has my leash. I'd have to suffer drinking from the Lethe to forget what that pendant looked like. Little amethyst without a setting.*

"I may have to, if she's kin." James's voice was bland. "Ask your questions and let me go. You have three of them, no more than that."

Three, one for the maiden, mother and crone. Or for the fates, depending on the telling. Aran hesitated, choosing his words carefully. The shade wasn't obligated to answer them truthfully, just give an answer after a fashion. James could lie, unlike the ordinary shadows of Agesander's realm. *I drowned someone's daughter the summer before, trying to protect my brother. At the time I thought she was a witch's child but now it seems... not. His curse was meant for me, but I deflected it onto the pup. Since then...*

"He's been unable to control his changing, trapped at dusk." James's brows furrowed before he raked a hand through shoulder length hair. "Don't ask me how I know that. I couldn't say even if I wanted to, and it would be a waste of your questions. It's your life, or your brother's if you want to break the curse. I cannot say more than that."

He'd expected as much. Aran sighed, briefly touching the base of his throat out of habit. *And the woman who took my voice?*

James grimaced, scuffing a modern combat boot across the ground and even in the darkness of the tunnel he had no shadow, or the scent of a living man. "I'm afraid I can't say directly but the affairs of... his brother aren't the sort of affairs Hades concerns himself much."

That seed of information was disappointing but more than he'd expected of the ghost. Aran flexed his fingers, wincing a little at the minor ache in the joints. *Echo is involved, somehow. But you're forbidden from telling me.*

"Quite." James ducked his head in assent, mouth thinning in distaste. "I would, willingly but I lost my life over two hundred years ago—the rules that govern the dead and your kind are different from mortals."

That much he hadn't needed to be told. Spirit kind and shadows were the light and dark of the same coin. He had one last question left to use. Wasting it on a trivial inquiry wouldn't do anyone any good.

There was only one thing he could ask and get a sure answer on, absent James's geas. *Will you be willing to help?*

"Within what's permitted of me, yes." James looked away, seeming untroubled by the lack of light within the tunnel. "If that means playing psychopomp for your brother and his fiancée or aiding you with your war, I will, but you must know I cannot tolerate daylight. Any action against your master will have to be at dark."

I understand. Aran said.

He wrinkled his nose at the faintest hint of bitterness and rot that reached him, one hand dropping to the sword at his waist. There was more than dust and memories in these tunnels and he'd wasted enough time in conversation with a shade even if it had been a necessity.

James's eyes narrowed as he pulled the handgun from the waistband of his jeans. "I'll forgive the summoning, you called me unwillingly from the crossroads for advice, but not abandoning my granddaughter to a vrykolakas. If she dies here, it's on your head, *Amyntas*."

The name again, centuries after abandoning it. Aran bit back on the soft snarl that threatened and broke into a run back the way he'd come. James was at his side, step uncanny in its silence, and his ability to keep pace with him. A human would have been winded, stumbled or misstepped, a shade rarely did any of that.

He reacted without thinking, putting himself between the long worm like creature and the two cowering in the shattered remains of a shop doorway. The lettering above the broken glass of the nearby window was as clear as they day they had been painted, now lost.

Susannah was whimpering, holding too tightly onto Tristan as he lay against her shoulder, small ears flat against his head and fur puffed with fear of his own. Neither of them had seen one of the slug like vampire things before.

It was an unpleasantly familiar memory for him. Aran snarled softly, dropping into a crouch as the thing reared overhead, circular mouth lined with too many teeth for anyone's comfort. The things rarely ate whole human flesh or drank blood, but they did favor the livers of their meals above all else.

He blurred, narrowly missing the creature's bite as he unsheathed the sword and slashed at its unguarded side. The blade bit deep, wrenching from his hands as it twisted away from him. Aran cursed silently, trying to stay one move ahead of it as it writhed. The one good thing about Mariko's father's weapon was that it had been crafted better than any Japanese smith could have made it, and the closest thing to real magic woven into its steel. It would survive the abuse and the vampire beast's blood.

The vyrkolakas shrieked and the sound had him gritting his teeth, resisting the urge to wince or stumble back a step at the thin, nearly high pitched teakettle sound it made at being wounded.

Susannah was visible out of the corner of his eye, trying desperately to protect her ears, and huddle deeper into the safety of the abandoned shop, with Tristan curled up in her lap.

Blood splattered as he went down, flat out on his stomach as it did a thing unlike a normal worm, inched itself up into an arch and twisted around upon itself, fleeing down the tunnel to wherever its nest or den was. The sword still half buried in its side. Aran groaned, trying not to wince at the burning across his back. The vykolakas's blood was more acid than anything human in origin, it stung, eating through the wash abused cotton t-shirt. If he was lucky, it would only scar. If not, he was in for another drawn out, painful death again.

The only mystery was its sudden flight—the beasts rarely abandoned their prey unless it was powdered bone and dust. Aran sucked in a pained breath and climbed stiffly to his feet, looking towards James. *Your doing?*

James's arm was extended, a handgun gripped in it before he shook his head, lowering the gun and placing the safety back on. It was tucked out of sight, covered by his shirt. "Not this time. I was prepared to, yes. But..."

He trailed off, grimacing. "It must have smelled fire."

Fire? There had been none which had been an oversight on their part, but no one had expected one of the slug like beasts to hunt tonight. Aran went still, striding over to the open space where there had been a door once. Susannah was still crouched in her corner, eyes wide and blank with shock, dust streaked as she held a little ball of fire cupped between both hands.

Aran drew back and forced himself to kneel, folding Susannah's hand over the flame. It went out, leaving unburned skin behind. *Translate for me?*

James hadn't left his side though his expression was unhappy. "Of course. But you must know I've about as much fondness for fire as that beast did."

Aran dismissed half of the remark off hand. It wasn't his business to know what a shade liked or not. Just what Susannah had accomplished. *How did you call fire to hand? Only a witch could have done that.*

There was a pause as James spoke his words before Susannah answered him, voice shaking. "I don't know. All I remember is you fighting... whatever the fuck that thing was. Then it was doing its nails on chalkboard sound and..."

She trailed off, reaching up to touch her ear with a small whimper. Her fingertips came away stained with blood. "Crap."

Tristan chirped something that sounded somewhere between irate and fearful as he skittered out of whatever place he had been hiding within. Aran made a face and gestured pointedly back the way they'd come. Susannah's little mystery could wait for another day—or they could wait for James to answer it, if he was of half a mind to. Now, it wasn't wise to stay longer than necessary.

The vampire thing had smelled like a female, and it wasn't certain if she had larvae nearby.

Like it or not, the house was safer than anywhere else in Seattle, in spite of the danger his former master was to them. *We go home, talk there in safety.*

TWENTY-ONE

Susannah

Her hand was still trembling when she lifted it to eye level. Susannah swallowed, wrapping both around the coffee mug of tea that Aran placed before her. Claustrophobia and darkness had never bothered her until the slug... thing had come out of nowhere. Too many teeth and slime for comfort. Slugs weren't supposed to have teeth, were they? Nothing that looked like out of a bad horror movie.

She squeezed her eyes shut tight and took a sip of the tea, grateful for the warmth, more than the taste. Aran's tea was better than his coffee but she normally avoided anything but coffee. Tea just looked like murky yellow piss with black flecks floating in it to her. "That... that happened."

The question of Aran's new 'friend' could wait until her breathing and hand steadied. If they ever did.

Aran brushed a hand over her wrist, gently forcing the mug down to the tabletop before the hot beverage could spill over the edge of the cup. Susannah shuddered, wrapping her arms around her body. "Supernatural's fine in the abstract but I don't want to know what that thing was. Why the fuck was it living in Seattle's sewer system?"

She looked away, glancing towards the stranger at the table. With Tristan's parents out, it was just the three of them in the kitchen. Four, as soon as the sun rose again. Tristan still had a couple hours stuck in otter form until then. "And you came out of nowhere, surprisingly quickly. It was... too convenient a rescue."

He acknowledged her with a look of apology and a brief duck of his head. "It may have been, yes. But your brother in law had a few questions for me. I was the only one he could find on such short notice. He needed a soldier and information only I could give him."

Susannah winced, tasting blood as she bit the inside of her cheek. "Ow. He's—Aran's not my brother-in-law. I'm dating Tristan, I'm not married to my boyfriend. And none of that tells me who you are, or your name."

By his accent alone, he was a Brit but that didn't tell her more about him than that. She buried her face in her hands, blocking out the light before she slumped in her chair, giving into his presence, if not the story yet. "Can we start over, please? Who the hell are you and why did you come here?"

194

"Aran was rather... insistent on my aid." He said it delicately, grimacing a little. "As for my name. James Gray."

Gray. Just like her own. It was far from an uncommon last name but the familiarity of it had her sitting up and glaring at him. "It's one thing to make up a name, I'm pretty sure Aran does it all the time, it's another to use mine and expect me to believe it."

"Then I apologize once more." He looked down at the plate, tracing an invisible pattern on its surface. "I was no less... surprised than you are but I didn't think any of my family had survived over the years. Much less look so much like my sister had."

Susannah opened her mouth and closed it again, scraping the chair against the linoleum as she pushed away from the table.

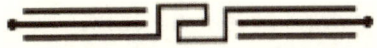

Aran found her sitting on the back step, watching a few silvery white moths fluttering around the yellow light of the rental house's lone porchlight. Susannah sighed, glancing in his direction. "Shapeshifters, gods and god knows what else out there. This isn't my world. At least not the one I thought I knew. And now I have a random stranger trying to imply he's family. Sometimes..."

She trailed off, rubbing at her eyes where the headache was beginning to form behind them. "I'm never going to go back to how things were before, am I?"

Aran's mouth thinned for a moment, and he held a single sheet of paper out for her to read.

Unfortunately, no. I'm not sure any of us can. Like it or not, you're a soldier now.

"Some soldier." Susannah snorted. "The biggest fight I was in was a few hours ago and I still can't get that thing out of my head. If I remember correctly, you did most of the fighting. I hid and somehow managed to hold a ball of fire in my hands without getting burned by it."

She looked down at her hands, chewing on her lower lip at the memory. The soft orange glow had been warm without burning, no blistering to show she had held an open flame for a few minutes.

Aran's hand slipped over hers, briefly reassuring before he released it. Susannah made a face, watching as one of the moths wandered too close to the light and fell to the ground with singed wings, a bit of smoke rising from its body. "Can I?"

Tristan's brother must have anticipated her unspoken question because he handed the paper over, the words neatly written below the answer he'd crossed out with ballpoint pen. *It may not last, whatever it was. If that's what you're worried about.*

"Good." Susannah said. "I don't want it."

She quieted, scuffing a foot across the cracked pavement at the base of the porch steps. "It's still convenient how—how James chose now to show up and help."

Aran looked down, bracing the paper on his lap as he wrote again. *He didn't choose it, I called him here. It's a Greek funerary rite and I don't regret the act.*

"Funerary...." Susannah swallowed back on unease, grip tightening on the hem of her t-shirt. "What's the implication with that one?"

"It means I died two hundred and fifty years ago." James's voice sounded behind them, from where he leaned against the doorframe into the house. "Aran Gallagher summoned a ghost, so to speak."

"I want to call bullshit, but I can't." Susannah flushed as her voice came out as a timid squeak. That really wasn't her at all. "Not after everything else I've learned this summer."

She lifted her hand, briefly touching the amethyst pendent at the base of her throat for reassurance. And squeaked, drawing back as James suddenly appeared in front of her, never having appeared to edge past her on the occupied step. "Jesus! Okay, okay, ghost thing is real."

He gave her a bland look and held a hand out for the little amethyst stone. "May I?"

Susannah swallowed again, trying not to acknowledge the twisting knot of discomfort in her stomach at what her eyes were telling her. James looked like solid flesh and blood to her but there was no warmth to his skin, or substance to his touch as they made brief contact with each other. "Sure."

James let the pendent drop back to the base of Susannah's neck. His expression was impossible for her to read and she didn't even try, covering the little stone with her hand. It still felt cool, colder than it should have been for the time she'd worn it. Whether that was James's touch or the lack of it remained to be seen but it still sent a shiver down her spine.

The discussion had drifted from the kitchen into the weed choked backyard. Aran still seated next to her on the porch steps, James standing opposite her, looking softer around the edges than he had a few minutes before. The only one missing from their little war party was

Tristan and she had no idea when he'd be able to shift back to human form.

Dawn was just on the horizon, but she wasn't sure what constituted daylight enough to give him back his natural shape. James by contrast was watching the same sky with just the faintest look of unease in his eyes.

Aran signed something and James shook his head, expression clearing. "No, but it's been years since I've seen dawn and even if you let me borrow a coat, I would still burn under the sun's light. My help is best served at nightfall, or just after it. Never before."

Aran grimaced, gesturing something else and pointed at the sky.

James followed the sweep of Aran's hand before he took a step away from them. "Not even your protection could save my, ah, life if I were to try. I am sorry for that, but it won't be long again, before we can regroup. Just a day of your time."

As long as it was just a day. James had only called her a soldier, she was leaving the real battle plan to the two men. Susannah nodded, fidgeting with a stray thread in one knee of her jeans. "Can we count on... your parents?"

Aran glanced at her, mouth thinning in distaste.

Susannah twisted the end of her plait between her fingers, not needing the sign language to understand that message. "That's a no, I guess. So it's down to us, and Tristan. Whenever we decide to deal with Poseidon."

No one had mentioned the mutually exclusive situation they'd found themselves in. Tristan couldn't do nights, James for whatever reason, was incapable of seeing daylight. Her boyfriend's curse wasn't broken yet.

TWENTY-TWO

Tristan

Tristan pulled the t-shirt on over his head, grabbing a jacket from the pile of laundry at the bottom of his closet. He'd listened to a little of the conversation before getting a couple hours much needed sleep, curled up beneath a corner of the ratty pillowcase he'd used as an otter sized coverlet.

The hours between creeping through Pioneer Square's tunnels, the slug thing and the three—four of them staggering back home before dawn were too sharp edged in his memory, too much crystal clear. Susannah had been soot streaked and smelling of ash by the end.

Her scent was fainter in the kitchen, stronger by the still ajar back door. Tristan poured a glass of tepid water from the sink and took a swallow of it with a grimace before leaving it in the sink. There were three people in the backyard. Susannah, his brother and an unfamiliar newcomer but only two of them had scents. Tristan snarled softly, briefly baring his teeth at the disquieting lack before he covered the reaction. The only other time he'd smelled something like that before, had been when he had been five. The college student that had babysat him for a night had been just as dead as the newcomer was. "Susannah?"

She turned to look at him, blonde hair catching the thin sunlight with a brief flash of gold before she stood. "We were just trying to figure out what to do next. Well, it was mostly me and James talking. Aran didn't really say much I could figure out."

Susannah's attempt at a smile was weak. "Jamie translated for him. I just filled in the blanks in that conversation. At least that was before it turned out he was a dead guy walking. And... family, apparently. Same last name. Doesn't matter, he went back to wherever he calls home for the night—day, god, whichever works for his schedule."

"James." The newcomer corrected her abruptly. "And I understand your... uncertainty but don't speak like I'm no longer within hearing while still present."

"Right." Susannah said. "James. Erm, meet Tristan. My boyfriend."

That was about as awkward an introduction as things could get. Tristan shoved his hands into his jacket pockets. "Fill me in later. If we've got a plan for dealing with Poseidon—I'm still not clear on it."

"Yeah, me too." Susannah dared a look over her shoulder towards Aran and James. "Seems like it's more their area than ours anyway. We're... just civilians playing at being soldiers here."

The only thing that could be said was that she was right, they were just pretending to be something they weren't, just to impress his brother. Tristan grimaced, feeling grateful when Susannah produced the keys to his car from her jacket pocket. At least someone was around to keep track of the things when he was otherwise occupied at night.

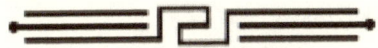

Susannah's mother smelled of antiseptic and lavender hand soap. Tristan looked away, covering the sneeze that threatened with his shirt sleeve. It figured that Janice Gray was a doctor and a germaphobe. The whole house smelled of bleach and artificially scented cleaning agents. She was also regarding him with a little furrow between her brows, mouth thinning as she took in the black jacket and untied-back hair.

Susannah's hand slipped over his, trying to be reassuring before she dropped it. "Mom, meet Tristan. Tristan, my mom."

"Nice to meet you." Tristan offered his hand to Susannah's mother, mouth going dry as she clasped it, studying the webbing between his fingers. The brief look of unhappiness in Janice's eyes replaced with curiosity.

Susannah saved him from further 'examination' by clearing her throat. "That's Italian, right? Your own or storebought?"

"Storebought." Janice drew back, barely hiding the disappointment in her expression. "Come into the living room, please."

Storebought was fine with him. Tristan exchanged a look with Susannah, letting her pass him. She knew her mother better than she did, and the thin set of Susannah's mouth hinted at unhappiness of her own. They hadn't given Janice much notice, so the pre-packaged stuff was fine with him. Better than that even, given how often he'd had to improvise from things found from the foodbank.

"Susannah's told me so little about you." Janice said, sitting down on the cream-colored leather couch.

With good reason, as far as he was concerned. Tristan grimaced, seeing the interview for what it was. Janice would never be satisfied with vague answers and deflections. She was too much the doctor for that but she wouldn't believe the truth either, if faced with it. "She just wanted to respect my privacy, I guess. Things are kind of... complicated at home but I'll give you the same story I told Susannah when we met. Grew up around here, dropped out of college to help my family. It's boring, really."

"I see." Janice looked disappointed, looking towards the door into the hallway. "Susannah, do you mind fetching the coffee and a cookie or two?"

"I'm not your—" Susannah bristled and cut herself off midsentence, stalking out of the living room. "Fine."

Janice rubbed a hand across her eyes, looking older and more tired than she was. "You see what we have to put up with? All we want is for her to have a good job and more of an opportunity than what was available in Kingston. She's still fighting us over it."

Us had to be Susannah's parents. Tristan made a face, hastily putting the paperback down on the coffee table. "She loved Jamaica..."

In a way he'd only ever seen in his brother when Aran talked about the Aegean. The sea had been his brother's home in a way he couldn't understand. Not even Aran seemed to have the words for it, only that it was. He cleared his throat, looking down at the paperback again. "I know that cover."

Books were a safe subject, safer than discussing the prospect of gods, or monsters in Pioneer Square.

Janice blinked, running a hand over the worn pages. "I didn't think very many people had heard of the book."

Tristan snorted, leaning back against the couch now that the subject had shifted towards something a little less personal. "Just luck I guess. I got bored of the big names and went a lot smaller than that. Martin Carpenter's one of the last independent bookstores in Seattle. Likes supporting new writers or something. I just didn't think you'd enjoy a Soviet werewolf story much."

The irony wasn't lost on him. A shapeshifter discussing fictional werewolves with his girlfriend's mother but at least it was letting him control the conversation more than he had, a few minutes ago. "Wasn't bad, I just thought it was a bit... brutal when my brother loaned me a copy. Didn't really like the parents or the kids much, to be honest."

"Really?" Janice was looking at him with something more like open curiosity in her eyes.

Tristan pulled the book out from under her hand, studying the pair depicted on the front. "I got through it at least but I'm mixed on feelings for the book. Some parts..."

He shook his head. "They just struck a little too close to home for comfort."

They were interrupted by Susannah's reappearance with chocolate chip cookies and the coffee balanced on a tray before she set it down on the coffee table. Janice looked at her disapprovingly. "Tristan is a guest. Shouldn't you...?"

Susannah sighed and poured some of the steaming drink into a mug. "Want coffee?"

Janice's expression could have melted steel at her daughter's question. Tristan winced, shaking his head. "Thanks, but no."

The last thing he needed was to be a source of conflict between mother and daughter. "We ended up talking about books."

As if that was any better or relevant to an oncoming war with Poseidon. Susannah sipped at the drink he'd declined, setting it down on a coaster. "I heard a little. Which one?"

Tristan flipped it to its front cover, showing the couple standing on the train station platform and the hammer and sickle printed beneath the title. "The werewolf one, apparently."

"Oh." Susannah's interest seemed to evaporate just like that as she stirred a teaspoon aimlessly through the still black liquid. "Well, it's better than interrogating Tristan about everything else in his life, I guess."

"Susannah." Janice's voice was sharper than it had been a few minutes ago.

Susannah rolled her eyes and stood, striding for the living room door. The front door slammed behind her a second or two later. Tristan sighed, giving Janice Gray an apologetic look. "Maybe she just got up on the wrong side of the bed lately. I'll talk to her. And I'm... sorry."

Janice managed a wistful smile at his apology. "Don't be sorry. That you made an effort to apologize tells me all I need to know about you. You're a good one, if nothing else. Maybe if we're lucky, you'll be able to get her to see some sort of reason here."

Maybe, maybe not but he wasn't going to put all his trust in luck right now. There was only one person better at holding a grudge as his parents or his brother's old master, and that was Aran. "I'll talk to her."

What else could he do?

Susannah sat on the front step, head resting against the white picket railing of the porch before Tristan joined her there. "What's this really about? I think you mentioned feeling trapped by your parents before but seeing it..."

He trailed off, watching as a car rolled through the intersection at the end of the street and turned the corner out of sight.

Susannah sighed, playing absently with her necklace. "I've told you everything I could. There's nothing else to do about that. As soon as summer ends, I'll be applying for a hold on my place and going into nursing school the year afterwards."

"What do you really want to do?" Tristan asked.

She sagged, toeing her runner against the sidewalk at the base of the porch. "Marine shit. I can't draw a line to save my life, but I love being out on the water. Or in it."

Susannah cracked a bleak, nearly brittle smile at her own words. "Guess I share that with your brother, huh. C'mon."

She stood, helping Tristan to his feet. "We have a war and a god to fight. Might as well do what Jamie—James says we are now. Like he said, we're soldiers whether we like it or not."

"Yeah." Tristan said.

It went unsaid but he was hoping wherever Aran was, whatever his brother's unmentioned plans were—that he would be safe doing it. They'd all seen too much lately since everything had begun. "Let's go."

TWENTY-THREE
Aran

Aran pushed the bookshop door open, suppressing the urge to sneeze. The dust and sickly perfume scent was no better than it had been before, overlaying something unpleasantly metallic. It took a moment for him to identify the reek. Aran dropped to one knee before a puddle of red, teasing it between his fingers before he wiped his hand on his jeans leg. Blood, and no more than an hour or two old. Too much for anyone to lose and live.

He found the body curled onto her side; fear etched into her expression. Aran drew back wary and alert for danger. Eva shouldn't have been in any danger from her husband but the blood staining her blouse told a different story. Someone, or Martin himself had shot her in the chest before leaving her corpse untended.

The disrespect in the deliberate act had him hissing low under his breath as he forced a coin between her teeth. No woman or her shade should have been stranded on the banks of the river. A pity he only had a voice in Poseidon's realm. It would have been nice to address Martin for his crime aloud. *You tried to have me drowned. That's not something I'll forgive, no more than your attempt at binding me a year ago.*

Martin's chuckle was cool, humorless as he lifted a hand in a mocking gesture. "And I think you know me. Or you did once."

Aran froze, staring at the man in disbelief. Echo stood behind Martin's shoulder, a little smirk playing across her lips. *You...*

Echo only answered to one, and he was supposed to be imprisoned. Her lover—his daughter had been dead for nearly eight thousand years. He forced the fear away, signing with a shaking hand. *My daughter never had any love for you, it was Poseidon she wanted and a chance at being a goddess. He had no interest in giving that gift to her, she—we were playthings to a god.*

Echo scowled, signing in turn. *You may have been. I wasn't. And I'll never forgive you for her death.*

She was as stubborn as she was misguided but there was no reasoning with someone who was so lost in what she wanted to see. Aran opened his mouth and closed it, looking from Martin to Echo and back again. Fear and running from a fight weren't things he had been made for but a little bit of much needed discretion was better than challenging a tormentor, or two of them and dying for it. He had a family to protect and the only way he knew was by fleeing, luring the pair away from Seattle. Even if it was at the cost of his own life.

He turned on one foot, darting for the bookstore door. The little bell overhead tinkled as he stepped through it. Tristan needed to know, Susannah as well. A fight with his former master was something he could handle. They would be unlikely to survive the same.

Echo had hurt him, but she was the petty threat in comparison to his former master. If she could be reasoned with, there was a chance she could be convinced to find her own path. As unlikely as that was.

The only hope he had of drawing the god away was as if he left but there was something he had to show Tristan and his brother's girlfriend first. He'd let his own past bury itself in the sixteen years since his departure all those years ago. For a time he'd been allowed to live, forget the pain and fury in the aftermath of his loss. That time had run out on him.

He ran into the barrier before he sensed it, one hand not quite reaching for the door handle that was in front of him. Aran dropped his hand back to his side, turning back to face Poseidon and Echo. *Eva's murder. Was it your doing, or Echo's?*

Poseidon never would have dirtied his hands with mortal blood if he could have helped it. The god had his pets to take care of that messy, unpleasant service. Like Echo, like... *him*, so long ago.

Poseidon shrugged, making the gesture stiff, something mimicked without understanding its meaning. "Does it matter? She's gone onto Charon and over the river now. Once you would have done my bidding without questioning it, Amyntas."

That name again, as if he'd never had anything but that. Aran drew back in disquiet, unable to find the words beyond the ones he could sign. *I was little more than a child in those days, skill with a sword aside. All I wanted to do was please you.*

A trite way of saying how easily the god could have pressed his will upon him and bade him act without regard for who might die in the act but the only words he had in English to describe it. *I had no free will while I was your slave.*

Poseidon's expression went shadowed, a brittle smile curving his lips. "I made you, boy. I could easily undo that and send you back to the dark."

That was always the risk, but he needed answers only the god could give him. Aran stepped way from the barrier, cursing it. Poseidon knew him too well even after several thousand years locked in a corner of Tartarus. A mortal could have run through the barrier without even feeling it. For him, it was like a sheet of crystal-clear glass or ice blocking his way. Invisible but impenetrable, beyond his power to break through the bookshop's warding on his own. *The girl. My brother's girlfriend. What is she? She smells like fire and ash but her love of water…*

"Is like yours." Poseidon's chuckle was faintly mocking as he folded his arms over the brown suit jacket. "Shall I make a guess that she threw fire at one of Echo's pets?"

Even a god couldn't have known that without asking. Aran swept his gaze between the pair standing in the open space between the checkout and the first of the bookshelves. There was no point in denying what

Susannah had done to the vampire like slug thing. *She's no witch. I'd have known if she was.*

Poseidon cast him a sardonic look, striding around him to place a hand on the door handle. "She wears a necklace you gifted to Captain Gray, one, if I'm not mistaken, was crafted by a blacksmith. Who do you know with the skills like that? Water is your element. What opposes it?"

Fire. Aran signed the word flatly, once again searching for a way past the god standing in the doorway and not finding it. If he was going to escape, it would have to somehow be through the barrier Poseidon had created. *Tristan and Susannah won't stop until you're imprisoned again.*

As for him, there was only one way out that he could see. Whether it was just carelessness or a deliberate attempt at baiting him didn't matter. It was still an out as the sky darkened outside the bookstore from calm, pale sunlight to a gray better suited to an oncoming storm.

He drew the edge of the pocket knife hard enough against his throat for dark blood to stain his front and the collar of his t-shirt. It burned like fire and went deeper than that as he sank to his knees, choking on his own blood. Aran rasped, vision going gray in front of him as he braced himself on one blood-streaked arm. Poseidon hadn't been forthcoming in who or what Susannah was but if she was as tied to the ocean as he was—it shouldn't have been possible. The mortal girl was human in all the ways that mattered.

Echo's kick to his side sent him to the floor, the gray clouding to black a few seconds later. Life, and light fading until he woke again in his natural form, beneath the waves of the Pacific Ocean.

TWENTY-FOUR
Tristan

The storm broke up instead of dumping buckets of water on their heads. Tristan glanced at the sky, relieved by pale gray clouds rather than the ominously black they had almost become. That didn't mean what they were planning was any less stupid but at least they wouldn't have to contend with bad weather on top of icy ocean water.

He'd stripped down to swim shorts and a t-shirt. Susannah was wearing the wetsuit, hair pulled back in a French braid. "Ready?"

"Yeah." Susannah held her board closer to her body as if it was a security blanket and set it reluctantly on the ground. "You?"

She was either braver than he was, or she had no imagination to speak of. Tristan swallowed, looking out across the water. "Hell, no. I grew up around here and I'm scared. Poseidon was fine in the abstract. Real, shit. I mean I did hear Aran's story and believed it then, but I was little. I thought I'd outgrown that crap."

"Try finding out that your cousin died during the American revolution." Susannah gave him a disillusioned look. "And I know he's closer to an uncle or whatever, but cousin doesn't make my head twitch thinking about it."

"Point, I guess." Tristan made a face, sweeping his gaze over the surf once more as the black horse stepped delicately through the water towards them. "That makes that easier, I guess. Just hope he remembers enough not to drown us. Kelpies are dangerous. Can you ride?"

Susannah chewed on her lower lip uncertainly. "About as well as you, which isn't much. I'm the surf girl, you're the otter here. And the last time I was tempted to piggyback your brother, you slapped me for it."

At least she was trying to lighten the mood a little even if what she described hadn't quite happened in the way she pictured it. Tristan took a cautious step towards the horse, murmuring soft, nonsense words in Welsh as he scrambled onto its back. Susannah ended up seated behind him, clinging tighter to his waist than she needed to. He shifted uncomfortably, wishing that there was a bridle or something to hold onto but all he had was dripping wet mane for security.

Aran's ears went flat against his skull, balking for a moment before moving into a full out run. Tristan swore, trying to adjust his balance and hold on while Susannah shrieked something worse in Spanish behind him. The salt water splashed around them and then closed over their heads.

The light changed with it and Susannah's grip eased a little around his waist as her panic. "How—how are we not...?"

"Drowning or crushed under the weight?" Tristan looked down, brushing a hand across Aran's neck. "I think he's... protecting us. Don't ask me how. This is more his world than ours."

"It's beautiful." Susannah's voice dropped, almost respectful. "I've always wanted to go to Athens but there was never any money for it until my parents got jobs here. Seeing something like it here. Where are we?"

Tristan shrugged, trying to take in the ruins more than answer Susannah's question. It was beautiful but felt more like a lonely ruin than anything habitable these days, even if the light through the water made it feel like the Aegean. "Best guess? Aran's home, maybe."

Susannah slipped off first, keeping one hand on the horse's back as she watched wide eyed. "Again, still beautiful. Any chance we can explore it?"

"I wouldn't chance it." Tristan looked uneasily up at the watery light overhead. There was more to Aran's power than his brother had let on previously. Stories could only tell so much and Aran had been keeping things very close to his chest. Seventeen years absence hadn't helped matters much either. "We don't really know where we are but wherever this is, there's still a lot of water overhead. Maybe that's on your bucket list but I don't want to experience decompression sickness, personally."

He couldn't explain it to himself but leaving Aran's side felt like a bad idea, whether that was a small, subtle warning that the kelpie was giving him, or just something known in the back of his thoughts, instinctive. I think as long as we're close to or touching him, we're safer."

Safer didn't mean safe but he was trying not to dwell on danger right now. He swung his leg off the horse's back, trying to estimate the limits of how far they could leave Aran's side before real damage could be done. One timid step and another before the salt sting in his mouth and nose started and he coughed, backing off hastily. "I'd guess no more than two or three yards before we start breathing in water. That's our little... uhm, bubble of safety. Shit knows what's going to happen when we get back to dry land."

Aran's horse shape shimmered, looking more like a play of light on water before it resolved into something human, still dressed in the white tunic. Something like human, anyway. Tristan hesitated, hearing Susannah's gasp behind him. "Yeah, he does that sometimes."

It was hard for him to look at and he'd seen the oddly insubstantial effect before. Aran's body see through, fading to nearly one with the water around them. "I told you he wasn't human."

"I know." Susannah swallowed, slipping her hand inside Tristan's. "But it's—it's seeing it for real."

"And he can hear you." Aran's voice was dry, a mix of Irish and Greek in the light baritone. "I'm not deaf."

He glanced down at himself with a sigh and the translucent effect faded, leaving solidity behind. "Better?"

"Better." Tristan bit back on his discomfort at the sound of Aran's question, a hard knot forming in the pit of his stomach. There had been only a few times when he'd heard the light baritone of his brother's voice. None or few of them had been in the past year—until now.

He sat gingerly on a fallen column, relieved to find his t-shirt and shorts as dry as they had been before the horse's wild run into the water. "If I make a guess you're talking because this place has something to do with it..."

"You would be right." Aran's mouth thinned, unhappily before he turned away. "Stay close. My protection for you only goes so far. How much do you remember of what I told you?"

Not as much as Aran was probably hoping for but some parts were still sharp in his memory. Tristan dragged his gaze away from a chipped mural of a horse team and a charioteer on one wall. "Bits, mostly. I remember knocking my cereal bowl over on the table and putting a cheerio in my nose. You had a trick with collecting the spilled milk back into the bowl before Mom could mop it up with a dishrag. I was five. Everything else, the teachers had me convinced your story was something I'd made up after reading Greek mythology too late into the night. They sent me to the principal's office for too creative an imagination."

"Humans." Aran said.

Susannah looked offended, holding a hand up at his disgust. "As the human girl here, I object to that comment."

"Are you?" Aran gave her a lingering look and shook his head. "I wonder sometimes but it doesn't matter. We'll figure that out later."

He trailed a hand over the cracked mural and dropped it back to his side. "There's no time for the full retelling and I wouldn't even if there was but there was a war a long time ago. I fought in it, serving as a soldier to Poseidon. I thought I was doing well by him but all he wanted of me was a slave. Alongside my wife and daughters."

The knot in his stomach only tightened further. Tristan squeezed his eyes shut for a moment, trying not to see the raw pain in Aran's expression. The sound of it couldn't be avoided though. Or the sight of the mural from his brother's point of view. It wasn't pretty now and the damage across the black tile horse's back could have been echoes of the scarring Aran still had marked on his back. "I'd... forgotten."

He drew back, picking up a rounded rock and threw it hard at the mural, shattering the tile where the black horse was in a spider's web. "When I did well, he occasionally let me sit in the hall with some of the other favored warriors. I lived for those days, until I couldn't. Pray you never find out what it's like to have your will taken from you and forced to your knees while he watches. He never did the beating himself; it was always someone else he thought was showing a little too much independence. I was his message to them. For centuries."

Even Susannah was looking green at that, sickly as she turned away and retched into a corner of the hall.

Tristan swallowed, trying and failing to find the words he wanted. An apology was too small and poor to say to the story Aran told him. "I thought Poseidon was supposed to be nice."

"Mythology doesn't get a lot right." Aran said. "And he was better than Zeus for treatment of his... pets. I was his once, I won't go back, even if it kills me."

He strode for the hall entrance, forcing Tristan and Susannah to keep up with him. The alternative was drowning or decompression sickness, staying close was preferred. There were horse bones tangled in among rotted hay. Tristan gagged, covering his mouth and nose as a fish nosed among them and swam away. "What was—"

"Who was that." Aran knelt, lifting the skull from its resting place with a shadowed look. "No one you would know but she was one of my lovers before I met my wife."

He sighed, brushing straw dust from the bone before placing it back where it had been. "I don't remember her name these days. My memory's good but it isn't perfect. She must have tried to hold on after he was imprisoned but died anyway."

Susannah spoke up timidly, looking from the skull to his back. "You said something while we were camping. Poseidon created you, that you didn't have parents. What about a... childhood?"

Aran stood, hoisting himself onto an intact stall door. "Not that I recall. My clearest memory is fighting for him. It could have been decades before the war, it could have been hours before they fought the titans. All I know is that I was made for him to use."

"Hurt." Susannah's voice dropped, barely hiding fury in it. "Don't call it anything but abuse. You—you're kind of an asshole sometimes but I like you. Poseidon's picture is worse than that. I don't see how anyone could forget that."

"Time, and people like their stories." Aran rested the back of his head against the splintered wooden column. "They want to remember the good parts, not the bad. And it was eight thousand years ago. Your memory is short."

"Can we go?" This was almost more than he could handle. Tristan gulped, fighting the hard lump in his throat and the prickling in his eyes. "If there's a point here, you've made it. Poseidon sucks and he's dangerous. I just want to go home now."

It sounded childish to his ears but if this was the world Aran was caught up in, he didn't want any part of it. Even the concern over his curse seemed small, pointless after learning about this.

"Not yet." Aran glanced at him, barely hiding the weariness in his expression. "I've got questions about the Pioneer square incident with the vrykolakas and Susannah's little fire trick. You're still protected if you want to explore a little, but I need to have a word with her in private."

There wasn't a lot to explore but he could appreciate the dismissal, and the trust Aran was giving him underneath it. "Thanks."

Susannah looked ready to object and quieted, lowering her gaze to the sandy ground beneath their feet at Aran's pointed look. Tristan scuffed a foot through the sand, stirring up a small cloud before he turned his back on the two and strode out of the stable. Whatever Aran wanted to discuss was none of his business. Aran would tell him in his own time, or Susannah would. Right now, that conversation was just between his girlfriend and his brother.

TWENTY-FIVE

Susannah

She couldn't share Tristan's worry about the water overhead or decompression sickness on the other side. Aran's place—or his home, there was only beauty in the ruins. How it might have looked while intact, she could only guess at. Susannah shook her head, trying to force her thoughts away from the small pang of loss as she sat on the stump of a marble column, breath catching in her throat. "You wanted to talk, so... talk."

Aran opened his mouth and closed it again, uncertainty making him look younger than thirty-four for a moment. "I don't understand it fully myself; maybe we're not supposed to but you're born from James's bloodline, but he was mortal once. You should be panicking like Tristan is, more concerned about this corner of the spirit world. Why aren't you?"

Susannah smoothed her hand over the wetsuit's cloth, trying to see the 'fear' Aran mentioned and failing. "Because I was swimming before I could walk. Maybe I take a few too many risks in water I don't know but I always felt safe in it, protected."

She lifted her gaze, taking in Aran's face and the dark hair he'd left loose around his shoulders. "I—was some of that you?"

"Maybe." Aran looked hesitant, dropping to one knee on the sandy ground. "But I don't have all that power. Even as strong as I am, I still have to be in the area to do something. I was in Ireland with—with my daughter's people and part of the south of France for those years. Jamaica never crossed my mind."

"But it could have been possible." Susannah said quietly. "Didn't you say it wasn't always by your choice if you—when you accidently took your own life?"

"It could have been." Aran's mouth thinned unhappily, the Irish accent at odds with his Japanese heritage. "The necklace you have was Steffon's few attempts at jewelry but he had a bit of an eye for it when he wanted to."

Aran had mentioned that before. Susannah bent down scooping up a handful of sand in her hand before she let it slide through her fingers. It didn't flow like a steady stream; it drifted like it was being carried by an invisible current. "I never mentioned this to Tristan— maybe I should have but between the war thing or whatever it is with your ex-boss and Tristan's curse—it never really felt like the time. Besides, it isn't really rape if it's a guy on the receiving end, is it? Mom—isn't really mom for me."

Susannah took a breath, continuing before her resolve could fail her. "Dad never talks about it, but he was in university when *she* found him. No clothes, no ID and very muddy. Nine months later, he finds me on the front step, wrapped in a borrowed ratty blanket and a basket. There was no note. And I never heard anything else about the woman."

"We'll argue the semantics around male rape later." Aran gave her a dry look, the sarcasm fading from his expression. "But the rest..."

He trailed off, murmuring something soft in Greek. A prayer or a string of unfamiliar expletives as Susannah watched him. She swallowed, feeling a knot of unease that had nothing to do with feeling like this was 'home' for her. "Aran?"

He shook his head, silencing her. "The fire trick was inexplicable, but I'll assume that was just because Steffon has a bit of... dragon in his heart. He would have used his own power to bind me. Some could have lingered for a bit, long enough for you to drive the vampire off."

He swiped a hand through the pale sand, stirring it up into a cloud. "I've been too long around my family if this didn't occur to me right off the bat. It should have been obvious from the first time you went after Tristan, and I pulled you from the water."

His voice dropped, an edge of frustration in the words. "Gods take it. There's a bit of siren in your blood. Half maybe, or a quarter but it would explain why you're at home here. Because you know it instinctively."

Susannah shuddered, thinking of the creature she'd seen below the water during her attempt at a rescue.

223

"I'm... related to that thing? It—she didn't have any color in her body."

"No, you're human. More or less." Aran's hand cupped hers, squeezing briefly before he let go. "It just means you have a connection here that Tristan doesn't."

He gave her a rueful look, standing and taking a step back. "And that you likely won't suffer decompression sickness when we return."

That was... good to know. Susannah slumped, bracing herself with one arm on the stump. "Great. Now what? You've shown us your home but how safe is it really here? Poseidon, god of the sea or whatever, we're in his palace. Won't he know about trespassers?"

"I died to break his warding." Aran's voice soured midsentence. "He won't think I was brave enough to come here—with my mortal brother and his girlfriend in tow. I'm sure James will be keeping him occupied—or have gone off by now to tell Ha—Agesander about the prison escape. And even if he denies it, he's still weak from the captivity."

That wasn't comforting in the least, but she had no good way of putting her concern into words. "Alright. It's your war with him. I'm just trying to muddle my way through this and survive whatever it is."

She tilted her head back, batting at a curious fish that swam too close for comfort with her free hand. "Are we really soldiers in your war or did you just say that to make us feel useful?"

Aran seemed like a good guy, for a shapeshifter but it was hard to tell how much he was ever telling of the truth these days. Lying was a bit more than a habit for him and he didn't seem completely aware when he did it.

Susannah watched as Aran turned away, hand slipping over the toppled column a yard or two from the stump of the one she sat on. She was willing to be patient but only up to a point. "Aran?"

He sighed, knuckles going white as he tightened his grip. "I wasn't just saying that to comfort you. Poseidon won't stop until he has me as his again. I'm not used to relying on others in my fights, but I'll need you and my brother this time. Mortals can't be compelled or bound in circles. I... can be."

"That explains the scarring." Susannah winced, touching the same spot on her throat where she'd seen the silver line on Aran's neck. "I—I'm sorry. I mean, you said it before but it's another thing hearing as honest. I kind of doubted you."

Aran's laugh was short, bitter. "Because I'm not human or mortal?"

"Kinda." Susannah looked down at her bare feet, shamed. "Sorry."

That seemed to be the end of Aran's good mood for as long as it had lasted. She got to her feet, abandoning her perch. "Why don't we go back to Seattle? I'm not sure of the time here but it's getting late. Or... we're risking being caught by Poseidon the longer we stay, right?"

If Poseidon could trap and punish Aran, there was no telling what the god could do to someone without any of that power.

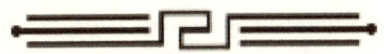

The journey to the hall or whatever it was had been terrifying. The return to the real world was easier though no less disconcerting. Susannah scrambled off Aran's back, grateful her surfboard was where she'd left it, untouched by people or the waves. "That was... interesting but I'm not sure I want to visit the spirit world again."

Tristan tightened his hands on the horse's mane, swaying slightly before he forced himself to sit straight and swing a leg off the horse, stumbling as he landed. Susannah frowned, offering her hand to him. "You alright?"

"Fine." Tristan said.

He didn't look fine, limping back through the shallow water. Susannah brushed a hand over Aran's neck and hastily pulled away as he turned, attempting to bite. "Alright, no touching now. Tristan warned me about that little habit of yours."

Tristan was visible out of the corner of her eye, rummaging through his knapsack before he went down, curling into a tight ball on the surf smoothed rocks. Susannah moved before her thoughts could catch up with her, dropping to her knees at his side. "Tristan?"

It couldn't be his curse, as improbable as it was to see how little time had passed overhead. They'd been in Poseidon's realm for hours.

Tristan squeezed his eyes shut tight, saying nothing to her question. Susannah swore under her breath, giving his shoulder a whack. "Hey, c'mon..."

He only rolled away from her touch, flinching at the brief contact. Susannah sat back, shaking. "Shit."

If no more than a few hours had passed and they'd had only had Aran's protection from the weight of the water... "Double shit!"

Aran's little bubble of safety had been like a bit of dry land taken deep below. However distant it was below the surface, the lack of time taken in coming back to the real world could only mean one thing. "Aran!"

Tristan's brother had warned her that this might be a possibility but she hadn't considered that it would happen. And if Aran had done it just to prove a point, to his own brother...

He was at her side in a minute, shifting from horse shape to human. Susannah gave him an agitated look, playing with the end of her plait. "Did you do this? You said it was a possibility that Tristan would be more affected but Jesus! Why take that chance with your brother's life?"

Aran gagged, retching into the sand though thankfully nowhere near his brother's body before he signed something incomprehensible at her. Susannah groaned, cursing him under her breath. "Right, sure. You're back to mute again. Whatever, just help him. I'm pretty sure no Seattle hospital has the equipment to deal with the bends these days. People should know how to prevent it. I can't even ask you how deep we were because we didn't have paper or a pencil with us. This thing used to kill people, you know."

Bad luck that their translator was the one suffering from the illness. Aran gave her an impatient look and gestured roughly to move off. Susannah opened her mouth to object and quailed under the hard look he gave her, watching as he rested a hand on Tristan's chest. At least one of the gestured 'words' had made sense to her now. "What are you doing?"

Aran shook his head, dark hair falling into his face as he closed his eyes. His lips moved though there was no sound. Susannah watched anxiously, clutching the phone in her hands. If there had been words, she almost would have called it a prayer though to who, she didn't know. Aran had never really said what he believed in. If he believed in anything.

All she could do was sit and watch, wishing she was more use than she was being next to Aran's side. "Is— Can I help?"

He subsided, sweat dampening his hair to his forehead. His breathing was ragged as he wiped the back of his hand across it. Susannah swallowed, looking from him to Tristan's still unconscious form. "How are you feeling?"

She would have pressed further but for the good look she got at his eyes. The gray of them was so washed out he nearly looked blind. No color or a visible pupil to be seen. Susannah turned away, stumbling a few steps before her knees gave out underneath her weight. The only time she'd seen that particular little gem was in a year-old video game a friend of hers had shown off. It hadn't looked natural then and it didn't look natural now, seeing it in real life. "All we need is a fucking dragon to show up."

"Susannah?"

Tristan's voice started her out of her queasy thoughts, and she scrambled backwards, looking up at him. "What the fuck was that? Aran's eye color. It—it was all white."

All white was the best description she could use to describe the sight she'd glimpsed of Aran's eyes. It had been like he was completely blind, or worse.

She dared a look over her shoulder seeing Aran on hand and knees, one arm pressed against his side. Tristan followed her glance, sitting in a vomit-free place on the ground. "He... does that sometimes. It's probably best if we stay out of his way for a bit. When he's like this, he's not always in control."

"Should we help?" Susannah asked.

Tristan hesitated, gaze still on his brother. "He'll manage. He's kind of right about one thing even if he won't go out and say it directly. We're both looking for danger. I'm pretty sure he'd count himself in that category right now. Right now, I'm kind of looking forward to a decent cup of hazelnut coffee at the Blue Cat. It was one of the few things I liked about the diner."

As tempting as hazelnut coffee was. It wasn't the time or the place for that offer. Susannah grimaced, wringing water out of her hair. "I'm still in a wetsuit and Aran just healed decompression sickness in a matter of minutes for you. I don't think that's the best decision to ask for right now. We need to get you home. The both of you."

In case Tristan tried to object again, she was using the nurse's voice her mom had forced her to learn over the years.

He subsided, looking away and strode over to Aran's side, murmuring something almost out of earshot in an unfamiliar language before Aran climbed stiffly to his feet, most of his weight supported by his younger brother. Whatever passed between them was none of her business but at least she had the keys. Neither brother was completely in the position to drive right now. It was on her and her still shaky navigation around Seattle. Luck willing, she wouldn't get lost trying to find home.

TWENTY-SIX

Hades

Cassandra was no seer despite her name, and she was more abrasive than the woman she'd been named for. He set the menu down, leaning back as she set a slice of apple crumble pie in front of him. "The last time I was here, it was your father managing the Cat."

She gave him a humorless look, folding her arms over her chest. "That was twenty years ago, and he died since. You don't look a day over forty."

"Luck." He broke a piece of the pie off with his fork, savoring the cinnamon and nutmeg in the filling. "And just as good as I remember."

Cassandra looked away, the ice in her tone thawing a little. "It was his recipe. He wanted it to be used. So why come here? It doesn't seem like a place a biker would enjoy much."

"Because it isn't noisy, smoke filled or racist?" He set the fork down on the plate, glancing at her curiously. "Most bikers are teddy bears. They just like to act tough. And I was kind of looking for family."

"Who then." Cassandra sat on the edge of the booth, looking charmed despite herself.

He shrugged, stirring the fork tines through the melting vanilla ice cream that had accompanied the pie. "Family, mostly. I heard that my brother was running a small bookstore in Seattle, and I wanted to see how he was doing."

It wasn't a lie, but it wasn't the whole truth either. He was tracking down his family, but not for the sweet little reunion Cassandra was thinking of. The other man had done what should have been impossible and wriggled his way out of prison. Echo had bragged about it, unknowingly to Thana. And Thana had told him in turn. One way or another, his brother would have to return to Tartarus. His crimes weren't yet forgivable. "He had a chance, but he blew it in the last year or so."

"For what?" Cassandra was sitting straight, posture stiff as she drew away from him.

He sighed, twisting the motorcycle helmet strap around his fingers. "It's complicated. We weren't exactly on speaking terms with each other, but he wasn't... a very good employer when I knew him last. Emotional and physical abuse. Rape of one or two of his underpaid female employees. He wasn't exactly sorry for his mistreatment either."

"Ah." Cassandra's expression soured as she lit a cigarette and blew the smoke away from him. "Hope you find him then. And that he gets what he deserves."

"He will, count on it." He stood, laying a ten on the table and placed a five on top of it. "Keep the change and thank you for the pie."

It had been delicious, almost comparable to anything Demeter or Persephone could make and the Blue Cat was worth coming back to for that. If there was time to. He'd have to give his compliments to Cassandra's father later. The man knew how to bake and seemed to have taught his daughter well before his death.

As for the young fair-haired soldier who had chosen to wait outside rather than set foot inside and risk revealing his own nature—there was always pie.

TWENTY-SEVEN

Aran

He drifted in and out of awareness, only vaguely aware of the voices just out of range. Their owners blurred, pale shapes through half closed eyes. His throat felt like sandpaper and the weight of the light blanket was too heavy for him, draped over his body.

Voices. Mariko's was soft, her husband's harder. Tristan and Susannah's muffled tones sharper. Once, an abrupt crack of someone's hand striking wood. It sounded like wood anyway. Aran pushed the worn flannel away, sitting up as the world spun in front of him. Thana had come for him once already, easing the path into the dark before he'd reawakened from it. The second time, she hadn't. Now... she was staying out of the way for the respect of his family.

The tunic was crumpled at the foot of the bed, not folded in the chair as he pulled it over his head. It brushed against his back, and he snarled softly at the friction across raw skin. It burned even under the slightest movement. Standing was no better, pain shooting up through his legs with each limping step down into the kitchen.

The voices broke off midsentence. All four of them looking towards him as he leaned against the doorframe. Tristan was the first to move, vacating his chair for him. Aran shook his head, refusing it. If he tried another step, he was going to end up on his knees again, from the way the room spun in front of him and the buzzing in his ears intensified.

Tristan and Susannah exchanged worried looks with each other before glancing back at him. She was the first to speak, uncertainty in her voice. "Are you... sure you're okay?"

Dying, most likely, and not for the last time, the way luck had turned out for him since his return a year ago. Or maybe it had been one long, slow death since then rather than several. Aran shook his head, gritting his teeth as the wave of sparkles threatened his vision again. It was an effort to sign his adoptive father's name. *Steffon*.

The older shapeshifter's eyes narrowed at the gestured word. Irritation or annoyance crossing his face instead of concern. "There is only one cure for your illness, boy. And you well know it. You brought your war here; it wasn't just something that happened by chance."

Steffon stepped around the edge of the table, ignoring Tristan's objections and stalked out of the kitchen but not before he spat on the floor at Aran's feet. "You were never a son of mine. God knows I tried to be your father."

God, not gods. Aran swallowed back on the bile that threatened in his throat as the mechanic vanished out the back door. It was like Steffon to deliberately insult his faith. Darkness clouded his vision before fading. He could taste blood in his mouth and bowed his head, trying to breathe as shallowly as possible. Anything would be better than vomiting in Mariko's clean kitchen.

White fire exploded in his head instead and he didn't feel it as he hit the linoleum floor.

TWENTY-EIGHT

Susannah

She grabbed for Tristan's arm before he could drop to his knees next to Aran's side. "Don't. Let the seizure run itself out. There's nothing else we can do."

He pulled away from her touch and ignored Susannah's words as he put a hand on Aran's shoulder. "C'mon... please come back to us."

Tristan meant well but Aran's condition was nothing they could deal with, except making him comfortable. Susannah threw a look over her shoulder, seeing Mariko frozen behind the table, a thin set to her mouth as she watched them. The plastic of her phone was warm under her touch. Susannah looked down at the device and cursed, praying silently that one or both of her parents were at home as she dialed their numbers. Home went to voicemail, followed by two more ineffective attempts to their cell numbers. "Damn it!"

Of all the days both her parents were in surgery, it had to be now. Her hand dipped, briefly below the surface of Aran's shoulder before she shuddered, pulling away. The seizure had passed but not the other thing. He was losing the thing that made him seem a little more human, if not mortal. Susannah lifted her gaze, meeting Tristan's eyes. "You know him better than I do. What can we do?"

"Get him into Tristan's room." Mariko's voice cut across her son's before Tristan could speak. "I'll have a word with my husband."

What would that do? Susannah cast Mariko a strained look. "He's already pretty much disowned Aran. Why would he help?"

Steffon had made his feelings clear by the way he'd spat at Aran's feet before stalking off, a black cloud hovering over his head.

"I'll speak with him." Mariko said. "Just do as I asked, please. Tristan's bed will be more comfortable than the floor. He left it too soon."

If that wasn't clear enough. Susannah nodded tightly, trying not to get too close again. As much as she wanted to help support Aran's weight, she didn't want to experience the more spirit critter thing he was doing. It would have to be on Tristan since he was more used to seeing that side of his brother than she was.

She stayed a step or two behind both guys, heart in her mouth as she watched, spotting from her position on the stairs up to the second floor. They made it without incident though whether that was because Tristan was stronger than he looked or because Aran had less physical substance than he'd had, she didn't know. She didn't want to know which was more accurate. "Will... he be alright?"

Tristan sat on the edge of the bed, brushing sweat dampened hair out of Aran's closed eyes. "Honestly, I don't know. He's been open about a lot of things but that only says how much we still don't get about him."

At least he'd included her in that we. Susannah sighed, reaching out for Aran before reconsidering the gesture. "That wasn't really a death threat, was it? Whatever your dad said to him."

"I don't know." Tristan smoothed a hand over the coverlet, picking at a stained spot on the cream linen. "I think he just wants to protect me, but I didn't think it meant he actually hated Aran. I—"

"Bind him to human shape." Steffon stood in the bedroom doorway. His arms were folded over his chest. "If you want Aran to live, it's the only way."

Susannah looked reflexively over at Aran, biting down on her lower lip. He took no notice of her, still deep in unconsciousness in Tristan's bed. She couldn't say she really knew Aran, but this felt like the wrong answer to their current problem. "He won't like it. I can't say I know him that well, who does, around here? But it doesn't feel like a solution he'd be happy with."

"Then don't, and he dies for good." Steffon's lip curled at that, looking from her to his adoptive son. "I knew him briefly, once. A long time ago. This is the only way to leash him, and the power he has. Do you want to save his life or not? He won't last long in this state."

"It's still his choice." Susannah said weakly. "He deserves the chance to decide for himself. It isn't something we can do for him."

"Is he capable of making that decision?" Steffon asked dryly.

"Well, no... but..." Susannah trailed off, hating herself for the answer. Just because Aran couldn't speak, didn't give them the right to make a big decision on his behalf. It was his life after all. "We'll need him. He's... kind of the only guy I know able to stand between Seattle and a pissed off god. Neither Tristan and I have that kind of power. We're mostly human here."

"So be it." Steffon dropped his arms back to his sides. "Binding him to human form is still the only path but if you're set on letting the... creature keep its freedom, I hope he's in a good mood when you let him go. It— Aran is nature untamed and the sea is the worst of it all."

That may have been true, but Aran was still a friend, even if he was unpredictable. Susannah swallowed, fingers tangling with the necklace chain as she zipped the little amethyst back and forth on it. "I believe in consent, and the Hippocratic oath thing my parents taught me to read when I was little. They don't have to be mutually exclusive. Let's wait a couple hours and see if he wakes up. Then we ask if he's willing to have this... binding done to him."

Only then would she push her reservations into the little box they belonged to. The binding whatever it was just felt like another way of controlling someone without consent. And Steffon didn't sound like he was suggesting it as a good thing for everyone. What had Aran told her about the man? The dragon in his heart? It might have been that if she was remembering it correctly.

Tristan's posture behind her was stiff, fingers interlacing with hers as he watched his dad over her shoulder before he let go of Susannah's hand and pushed past the man. Susannah followed reluctantly a moment or two later. "Where are we going?"

He didn't answer her and she found out the where half an hour later as he shoved at a piece of corrugated metal and scrap plywood away from the back door of a brick building. Susannah ducked through the low lintel, nervously looking up over her head. The ceiling was lost in the dim light and thick dust still floating in the air. She sneezed, wiping her nose on her shirt sleeve. "Tristan? Talk to me. Why are we trespassing in an abandoned building?"

"It isn't abandoned if we're here, is it?" Tristan's answer was flippant before he sighed, guiding her around a hole in the ancient floor. "I haven't been here in years, but it used to be my place. Used to come here just to sit in the window or the rooftop to think. Mom and Dad didn't know about it and Aran didn't care to stick around to learn about it either."

That was something to apologize for or pity Tristan for. Susannah kept her mouth shut, changing her mind about putting that into words. "Did it help?"

"Kind of." Tristan hoisted himself into one of the windows, resting the back of his head against the crumbling window frame. "At least no one bothered me here. Other kids had their play forts and swing sets. I had Chinatown and some of its older places most hu—people thought wasn't safe to play in."

"You can say human, since we aren't really that." Susannah said awkwardly. "I mean... part bloody mermaid thing for me and you're a shapeshifter. It's just something I'm going to have to get used to saying."

"Yeah." Tristan's mouth thinned, making him look like a much younger version of his father for a second.

He looked away, wrapping an arm around the knee he drew up to his chest. "I don't want to bind Aran to human shape. It might save his life, but he'll hate me for it. I think we've seen that movie enough times to see what happens when you trap someone like him and take their power away from them."

Susannah winced at the veiled reference and scuffed a runner through dirt and an unused coil of rusting electrical cable on the warped floor. "You know I hate that movie series. Doesn't do Port Royal justice or accuracy."

She forced an attempt at a smile, half quoting one of the movie's lines. "Though, I guess if we're in a ghost story. Might as well believe in the rest of it, right? Bloody undead monkey and all that."

"Was that a part of it?" At least her reference to the monkey did enough to distract Tristan enough from his brooding.

Susannah rolled her eyes, half turning away from the window. "It was. About the only thing I liked about them. And the dog. Question is, now—where did James bloody Gray go? If he's supposed to help, he sure isn't showing it."

She quieted, sobering. "There isn't some kind of magic circle thing we're supposed to do, or something to bring him back here, is there? We need a witch and the only one we thought we knew turned out to be an insane god. I'm pretty sure we aren't capable of calling the dead back to life here."

It wasn't within her abilities, and she was pretty sure it wasn't within Tristan's either.

Tristan's expression clouded and he shifted position, bracing himself so he didn't fall from the third story height. "I'm not going to suggest anything we can't do but maybe we should go back to Pioneer Square again. I'm pretty sure Aran did something to bring your cousin here. How hard would it be to do that again?"

"And face another vampire slug?" Susannah asked. "Sure, I'm game. Because it was fun the last time we went. I hid, you squeaked and huddled in my backpack and Aran did most of the work."

She tightened her hands in the hem of her shirt, trying to still the slight tremor in them. "At least it'll be daylight this time. We can call Jamie back here and if he's really a ghost, wait until nightfall if the sun is a problem for him."

Wandering unfamiliar tunnels wasn't on her bucket list for a good time but there was no choice about going. They needed answers and someone more experienced in dealing with angry gods. Or vampires. "It's just honey and blood, right?"

"As long as we do this and get out of there." Tristan said. "Aran..."

She hadn't forgotten anymore than he had. Aran was a friend of hers as well. "We'll save him and break the curse, okay. We're in this together now."

For better or for worse.

TWENTY-NINE
Tristan

The lesson had been learned from the last time they'd visited the tunnels beneath the square. Tristan knelt, flicking a lighter at the gasoline-soaked rag tied around a stick before he lifted the crude torch high. This time they had fire, not just a flashlight for protection. "Hope whatever's out there will accept a meets expectations grade because we're going to be putting a lot on a faith we don't believe in. Plus vampires."

"Google is our friend." Susannah's quip only belied the strain in her voice. "It's an old Greek rite, we're in an underworld—kinda and we have honey and blood.

It should be enough. I hope. Now we just need to find a crossroads down here."

That was easier said than done without a map. Tristan struck chalk against the side of one abandoned storefront and stepped carefully around a pile of rubble in their path. They could be down here for hours and never find what they wanted, or a way out without some kind of marker showing the path behind them.

The torch guttered as Tristan cursed, sweeping the fading flame around the tunnel. "Settle for a T-intersection?"

Their path ahead was blocked by a cave in but three of the four arms of their crossroads were clear of debris. Susannah swallowed, kneeling in the rubble as she held a plastic dog bowl in one hand, squirting just enough honey in it to coat the bottom of it before she pricked a finger with a pocketknife. A few drops of blood fell, dark against the sweet, slightly sticky treat. "Hope this works because we're lost if it doesn't. Or we'll get eaten by a vampire slug down here."

That was no argument from him as Tristan abandoned the torch for a flashlight. Batteries would last longer than flame and an oil-soaked rag tied around the end of a stick.

Susannah had done most of the research, she knew more about the rite they were trying to attempt beneath the light and safety of Seattle's modern streets. She looked back at him nervously before tipping the bowl sideways and let its contents flow onto the dusty path in front of her. "We don't know the words but we're still counting on your help, Jamie. Please—if you're one of Aran's friends, help him. Help us. We're in the middle of something with his ex-employer and the guy is pissed. Aran's too sick to help us fight a god."

The back of Tristan's neck prickled, and he turned as he white knuckled his hand at his side. Holding a pocketknife would have been more comforting but Susannah had their only weapon. And it was all but useless against anything bigger than an individual rat. "Jamie?"

"So to speak anyway." James cast a disillusioned look across both of them, lingering on the bowl still in Susannah's hands. "And I daresay that was the worst attempt at summoning a shade that I've ever seen, or experienced. Good lord, I've seen better from a cat that spilled blood over a pot of honey in a fight."

That had to be a metaphor because it didn't sound real to him. Tristan forced himself to relax and not strike the soldier. "So... it worked?"

"No." James gave him a bland look in return. "But I'm obligated to stay for a while, thanks to Aran's previous summoning. And I must confess your brother's attempt was more successful. He knew what he was doing."

"Someone had to." Tristan forced the words out. "But we really need your help and you came through for us with the vampire thing the last time. Aran's the sickest I've ever seen him, and Dad's best solution is binding him to human shape. It might help but it'll piss Aran off if he realizes what was done to him."

"Show me." James's voice hardened. "Just let me borrow your jacket before we reach the surface. I can't chance daylight unless I'm incarnate."

He didn't wait for them to agree to the request, just turned on one combat booted foot and broke into an eerily silent run with Tristan and Susannah trailing behind him. Somehow navigating the route without slowing to check the chalked marks Tristan had left behind for that purpose.

Tristan braced his hands on his legs, panting as he caught his breath. Susannah looked just as winded as he felt, hair escaping her plait. The only one who didn't seem affected was James, standing just out of reach of the light in the entrance tunnel. Tristan forced himself to stand straight, wiping sweat dampened hair from his forehead. "You're fast, Jesus."

James gave him a shrug, slipping his arms through the jacket Tristan handed to him. "One of the few advantages of being a dead man. I don't tire. Now, let's protect your brother from what will be an unpleasant fate for him."

James was the first out of the tunnel, hesitating only briefly before he stepped out into the cloudy Seattle daylight. Tristan frowned at his back. "It's—is Aran still protecting you? I think he mentioned he was the first time we met."

"Not this time." James shielded his eyes from the sunlight, wincing a little. "I'm pretending I know who gave me this little reprieve, but I should have been banished back to the crossroads even with a coat for daring daylight. Come, let's go before Steffon takes matters into his own hands, beyond stripping Aran of his power."

No time to waste, that was fine with him. "The car's this way."

Tristan turned the wheel hard, startling a squeak from Susannah in the passenger side seat at the abrupt swerve of the car. He couldn't look back to check but it sounded like James was clinging to his seatbelt and praying in a soft undertone.

He ignored it, cutting off one driver and earning himself an irritated honk before he turned off the main street onto the alley where the detached garage was. This time he didn't bother with kicking his runners off as he wrenched on the door. Mariko was seated at the table, a small cup of tea cradled in her hands. The tip of her nose an alarming shade of pink. Tristan faltered at the sight. "Which side is Dad on here?"

This wasn't his parents' fight, but Steffon had never really hidden his dislike for Aran or his lack of trust for his adopted son. Mariko set her teacup down on the table, blowing her nose into a tissue. "Neither. He wants little to do with Poseidon, but he trusts Aran even less. He is upstairs."

She hadn't specified one, the other or both but that was enough for Tristan to turn away and take the stairs two at a time up to his bedroom. "Dad!"

Susannah and James weren't far behind him as he saw his father's back through the ajar bedroom door, leaning hard on a pillow as Aran thrashed, somehow finding the strength to fight against the mechanic's hold.

Tristan moved without thinking, trying to pull Steffon away from the bed. "Stop it!"

The blow came out of nowhere, connecting with his jaw before he could duck out of the way. Tristan stumbled, hand against the ache as he tasted blood in his mouth. "Dad—"

Steffon stood, breathing hard. "He started this war when he came back to our home. If he hadn't there would be no curse, no reason for you to have suffered each night. And Poseidon would still be in prison."

"You would be visiting a cemetery instead." Tristan tried not to wince, rubbing at his jaw. "Irene wanted to kill me that night. She would have if Aran hadn't... stepped in. He saved my life. Can we just talk about this instead of starting something that ends with the police being called? It isn't too late to stop this."

"It is already too late." Steffon spat his next words in Welsh, looking past Tristan's shoulder. "And the man is gone."

Tristan swallowed, all too aware of Susannah and James looking on from behind him. "Dad..."

There was disinterest and dislike, and then there was outright murder. Steffon's mouth was a hard line, darkness in his eyes. "Why, exactly? The power Aran has, maybe. That scares the shit out of me too sometimes but he's family, You can't even call this mercy anymore. He'll be more pissed when he comes back, not less. The war would be between Aran and you if Poseidon wasn't being

252

a distraction. And there's no fucking point to it when we're supposed to be a family."

"Believe what you want." Steffon's answer came through gritted teeth. "But Aran is no son of mine and never was. Once more, it is too late for the boy."

He stalked past Tristan, barely suppressing a shudder as he brushed past James and stomped down the stairs to the main floor. Tristan sagged, going to his knees next to the bed as the prickling sensation in his eyes spilled over into wetness. "I—I don't understand why..."

How could his father have done this? It was beyond his understanding as he brushed a hand over Aran's too still wrist. "He's always been quiet, but I didn't think he'd do this. I don't—"

Tristan broke off, shoulders slumping in defeat. "He's my dad. Family was supposed to matter here."

"Is he devout?" James's question came from behind him as the soldier edged into the bedroom. "I know your brother didn't always hold to Christian beliefs. That may have been Steffon's reasoning for the pillow attack."

"Maybe, I don't know." Tristan swallowed past the hard lump in his throat. "Mom never went out on Sunday mornings. Dad did but I never asked where."

"Use the hurt." James said gently. "Remember it for when you need it most. Your brother may be gone briefly but Poseidon is still out there, a threat to a sizable portion of Seattle and the coast if he isn't confronted."

"I know." Tristan averted his gaze from the bed as Susannah draped the coverlet over Aran's face. "Angry gods are shit for people to deal with."

The attic was more thickly coated in dust than the guest bedroom, but it held a measure of peace that his bedroom didn't. Tristan knelt in front of the old steamer trunk, more interested in playing with the rusting brass key than unlocking it.

A creak of the worn floorboards announced Susannah's presence before she dropped to her knees next to him. "You alright?"

In all honesty, no. Not after trying and failing to do CPR on his brother in the hopes that it might do something for him. Tristan scrubbed a shirt sleeve across his eyes and dropped his hand back to his side. "I didn't think Dad would actually kill him. It just..."

He trailed off, glancing away. "I thought family meant something to him. Guess I was too stupid or naïve to see the cracks here."

Susannah forced a smile, shaking her head. "Not stupid. Just... hopeful. You were the glue or whatever holding your family together for the last year but that'll never last. It's not supposed to. One family's lost—you found another. I hope anyway, you've got me and Aran."

Her words were meant well but it was going to take more than that to make him feel better. Tristan sighed, twisting the key into the lock with the right amount of force before he lifted the steamer trunk lid. There wasn't much to show for its contents other than the katana and the photograph from 1938 lying beneath the sword on a bed made from an old moving blanket. "Mom wanted me to have granddad's sword. I said no— Aran's the real warrior here, it belongs to him. Shows how much I know about her. As much as I thought I knew Dad." Tristan's voice soured as he closed the lid again.

Susannah slipped her arm through his, resting her head against his shoulder. "If there's time after this, give it to him. I don't want to make light of his death, again. But it isn't like Aran can stay dead, right? If your mom meant for you to have it, there's no reason why you can't return it to someone who knows how to use it."

"I guess." Tristan didn't pull away from her touch. "I always preferred a handgun over a sword anyway. Not that it'll do any good against Poseidon."

"That's cynical or a very bitter realist." Susannah said dryly. "Look, I don't know if we're on the right side of things, or even if there is a right side here but Poseidon's still out there and as long as he is, he screws everything up for you and Aran. He needs to be dealt with."

THIRTY

Aran

Steffon had placed a pillow over his face and smothered him. It was death again, for the third or fourth time this year and this time it couldn't be forgiven.

Nor was he alone this time. Aran steeled himself, trying to keep his expression neutral in front of Poseidon. The god hadn't yet abandoned his identity as Martin Carpenter yet, but it hadn't taken him long to make some changes, rebuilding the realm he'd been forced to vacate centuries before. Aran stopped to brush a hand or two along the nearest column, feeling a bit of homesickness at the reconstruction but he was daring the god's anger for a word. And a promise.

He dropped his hand back to his side, unsurprised to feel the weight of the sword at his waist this time. He hadn't worn that blade for decades, but he'd missed it. Staying in practice with a borrowed katana wasn't the same thing by far. "Do something for me and I'll come back to your service, whatever it is."

Martin's eyes narrowed as he braced his chin on a closed fist, the elbow resting on one arm of his seat. "And why should I trust you? It was a betrayal when you left me the first time. There's little to stop you from doing that again."

"My brother." Aran said. "You put the curse on him, you're the only one who can take it off. I tried and all I did was hurt him in the attempt. It's... my life for Tristan's. And I'll swear on the Styx if I have to. You'll have me, body and spirit if you agree to this. I won't fight you."

"Tempting." Martin gave him a long look. "But I always liked you a little wild. A pet soldier is useless to me. I learned that an age ago. There was too little creativity for the price of obedience from you. I missed seeing that until you drowned Irene last summer. Then again, I spent too long imprisoned until my sibling decided I could spend a decade or two on probation."

He propped his chin on his hand, resting the elbow on the armrest. "Your body then, not the spirit. And I'll think about releasing your brother from my curse."

"Swear it." Aran took a step forward, daring the challenge in the little words. "Please."

Martin glanced at him, unreadable. "Maybe."

That wasn't a promise. Aran swallowed, dropping to his knee with head bowed. "You'll give Tristan his freedom back if I agree to your service again?"

"Fine." Martin looked away, annoyance crossing his face. "I'll swear it on the river, I'll free the pup if you come back to my side like you used to be. This time I won't make the same mistake I did all that time ago. Your body is mine but the spirit, I'll leave that to you."

Martin stood, brown slacks and shirt shifting to an undyed tunic as he made a small circle around Aran, appraising. "C'mon then. Where's the storm I remember?"

Aran lifted his gaze to look at the god. If it was defiance Martin wanted, he wasn't obligated to answer the question. It was an effort not to pull away and snarl softly as Martin's mouth pressed against his. This was for Tristan's sake if nothing else. An oath on the Styx didn't have to be spoken aloud for it to be binding.

It was easier not thinking, pretending the memories belonged to someone else as he looked into the washroom mirror. There was no one to call even if he'd had a voice and he didn't have an ID card for identification. The police were out of the question, even if there were an unlikely handful willing to believe in thegods.

A knock sounded on the other side of the door, the footsteps retreating a moment later. Aran splashed water across his face, slumping against the vanity below the sink. He'd barely recognized the boy in the mirror as himself. Half the age he'd chosen for the sake of blending in as Tristan's older brother, and too delicate this time. Martin liked them pretty.

He shoved the thoughts away, drawing his legs up to his chest. What good was sign language when no one else could speak it?

The knock came again, impatient as the doorknob rattled. Aran swallowed, fighting the lump in his throat and turned the lock, stepping out of the way of the grumpy man on the other side of the door. A lack of shoes and dressed in a tunic, without jeans beneath it was the least of his worries. Getting home, as much as the rental house was, was more important.

If anyone was there, it would be Mariko or Tristan. James found him first, stepping out of the darkness cast by a broken streetlamp. "It's been three days. Your family was worried about you."

It didn't feel like three days. Aran looked away from the English soldier, failing to find the words he wanted. There was nothing he could say anyway.

James's sigh didn't leave a little puff of fog behind as he gestured to the car idling by the curb. "Come, please. You're lucky Mariko gave me one of Steffon's jackets or we would be traveling differently. If you lived to tell the tale about the crossroads. Let me take you back."

It wasn't like he had anywhere else to go and very few places would let a barefoot seventeen-year-old into them without a drivers' license. Aran sat in the passenger side seat, staring out the window as James navigated the streets with an ease that came from experience. Or something natural to whatever he was.

"Psychopomp, and occasionally hunter but you knew this from before." James glanced into the rear-view mirror, taking his gaze off the road long enough to glance at Aran. "Hades is aware and he'll come when he thinks it best."

Aran slumped against the seat, turning away from the small mirror between them. The only reflection visible was his own and it was still of a boy too young to defend himself. Three days missing was three days too long. There was no answer he could give that would satisfy the English soldier and any mention of service was only a reminder of what he'd sacrificed to protect the little family he'd found in Susannah and his brother.

James quieted, focusing on the road in front of them until he slowed, parking haphazardly in the cracked driveway. "Mariko went to bed hours ago, but Tristan and Susannah insisted on waiting for news. Shall I tell them, or will you?"

Nothing about Martin's activities or what he'd done in an attempt to break Tristan's curse but the least he could do was say he was safe, safer anyway. Aran shook his head, one hand on the door latch. He'd say, if he could. Aran rummaged through the glove compartment, coming back with a pen and paper. *I will*.

James had no right to take that from him when so much had already been taken.

Susannah was holding a one-sided conversation with the otter sitting on the table until she broke it off, seeing him. Aran faltered seeing it there as a nearby glass of water shattered, sending liquid across the table. Martin had promised to remove the curse, but it was night and Tristan was in otter form. The god had given him his word and broken it despite all he'd given Poseidon. If he'd had a voice, he would have been swearing in Greek.

He slumped in the remaining unoccupied seat, exhausted. Martin had sworn on a river, he hadn't explicitly mentioned the Styx. It was clear in hindsight; it hadn't been three days ago.

Tristan chirped, putting a paw on his hand. Aran sighed, petting the small head and looked away, pulling the notebook closer to him. *I thought—I tried to bargain with Martin. Forgive me?*

Tristan hissed, showing his teeth and settled against Aran's arm, pushing the pencil away. He was wordless but the opinion was clear to anyone who could understand him. It wasn't his fault. If only it didn't feel that way. Aran looked away, signing a thank you to the otter.

"Aran?" Susannah's voice was tentative, uncertainty crossing her face. "You look... younger than I remember."

It had only been a few days; her memory wasn't that short. Aran snorted, tearing the sheet of paper free and writing again. *He likes them young. You're seeing me as I was when Tristan was a five-year-old kit. And the age I... was when Poseidon created me over six thousand years ago.*

"I—oh." Susannah blanched at the sloppy answer. "I'm sorry."

Apologies were just words, but Susannah sounded like she meant it, without asking for details he couldn't give. Aran closed the notebook cover on his last message and scraped the chair across the linoleum floor. Sleep didn't matter to him, but he was going to try finding a little rest, curled up in Tristan's unoccupied bed.

If he was lucky, he wouldn't dream of his former—present master tonight. Or his murder in the hours before his oath to the god.

No one stopped him or called for his name. It was almost a relief not to be addressed.

THIRTY-ONE

Susannah

Talking to an otter was one of the less strange things she'd seen since the move to Seattle. Susannah glanced ruefully at Tristan's other form, wishing he was here in person. She could have done without his answering chirps and squeaks at her questions. Still, maybe it was for the best that the curse hadn't been broken yet. His language had been foul in the last three days, alternating between the Spanish he'd picked up from her, Welsh and English after what Steffon had... done. Mariko hadn't stopped her husband, but she was less at fault for ending Aran's life than Steffon was. She hadn't been the one to hold the pillow three days ago.

Steffon had made his position plain with that attempt, backing the car out with a screech of rubber on pavement. He hadn't been seen since, much to Susannah's relief. "So he's back, I guess."

For what little good that was. Aran looked like seventeen now but there was a distant look in his gaze that barely hid whatever he'd experienced as a captive of Poseidon's. "And we're officially at war with a real god, yay."

That was one for the resume. Or for the long-term care facility depending on the employer. She buried her face in her hands, preferring darkness to the sight of her cousin sitting in one of the kitchen chairs as if he was flesh and blood—living instead of the see through shade he really was. "And fuck on top of it. Since whatever Aran tried *clearly* didn't work—we need an alternative here."

James opened his mouth to speak, only to be interrupted by the doorbell ringing from the front of the house. Susannah cast him and her boyfriend exasperated looks and answered it, seeing the girl standing on the step. "If you're selling cookies—"

"Do I look like a cookie girl?" The girl's voice was snippy as she pushed by Susannah without an excuse me. "That gods forsaken Echo told me, I told my aunt, and you don't want to get on Helen Takala's bad side. 'Sides, Aran's a friend."

"Well, yeah, but..." Susannah started.

Their new guest gave her an affronted look and stalked into the kitchen. "James's granddaughter. I heard that too. Look like his bloody sister to me."

"Lyra." James's voice was dry sounding as Susannah managed to reclaim or original seat at the square table.

Lyra sniffed, casting him a once over. "When did you die, Captain?"

This was too much and not nearly enough context for her. Susannah sighed, tempted to to throw Aran's abandoned notebook at someone's head. "Can I get some subtitles here, please? Who the hell are you and how do you know I'm James's erm... family?"

James made a face, hand briefly slipping below the surface of the tabletop. "We, ah, met for a time in New York during the war. The girl isn't really a young woman, she's a shapeshifter. She was a messenger during those years. Among... other things."

Another shapeshifter. Susannah groaned, settling for burying her face in her hands for a second time instead of throwing the coil bound notebook like she was tempted to. "Great, just what we need tonight. An uninvited guest. And how is her—your aunt going to be able to help?"

Lyra gave her a dirty look, tangling raggedly styled hair around her fingers before letting go. "She's a psychologist or something. I've seen Aran with a hell of a lot more spark in him and this ain't it. Never asked his story but I think I can guess, those three days he spent trying to break Tristan's curse thing. Didn't go well."

"Doesn't sound like it." Susannah said tiredly. "What do you think happened?"

Lyra snarled, sounding more like an angry cat than a girl at the question. "Rape. That's the only answer you need, Gray. Think you're the only one to see the scarring on his back, try again. He can tolerate a lot but not being treated as a plaything. Poseidon's a mad bastard if he thinks he can get away with hurting my friends."

Friends, well, that was a start. Susannah swallowed back on bile at the small, blunt word. It was easier to fixate on that rather than whatever Aran had experienced. "So how do we stop a god without Aran to help? He's the only one strong enough to try. The rest of us are mostly human."

Lyra subsided, exchanging an unreadable look with James before she spoke again. "If I'm good enough to fool my cousin into stepping into an empty elevator shaft and have him think that the stupid metal box is there when it isn't, I think I can fool Poseidon into a trap. I'm not a fighter though. I can't do that and be bait at the same time."

"And we would never ask that of you." James said. "It *is* Tristan's curse, not yours."

The groundwork for their plan seemed better left off in their hands but she still had a question or two. Susannah lifted her hand, feeling like a student about to be told off by a teacher for speaking out of turn. "Shapeshifting and illusions? Isn't that a bit overkill?"

James coughed discretely; Lyra managed to look smug as she put a boot on top of the kitchen table. "Aran's nearly a god, your boyfriend can do a bit with storms when he wants to and you're worried about *my* illusions being overkill? I don't have much to worry about if you know more about Greek mythology than Norse."

James sighed, discomfort flickering across his face. "And none too modest about it either. Susannah, meet Loki. Lyra Takala, my grand—my cousin, if we're to take her feelings into account."

"Loki." Susannah said.

"Yeah." The younger woman smirked, folding her arms over her chest. "Forget all you think you know

268

about the stories. Fenris was my father, not my son and that thing about the mare never happened. One night where the only clothes available were a pair of trousers and a stolen shirt, and I get mistaken for a boy ever since."

"Good to know." Susannah said slowly. "I'm just going to go over here and see how Aran's doing."

It was just an excuse to escape an overwhelming situation but the best thing she could come up with on short notice.

Susannah knocked on the door and pushed it open, not expecting an answer as she entered the room. "Hey, Aran."

The roughly human sized lump stirred as Aran sat up, dark hair looking mussed rather than brushed straight and loose over his shoulders. He couldn't have spoken her name if he'd wanted to and she wouldn't have understood the signing of it so she just sat instead, finding a spot at the foot of the bed. She spoke for him, keeping her hands to herself in her lap. "You didn't need to talk to Poseidon to break Tristan's curse if he—he was just going to hurt you for it."

Aran opened his mouth and closed it, averting his gaze from hers. Susannah sighed, wishing there was something she could say to make this better. Or take his pain away. "I can get a notebook for you if that helps. Not to tell about the... rape. But I do need answers that don't come from sign language."

Aran brushed a hand across the base of his throat and shook his head, rummaging through Tristan's nightstand for a little coil bound book and a pen. *It was the only way I could think of that would keep you and my brother safe.*

Aran fidgeted with the quilt corner, not quite meeting her eyes. *It worked, more or less.*

If that was his idea of working, she didn't want to know what failure was to him. Susannah bit down on her lower lip. "He used you. That's not sane, or safe. I don't care if you're one of the strongest shapeshifters I know, it never should have happened."

I'm one of the only shapeshifters you know. Aran looked down at his message. *Tristan is another of them.*

"There's a girl now. Calls herself Loki." Susannah said blandly.

Ah. Aran looked down at the notebook braced on one knee. *I know her, knew her once.*

"Seems like that's common." Susannah glanced away, taking in the undecorated bedroom walls and the boxes piled in a corner that were all Tristan had for a wardrobe. "So you, Lyra and James were a thing back then, whenever it was."

He had the decency to tilt his head at that, the barest hint of a weak smile playing at his lips. *And Malachi Blackburn but it was not a... thing. We just knew each other during the revolution.*

"Is that a story you'd be willing to tell?" She couldn't help just a bit of curiosity at Aran's written answer.

Aran raked a hand through dark hair, dropping it back down by his side. *I might but it would take too long, and I only saw a little of it during those years. If you want the whole story, ask James or Malachi if you meet the latter. They'd know their own tale better than I do.*

That was disappointing but understanding at the same time. Susannah hesitated, expecting something insubstantial under the touch she laid on his hand and relieved when it was flesh and blood, solid if cooler than her comfort would have liked. "Just get some rest. Everyone else's downstairs trying to lay a trap for the bastard."

She turned away with those parting words and rejoined the group in the kitchen. No progress seemed to have been made in their plans and Tristan looked like he'd given up, curling up in a brown furred ball on the table with his tail tucked up alongside his body. "How's it going?"

Lyra, she refused to think of the younger woman as Loki—it was too much of a disconnect for Susannah to be comfortable with—shook her head. "Not that much. Whatever we're going to do, we're going to have to do it in daylight. You didn't miss much except for an argument over the best place to do it in. A warehouse would be better. I can control things better in an enclosed space. I don't suppose you know anywhere..."

Susannah grimaced, pouring herself a glass of water from the sink and spat it out again at the taste of rust in it. "Sorry, no. I've only been in Seattle for the past month and a half."

Though at times it felt like much longer than that. And if it weren't for Aran and Tristan, she would have hated every minute of it. The state was still too cold and damp for her comfort. Her home was and always be in Jamaica.

"Awh." Lyra looked disappointed. "I'll scout something out on my own. Maybe James can help as well. He's got an uncanny sense for this crap, and it isn't like he can die for a second time. Everything else will have to wait for dawn."

"And you'll be on your own, I'm afraid." James said. "I would gladly help you then but daylight isn't safe for shadows."

"I understand." Lyra dipped a fingertip into a spilled pile of salt and teased an obscure pattern out of it. "Thank you. Whatever you're able to give, I—we'll be grateful for."

"You'll have it." James got to his feet, letting a borrowed jacket fall to the seat of the chair before he faded away.

Susannah jerked her gaze away from where the soldier had been standing a few moments before. "I almost prefer Aran's trick to whatever Jamie—James does and the two almost look the same to me."

Lyra shrugged, absently petting Tristan's side before she remembered whose boyfriend he was. "James is the oldest ghost I know. Aran's the closest thing to a nature spirit I can call a friend. Most of them don't have personalities."

"Most of them?" Susannah asked.

Lyra swept her pattern onto the floor before its design could be worked out. "Missy, Sieh, Coyote. One of them is the spirit of the Mississippi, the other two belong to Alaska and Washington state. There might be others but as a mortal, I try not to offend them. Do you think Tristan will mind being put in a backpack? I'd rather not go anywhere without him, just in case. If we're going to be challenging a god for his brother's sake..."

There was a bit of logic in the request. Susannah grimaced, brushing Tristan between his ears to wake him. "I'm still not sure if you can understand me but we're going on a field trip. Do you mind riding piggyback in a knapsack again?"

A spare change of clothes could serve as a bit of extra padding at the bottom of the pack. And give Tristan something to wear if their little excursion went past dawn. Tristan chirped, tugging at her shirt sleeve. She looked down, taking his attempt at speaking as a yes. "Alright then. I guess it's official. We're at war."

Three small words that never sounded as ominous as they were when spoken.

THIRTY-TWO

Tristan

Piggybacking in his girlfriend's knapsack wasn't the most dignified moment of the remainder of the night. He would have preferred draping himself over Susannah's shoulder but that had the danger of slipping off and hurting himself with a few broken ribs or a fractured spine. He'd be useless if he had to deal with paralysis on top of everything else.

The best he could do was squeak and tug on a loose strand of hair to get her attention before she shrugged the pack off and set it on the concrete floor. He rummaged head and paws first through it, seizing the t-shirt in his mouth before dragging the shirt across the floor. The jeans were heavier, harder to wrangle before he pushed his full weight against the splintered side door. Privacy might not matter to his brother, it did to him.

Changing from otter to human shape was always easier than the reverse and it was a relief to stand on two feet again. And speak in more than squeaks and chirps. Tristan pulled the shirt on over his head, brushing dust from it. No shoes or socks included but maybe that was for the best if he got his changing ability back. They would only inconvenience him. "Do we know this'll work?"

"No idea." Susannah twisted her hands in the hem of her t-shirt. "Neither of us have fought a god before, you know."

If he was reading her strained joke the way it was meant to, she was just as terrified as he was. "Yeah."

It was good to know he wasn't the only one worried about Lyra's illusion trick failing on them. Poseidon's abilities were unknown and the only who could have told them how to deal with the god, couldn't. Aran was still stubbornly silent on the matter. "Where is he anyway?"

Susannah glanced at a tattered safety poster on the warehouse wall. "Lyra said she was giving him some free therapy. She didn't say what kind or if she was trained for it."

Neither of them really knew the nineteen-year-old girl well but he was brave enough to make a guess at what Lyra's 'therapy' entailed.

"She's Loki. If we have to rely on mythology here, probably something with fire. I think Mount St. Helens is too big for her but there are other things she could do." Tristan said.

The only thing they could do was wait until the pair were back from their errand, however long it took. If they were waiting on Martin's schedule, there was no need to rush. The only person he seemed interested in was Aran. Everyone else was just collateral to whatever the god had in mind. "There isn't a lot we can do but wait, I guess. He won't come until he knows Aran's around."

"Lovely." Susannah's answer was bleak. "Which pretty much sounds like never since Aran isn't with us. I wouldn't either if I was in his position. If he does show, we'll get the curse off you, right?"

"I hope so." Tristan tore the poster advertising a long closed farmer's market from the wall, crumpling it into a yellowed ball of paper. "One year was hell, longer than that, I don't even want to think about."

He sat gingerly in a rickety abandoned chair, kicking the toe of his runner against the ground. "The only bit of poetry Aran liked reading was that stupid thing from Robert Frost. I think the book was a gift from one of his ex-girlfriends. Never thought much of who wrote a little note in the front of it but it was signed with Lyra's name."

"The one about the world ending in fire or ice?" Susannah said.

"Yeah." Tristan shifted position, wincing as the chair creaked under his weight. "That one."

Susannah barely suppressed a strained snicker at that. "I think I know what your trickster is up to then. She's Norse, giving Aran what she calls therapy and Martin owns a bookstore. She's going to burn it down, isn't she?"

"Don't know, she might." Tristan forced a smile he couldn't feel. "Wouldn't surprise me if you got that one exactly right. Lyra's not the most subtle of people, from what I've seen."

As long as she didn't stay to watch the fire or let it spread to other buildings in the area, he wasn't going to quibble over what Lyra thought was an appropriate therapy session. "Shouldn't be too long, I hope."

The sooner this was dealt with, the better.

THIRTY-THREE

Aran

It wasn't that much of a secret that Lyra had a fondness for setting things on fire, but the therapeutical benefit of arson was doubtful. Even if she thought he needed it. The bookshop smelled too much like gasoline to him. Something toxic, unnatural in its reek. Aran gagged, half turning away for what little the gesture did for him. It was everywhere and the only escape would be if he crossed the street before Loki dropped the butchered lighter she was holding. *Why do I think this is more for you than me?*

Lyra smirked, glancing into the small flame she carried. "Cause it wouldn't be the first time I've done this

279

to some rich asshole's home. First time I've done it for a god though. And hell, Grandfather will love the tale when I tell it to him. Almost up there with the time I dropped the red-haired son of a bitch down the elevator shaft, and he came back up as a wild chicken. Want me to do the honors, or do you?"

Fire wasn't his element, that particular knack belonged more to his adoptive father or to the long dead Hephaestus, but it wouldn't take much to let the lighter fall onto a pile of gasoline-soaked pages. They went up like so much kindling and he coughed, shielding his mouth and nose with one sleeve as they hastily vacated the building through the back door.

Right into Martin's path.

He looked between them as the pavement cracked underfoot and a few startled shrieks from passerby sounded. A set of squealing brakes followed as Lyra backed up, wide eyed and terrified, clinging to Aran's side for a moment before she scrambled through the silvery-green light of her gate. To warn his brother and Susannah, or just scared of a furious god before them.

Water hissed, spouting from the broken watermain as the earth shifted below the street. Aran lifted his gaze to look at Martin. *You knew it would end like this. That Tristan wouldn't want to see me hurt further at your hand. Not after what you did to me. He cares more about that than the curse you placed on him.*

"Short sighted and mortal." Martin said.

He's my brother. Gods, he shouldn't have become so attached to the kit, but he had despite his better judgement. *The fight you want is with me, not them. Break the curse like I asked you to, please.*

"Are you begging me for it?" Martin's expression soured as sirens sounded in the distance, attempting to deal with the fire and stopped by the broken watermains throughout the city. "I've got all I want out of you. I wasn't convinced then and I'm not now. I swore on the river but never said which one, boy. Once, you might have picked up on that."

He gestured in contempt as the crack marring the street beyond the alley widened into a sinkhole. Someone's car braking not soon enough to avoid half tumbling into the gap. "Even with half the power I once had, I could still drown part of the city."

Coyote wouldn't let you. Aran said.

Martin scowled, lowering his hand back to his side. "He's not obligated to interfere in a war, and I drove him off to his spirit world. He won't be stepping in to help you. Not until he recovers from his wounds. Come. Perhaps I'll remove the curse on your brother. After his shade wanders the underworld for a while."

Aran went to his knees, scraping them on gravel. *You can't…*

"Don't try me, boy." Martin picked up a handful of sand and threw it into Aran's face. "And remember your oath. You're still bound to it. Your body's mine."

It felt like fire running across his nerves. Aran curled up in a tight ball, wetness streaking his cheeks as Martin knelt in the dirt and brushed a hand over his shoulder. The touch was gentle, more of a caress, but that only made it worse. Aran choked, trying to find words he couldn't use.

The light surrounding him was too hot, too bright and fading sooner than expected. Aran squeezed his eyes shut tight, holding back the tears that threatened to spill again.

He was on his knees again, seated next to Martin with Tristan and Susannah standing opposite them. Both were disbelieving and horrified. Loki's face was turned away, buried in Susannah's shoulder as she trembled.

Whatever plan they'd had, had fallen apart before it could play out.

Tristan spoke first, knuckles going white as he tightened his hand at his side. "Let him go."

Martin gave him a long look and stepped aside, placing a foot or two between himself and Aran. "What makes you think you're a better protector for a soldier I created than I am. I tried to keep him safe, cared for until he started trying to make up his own mind. We can't have that, can we?"

Tristan bristled, snarling softly. "He deserves more than whatever you put him through."

"Indeed?" Martin shrugged, placing a hand on Aran's shoulder. "He came to me willingly, prepared to offer anything to break that curse on you. Irene, Eva. They were only for the sake of blending in. It was never really about their lives when all I wanted was your... brother back at my side."

He sighed, shaking his head. "Certainly not for his ability to entertain me in bed. That, he was a disappointment there."

"Aran isn't a plaything you can use and throw away." Tristan said flatly. "No one's at their best when someone just goes and takes them without permission."

"Enough." Martin said. "Do you want the curse removed or not, boy."

Tristan went still, mouth opening and closing before he spat on the ground in front of him. "I'll take the curse if you just let Aran go."

"That was never really his name, you know." Martin's voice dropped, lazily. "But it's done. You'll never suffer changing from human to otter again after tonight. *Amyntas.*"

His next words were in Greek, toneless as Tristan froze in incredulity. Aran blurred, pinning him against the warehouse wall, one arm against his throat before thought could catch up with reaction. And a smaller part of him screaming in the dark at the lack of control his brother had over his actions. This wasn't his choice, it was Martin's and he was watching, unable to stop it.

Susannah was swearing in Spanish, Loki adding her own words in Finnish. Words were all they had. The warehouse was too big, too empty to find something to throw at such short notice. Even if he could breathe through the pressure on his neck. Tristan choked, gasping before he did the one thing left to him. And bit down hard enough on his brother's arm to draw dark blood. Aran drew back, eyes narrowing as he spat something unfamiliar in Greek. Tristan blinked back tears, scrambling to his feet as he sucked in another desperate breath.

Poseidon was too calm, a little smile playing across his lips as he watched. He made no move to join the fight because he didn't have to. He had Aran to deal with that. His soldier. His *slave*.

The pain of Tristan's bite cleared his thoughts enough for him to take a half step back from the young shapeshifter. Aran shook his head, one hand on the sword at his waist. Poseidon's demands were wordless but that didn't make it any easier to resist the compulsion forced into his thoughts. "*Ochi*."

No.

Martin's smile slipped a little and he tightened the hand at his side into a white knuckled fist. "You won't disobey, you cannot. You swore on the Styx you wouldn't. If you won't deal with the boy, then deal with the girl instead."

Aran went to hands and knees, trying to resist the migraine that threatened to blind him as Martin strode to his side, one hand tightening on his shoulder hard enough to bruise through cotton cloth.

He watched helplessly and unable to move as the three fled, taking advantage of the respite to run for the entrance they had used to enter the warehouse. There would be no further fight now, but it wasn't as much a blessing of safety as they thought it would be. And in running, they were risking Martin's fury. The god had little tolerance for what he saw as cowardice. Running had just sealed their fates—and the fate for the coast as well. With him as the agent of that fate.

"Stop." This voice was new, a stranger as he stepped out of the shadows to join them.

Martin faltered, eyes narrowing at the sight of the man in the leather jacket. "What do you want, *brother*?"

The newcomer's mouth thinned as he looked in the direction that Tristan and the girls had fled, long since out of sight now as he switched from English to Greek.

"For a start, Martin. Don't compel your soldier into tearing the Cascadia Faultline in half. You'll have the likes of Coyote to contend with and a greater war than one against pups. Pups."

He shook his head, a flicker of blue fire dancing around his hands before he dismissed it. "When did mortals become more your concern? They were innocent and chances were—no threat to you. If I remember correctly, the responsible party for your daughter's death is kneeling at your feet. Why would you bother his own family?"

Martin scowled, saying nothing.

Aran kept his gaze on the concrete underneath his hands. Let Hades and Martin work this out in their own way, he was only the soldier here. Hades sighed, dropping to one knee next to him as he broke Martin's hand on his shoulder. The words were soft, barely above a murmur. "Tristan's curse was broken but he won't find that out until nightfall. Your oath on the other hand, I am... sorry. It was sworn on the Styx. Only a death will free you of that."

And since he was nearly immortal, it was unlikely to happen. Aran sagged, hair falling into his face. "I knew that when I went to M—my master."

"Call my brother by his name." Hades said gently. "It's a small prize but better than 'master'."

Hades stood, glancing at his brother. "You were sloppy this time, all for petty revenge disguised as justice for Irene's death. I thought better of you. I thought twenty years here, as a mortal would be enough to serve as probation and that you could go free after so long in Tartarus. I suppose I was wrong after all. More's the pity."

Martin's expression turned ugly at the words. "If I can't have him, neither can his brother."

"Every master justifies it the same way." Hades said. "It's over, Martin. Unless you want to spend your nights being hunted by Erinyes. She's not a forgiving woman for man or god."

Martin paled at that, but the scowl stayed plastered on his face as he cut an abrupt slash through the air at Aran rather than his brother. "I'll take my chances."

The conversation had been meant between the two but that didn't mean he wasn't unable to listen. Aran slumped on the cold concrete floor, already feeling the fire burning at him from within. At least this way it wouldn't be long and soon he'd be free to see his wife again. It had been eight thousand years too long since he'd held her in his arms.

Thana and Atropos were nearby, only seen to him. The younger girl in a gray hoodie and faded jeans, the older woman in a charcoal blouse and slacks. Thana knelt next to him, worry in her eyes as she placed a gentle hand on the burn scarred skin. "Is this... what you want? Peace with your wife after so long, or life with your brother?"

It was hard to say which was stronger for him. Aran coughed, bringing up blood as it tore at his throat. Martin had backed up, fear replacing the hate before he vanished abruptly, going somewhere Hades didn't seem inclined to follow him to. It wasn't his business and the black sparkles in front of his vision made it hard to focus.

"His silence should be enough." Atropos put her hand on Thana's shoulder. "He's outlived more than he should have, and you know his creation as well as my sister did."

Thana's shoulders slumped. "Not while there's still hope. I have to believe in the light even if you don't."

"Hope." Atropos gave her a chiding look. "The boy is suffering while we argue over his fate. You know as well as I do what was done to him. He hasn't been mortal for a very long time, may or may not have been but we both once loved the man—and the name he kept. He was, or he still carries part of Amyntas with him."

"All the more reason to help him." Thana said.

This wasn't a conversation even he could follow but not because of its subject. Aran swallowed with difficulty, trying to sit up. He only succeeded with Hades's arm around his shoulders, looking past the god. Even a little motion made his stomach twist in discomfort and as he shifted position, blistered skin cracked. Strength failing him with each labored breath.

Atropos let out a tired breath, tucking short dark hair behind her ear. "There is a way. He'll keep his self, but he won't have the attachment to the boy, or the girl he used to. It is best."

Thana bowed her head, resignation in her eyes. "They won't like it when we tell them but if it the only way, yes. Bring the water bottle."

Aran reached for Thana, brushing a hand over the line of her jaw before the darkness finally closed over his head. Drifting was easier, more painless than trying to hold on and watching his body break down in front of him.

THIRTY-FOUR

Susannah

Tristan was on hands and knees in an eerie echo of his brother's posture in the moments after he'd backed off from the attack. Susannah clung to him, trembling and half expecting to see a wall of water sweeping through the city. Drowning everything in its path. Lyra was cat shaped and perched on a half wall of crumbling brick, fur puffed out to three times her natural size.

  The two women appearing out of nowhere with Aran between them had Susannah shrieking and throwing a crumpled soda can at the nearest of the two strangers. Her target gave her an affronted look and caught the can before dropping it to the ground at her feet before stepping over it. "I would have thought you had more composure than that, girl."

Susannah gaped, staring wide eyed at the newcomer in disbelief. "Well, when you..."

"Atropos." The younger woman laid a warning hand on her older companion's arm. "We could have given some sign of our approach, but you chose the subtle way. Little wonder she threw a can at you."

She approached Susannah carefully, treading through a shallow puddle's edge. "And I am sorry for that, but she seldom sees the world I do. Just as the threads at the end of a life. And it would help much if she used your name—it isn't as if she is unaware of it after all."

There was a chiding note directed to the other woman before she returned her attention to Susannah. "You showed a little wisdom in fleeing, Susannah. Few people could have challenged a god and lived to tell the tale but I'm afraid to say your war isn't over yet."

"Thana." Atropos's voice held a hint of warning in it. "This changes my sister's weavings—"

Thana sniffed, touching mouse brown hair. "As humans say, fuck fate. Susannah and her friends deserve honesty, not more secrets or your sisters' mathematics."

She turned away, seeing Lyra still cat shaped on her perch. "And you can come down from the wall, Loki. Your aunt and grandfather want you safe at home in Valhalla."

Lyra hissed, still puffed up with fright as the silvery green light of a portal surrounded her and she vanished along with it.

"That clears at least one mortal out of here." Atropos's voice was acidic, bitter in its tone at being sworn at. "But that still leaves Tristan, Amyntas and Susannah in this..."

She trailed off, looking around the alley with distaste before gesturing pointedly towards Tristan still murmuring desperate Welsh pleas at his brother's side. "This street. And one of them is dying. I believe that is your duty, Thana."

"I haven't forgotten." Thana held a hand out for Susannah to take for the few steps it needed to pull her over to where Tristan and Aran were. "Come, sit a moment, please."

Susannah sat, still shaking at the sight of the goddess or whatever Thana was. "Okay, sure. Why me? I mean..."

Thana sighed, producing an improbably pink water bottle from a knapsack slung over her shoulder. "You should listen, Susannah. You as well, Tristan. This matters for both your sakes. And for Amyntas—Aran now, I suppose."

"What is it?" Tristan looked from Thana to the water bottle and Aran, swallowing as his grip tightened around Aran's hand.

Thana brushed dark hair from Aran's closed eyes, setting the water bottle down on the pavement. "Aran is dying, for real this time. Poseidon's last act after fleeing was to cut him off from the power that created him so long ago, but he doesn't have to be. There is a cost to it though."

Susannah took the water bottle warily, picking at the wax sealing the cap to the neck before the woman's hand caught hers, stopping her from pulling the cap off the bottle's top. "It's just water."

Thana looked at her, a shadow flickering across her face. "It's water from the Lethe. Drink or let a few drops fall onto your skin and you may not suffer an immediate loss of memory, but dementia will claim you earlier than it usually affects people. I've seen the effects of that illness far too often to enjoy it."

"Oh." Susannah stopped fidgeting with the cap and set it gingerly down once more. "Yeah. I want to remember this later."

"You always were too gentle, Thana." Atropos's voice was sharper than it had been a few minutes earlier. "Stop attempting to spare the girl's feelings and get it out. Unless you want to claim Amyntas's life after all. His wife is waiting for him."

Susannah cast Atropos a look of distaste mixed with hurt. "Look, I'm happy that you kind of think me and Tristan are a package deal here but I'm not sure if that's because you can't tell the difference between a couple humans here. This should be Tristan's decision. Not mine. I'm not family. Not really."

She stood, edging a few yards away and sat again on a stack of flattened cardboard boxes, kicking at a few weeds poking up through a crack in the concrete.

Tristan watched Susannah leave and sit, mouth going dry as he picked the bottle of water up, not daring to touch the cap in case it spilled. "Why that river in particular? And what does it have to do with Aran? I know my mythology, but I don't understand why you think this'll help."

She folded her hands in her lap, fidgeting with the drawstring on her hoodie. "Because Aran will still remember you, but it'll be like you're strangers to him. It isn't as contradictory as it sounds. He'll remember you but there won't be the affection there was before. It's... a death but only of memory. He cannot live while on land."

"Do it." Tristan said. "I'd rather have my brother than not. And it isn't like I can't teach him everything he's... lost."

Thana broke the seal on the bottle with a swift twist of the cap, carefully tipping the water into Aran's mouth as the alley faded around them, replaced by the small crescent of beach where she'd first met Tristan. Aran gasped, eyes widening in shock as he scrabbled at the rocks before he pulled away from Thana's supporting arm.

Watery light shimmered around him before leaving the kelpie in his place. It looked back over its shoulder at them and turned away, slipping into the trees edging the beach. Tristan scrubbed at his eyes, trying to pretend that the prickling in them was from exhaustion or grit rather than tears. "Where's At—Annie and Susannah?"

"Annie." Thana gave him an appraising look. "Atropos may not be fond of it, but I may remember that name and use it for her next we meet. They stayed behind. I believe she had a few words of her own for your girlfriend. We can stay a while and watch the water if you wish. It may take some time for Aran to return if he chooses to at all. That may not be certain."

"Can't be any worse than before. I've been waiting since I was five for him to come home to me." Tristan said.

"Poor child." Thana took his hand in hers, briefly holding it before she released him. "That cannot have been easy."

It wasn't—hadn't been. Tristan looked away, trying to find any hint of Aran's presence in the thin bit of woods bordering the beach or in the water. "There's still time. I've been waiting this long, a little longer can't hurt."

What was an hour or two compared to seventeen years, after all?

THIRTY-FIVE

Susannah

Mythology hadn't been her strong suit two and a half months ago, now her life had changed to include feuding gods, shapeshifters and the eldest sister of the three Fates. Susannah gulped, staring up at the dark-haired woman with her hands folded in her lap. "Where'd Tristan and Aran go?"

Atropos looked at her impassively, making no move to offer comfort by sitting next to her on the box. Or it would have collapsed under their combined weight. It was hard to say which was more likely. "Back to the beach where you met your sister."

It had to be a metaphor rather than the truth. She didn't have a sister that she was aware of. Susannah shuddered, memory drawn back to the pale haired girl in the water. "Sure, fun. Remind me about the half siren thing, thanks. You're scaring me more than Thana did."

Thana at least, had had the grace to be kind. There was little of that look in Atropos's eyes. Susannah took a breath, hating how her voice wobbled midsentence. "What do you want?"

"Simply to speak with you, girl." Atropos said. "You still wear Amyntas's leash around your neck."

Susannah put her hand to the little gemstone reflexively, feeling it there. "Yeah. I tried to get rid of it, give it back to him but it's back like a bad penny or whatever."

"Or whatever." Atropos gave her a long look, mouth thinning in distaste. "Mortal expressions in this age. I miss the days when Greek was the common tongue. Far more civilized a language. Wearing it makes you Amyntas's mistress—you must be aware of that now."

Amyntas. That name again. Susannah ducked her head, trying to reconcile the unfamiliar sound of it with Aran and failing. Tristan's brother would always be Aran to her, not what the Fate called him. "What if I don't want to be? You probably already know I grew up in Jamaica. It had a history of slave ownership in the old days. I don't want to do that to my boyfriend's brother."

More to the point, she couldn't. Morally or literally, it was wrong.

"You don't have a choice, little fury." Atropos said.

That left one more question than she wanted to hear for the day but at least it distracted her from the revolting tidbit that she was now Aran's keeper, wherever he was. "Little... fury?"

Atropos sniffed in dismissal. "You think Erinyes is the only woman to protect the vulnerable from harm? I was against it, but my sisters overruled me in this. They took your thread and tangled it with the boy's. Your life is as long as his now, bound to it."

The fate hadn't specified whether it was Tristan's life or Aran's that hers was tied to but one look at the woman's remote expression made her decide not to ask. Susannah gulped, folding her hands in her lap in an attempt not to fiddle with the chain around her neck. "Okay."

"So don't you get yourself killed, girl." Atropos said.

Susannah tucked blonde hair behind one ear. "But what does that—"

"Daylight hunter, girl, daylight hunter." Atropos's reply was tart. "You're the only hunter I know, and I know many of them, to see the light without needing sunglasses. Or facing her own death to earn it."

That didn't sound as much like a compliment as it did on the surface. Susannah looked away, biting down on her lower lip. "Thanks..."

The fate snorted, casting her an unimpressed look as she seized Susannah's wrist in her grip and tugged. Susannah felt her stomach drop at the unexpected pull, stumbling and retching as she landed on hands and knees on the rocky crescent of the beach. "Fuck..."

A little warning would have been welcomed, for the next time she was going to be dragged from one place to another in a matter of seconds. Particularly when they were miles apart from one another.

Atropos snorted, turning away before she vanished without a further comment. Susannah made a face, hoping the woman wouldn't take offense—wherever she watched from. "And goddamn."

Or were gods, plural, more appropriate? She didn't know. Susannah lifted her head, standing gingerly as she stepped around the mess she'd made on the rocks. "Tristan?"

He turned to look at her, hands stuffed into his jacket pockets. "There's no sign yet."

"Would there be?" Susannah asked tentatively.

Tristan's expression fell and he dragged the toe of one shoe across the ground, not looking at her. Susannah sighed, taking Tristan's hand in hers and released it a moment later, "Sorry. I didn't mean it like that, but…"

She faltered, continuing. "Isn't it time to stop waiting for Aran and start moving on with life? It's just me but it feels like you're stuck. Maybe that was the real curse, not the changing problem."

"Maybe." Tristan glanced towards the pale blue sky overhead. "But can we give it until dusk? If he doesn't come by then—he won't, and we can figure the future out at home together."

Together. Susannah managed a weak smile and pressing a chaste kiss to Tristan's mouth before breaking it off. "Thank you."

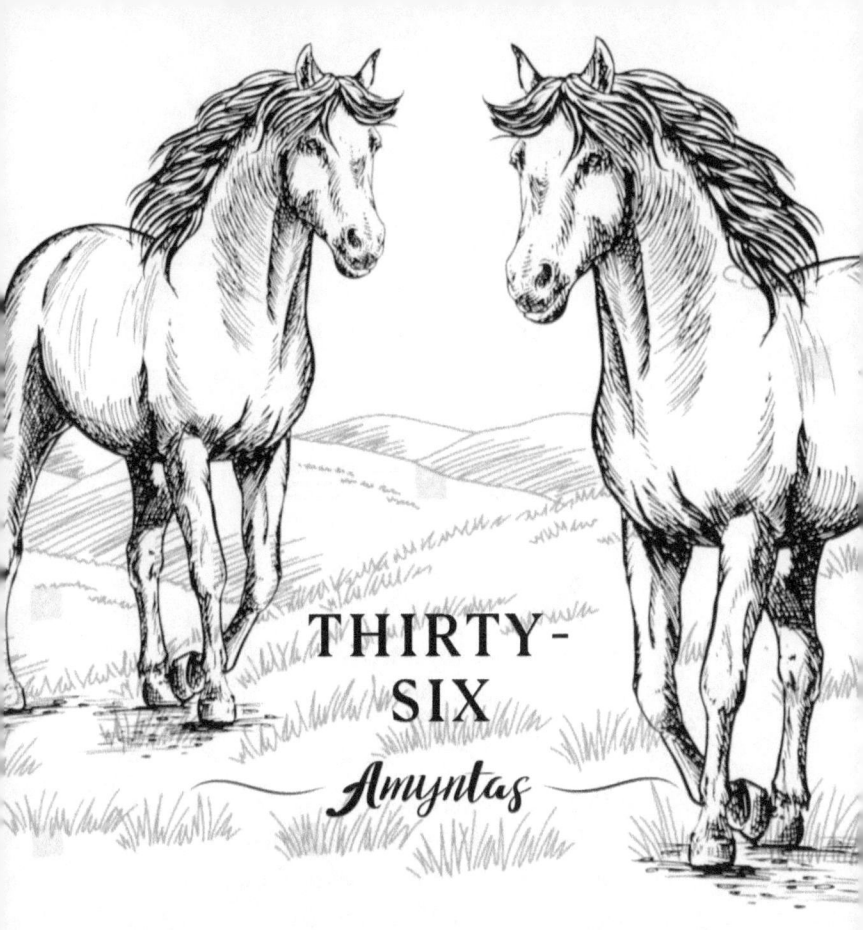

THIRTY-SIX

Amyntas

EARLY NEOLITHIC GREECE
APPROXIMATELY 5800 BC
Every child learned to at least paddle in shallow water, but this was a bit more than splashing through knee deep water to gather up nets and baskets with the day's catch. His head broke the surface as he gasped for air, fighting to drag himself to the pale sand of the beach. And to safety. He was a hunter and a warrior, not a fisherman. That oversight hadn't appeared to matter to the gray streaked,

heavily bearded man who had taken a liking to him over the course of a summer.

The sky overhead was dark with a coming, angry storm and he choked, inhaling water as weight coiled around his ankle, tangling him fast. Gray sparkles danced in front of his vision, going dim as the light faded around him.

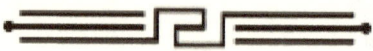

This world was too fine a place to be anything but a spirit realm as he forced himself to his feet, every step feeling like fire as he limped towards the largest and finest of the stone-built dwellings. It could have housed half of his village had they desired it.

The light was watery, echoing the play of light on the water of the land above. Eerie and beautiful at the same time. Its weight should have driven the air from his lungs, yet somehow, he was still standing, protected by the spirits.

The man from earlier sat on a bench made of the same pale stone, hair loose around his shoulders as he looked on at him. A small smile curving at his lips. "My young warrior..."

Three small words that should have pleased him, but for the way the fire twisted in his body, sending him to his knees and unable to cry out. Ancestors, he wanted to, but the scream was stolen away by the young woman suddenly by his side. Her hand a cool touch against the fire searing through his body.

It burned even in the stranger's watery realm, scorching through blood and flesh until the spirit was all that was left, forced into a new form by a god's will...

Poseidon's touch against his shoulder was unexpectedly gentle as he tangled a hand through the dark mane of hair. "I could rename you, young one but the mortal name still suits, Amyntas."

PRESENT DAY. SEATTLE, WASHINGTON.
The memories were sharper, oddly, without the emotional attachment to them. Free of the pain he'd long since blocked out. Every blow and punishment Poseidon had delivered for poor service still marked on his back, but they were the memories of a stranger's—not his own.

Hope flickered across Tristan's face, only to turn to defeat as Amyntas turned away, staying in the shallow water between land and sea. "Ari—Aran?"

That might have been a name he had favored once but it was just a word now, much like the half Japanese shape he'd used to wear. Some things hadn't changed for him as much as he'd have liked them to. Fairer haired now, as it had been in the days before meeting

Steffon and his wife, but the voice was still gone—stolen by Echo. He signed impatiently, spelling out his name. *Amyntas.*

For the mortal warrior he had been once. Tristan opened his mouth, closed it and turned on one foot, breaking into a hard run for the trees that bordered the northern beach. He watched, impassive as Susannah dropped her gaze, stricken. Following behind the younger shapeshifter as fast as she could.

There was always a price to be paid when it came to drinking the waters of the Lethe and Thana had warned them what it would cost.

"That was unkind, even for you." James Gray's voice was bland as he seemed to appear out of nowhere, stepping from the crossroads into the daylight world. "Tristan's your brother. It wouldn't hurt much to feign a little affection for the boy."

Amyntas gave the English soldier a disillusioned look. *Why? There was never any blood between us. His parents only took me in-*

"Out of kindness, at least that was Mariko's motivation." James's voice sharpened. "I cannot speak for Steffon but she loved you as much as she could. Tristan still does. Find him and apologize. You were born long before I, yes, and you forgot much when Poseidon stripped spirit from flesh and blood, but I'm told you learned it eventually. You can learn this again if you have the will to."

The shade cast him a bleak look, dropping the borrowed coat he wore to the ground. "And for God's sake. Accept the name Tristan called you by. Amyntas the mortal died long ago. Your brother doesn't know that man."

Amyntas sighed, picking a path through the narrow stand of trees, searching for Tristan more by scent than calling out the younger shapeshifter's name. It could barely be called a clearing and more of a small break in the trees with a fallen log between them. Tristan was white faced, trembling on his perch. *You were always that five-year-old child, where my...leaving was concerned.*

"Yeah." Tristan's answer was flat with the effort of keeping his voice steady. "So?"

No. Amyntas signed half-heartedly. *Stop. I can't promise anything, and I won't but that gods forsaken shadow suggested I go to you. At least for a little while. I—I'll be Aran for you if you want me to.*

Tristan wiped his nose on his t-shirt sleeve. "I don't know if I should let you off the hook that easily, but I want to, shit."

He sniffed, averting his gaze. "You still look seventeen but you're still my... older brother. Blonde, I know it's kind of your default look, but I liked it better when you were half Japanese."

The kit was asking for a lot but it was a smaller price to pay than his memories. Amyntas forced a smile, letting the light surround and warm him from the inside before it faded. Like before, his dark hair was loose and halfway down his back. Appearing in his late twenties was as much of a compromise as he was willing to make for Tristan.

"Close enough." Tristan swallowed, gaze sweeping across him. "Still wearing that damn tunic though, Am—"

Aran. He sighed the word tiredly, looking towards the water half visible through the trees. *James had a… point. Amyntas died a long time ago and you were always more comfortable with that name.*

"Died?" Tristan blinked, confusion briefly in his eyes. "Like really-?"

Aran snorted, raking a hand through his hair. *Or I was created to mimic the human's form and given his last memories. I'm not one to say one way or the other. Only that he… died, drowned at Poseidon's hand and I stepped into his place.*

"So he's kind of your dad. Sort of. At least when you're blonde." Tristan wrinkled his nose, looking for a moment like a rabbit. "That's... uhm, nice to know. The whole no parents thing kind of freaked me out, to be honest."

Come here. Aran got to his feet, ignoring the beginnings of discomfort prickling over his skin.

Tristan hesitated, uncertainty in his expression before he let himself be pulled into a brief embrace, resting his head against Aran's chest. "Wish you didn't have to go. I'm guessing that's the reason for the hug."

The ocean's song was something that couldn't be ignored even if he had been at his full strength. Aran nodded, taking a step back to give himself a little room to sign. *I would stay if I could, but I can't make that promise again. I'm still weak and recovery, this time, could take months.*

If not a decade or more given how close he had come to a true death this time. *Susannah still has that power over me if it helps. If she calls for me, I'll have*

304

no choice but to come. She has my leash. That's more than any oath I could give now. She's my mistress whether or not we like the thought.

"I—alright." Tristan's voice was steadier than it had been a few minutes ago but no less dejected. "Just so you know, there's no concrete plans to go anywhere but I think a random Greek archeologist offered Susannah an internship in Athens kind of out of the blue. We might not be in Seattle the next time you decide to visit again."

Or it may be sooner than that. Aran signed dryly. *Greece was home once, and I think I know the archeologist who extended that offer. Red haired, sunglasses—took her name from the ancient city.*

He didn't wait for Tristan's answer before turning his back on his brother and making his way back to the beach. The saltwater teasing around his legs eased the agony each step had caused him. He could have shifted form and let the light of the change take care of the tunic for him. This time he wrapped the cotton cloth in a plastic grocery bag with a note safety pinned to it. Tristan deserved a little closure if nothing else.

Aran closed his eyes and dove beneath the water, letting the weight of the human mask wash away with a feeling of relief. Time would heal his relationship with Tristan, however long it took. But for now, it was his time to rest and recover from his own wounds, regaining the strength he'd lost.

Rest would be much welcomed after so long without it.

EPILOGUE

Susannah

She was old enough to make her own decisions, even if it had come with the inexplicable offer of studying marine biology in Athens. And learning a whole new language on top of it. Her parents had fought the decision every step of the way, wondering what use that career choice was over something like medicine. They'd only shut up about it when she'd mentioned Hippocrates and that she wouldn't be using the time to lie on the beach with an iced coffee on a table next to her.

It wasn't the whole truth, but it was enough to make them grudgingly accept her choice—aided in part by the official looking scholarship letter in her email. Never minding that as good as it looked—it was still halfway forged. She was attending enough classes to make it seem real but the rest of the time was spent trying not to get herself killed. One battle against Poseidon had been won a few months ago. The war wouldn't end until he was back in the prison where he belonged, however long it took.

Tonight was one of the few reprieves they had from schoolwork and conflict, and one of the few days where Tristan was willing to let his feelings show. Susannah touched the little amethyst pendant resting at the base of her throat and sighed, looking over at him. He was still grieving the loss of his brother. It had never been a physical loss, but all the memories Aran had once were gone. The important stuff remained but his brother was a stranger to him.

A true death would have been easier to bear, in some ways.

Susannah looked away, giving Tristan and his brother as much privacy as she could on the small boat, resting her arms on the warm metal of the railing.

A woman's polite cough distracted her from watching the crystal blue water of the Aegean and the silver engagement ring on one finger. It was fairer to say that her parents had been more upset with her over Tristan's proposal than moving halfway across the world to somewhere actually warm for university but that didn't matter as much as it once had. "Sorry, Tiryn."

Tiryn glanced past her, a shadow passing over her face as Aran pulled away from his brother and turned away, making a perfect swan dive off the boat. The only sign of his brief visit was a shimmer of light beneath the water. Anyone could have mistaken his return home for a play of sunlight on top of the water. "It wasn't your fault; Tristan made the decision he thought was right at the time. You shouldn't feel guilty for it."

Those were the words of a soldier who had been fighting for far too long. Against a god worse than Poseidon. Susannah sighed, dropping her forehead to her folded hands. "I guess. But we bought Aran's freedom at a cost. Some days it feels like it was too big a price."

The Greek woman pushed the sunglasses back up to the bridge of her nose, wincing a little as the sunlight stung her eyes. "It's still freedom. And he still has his life. The loss of the emotions from his memories is a small price, as I see it."

"I guess." Susannah turned away from the water, mood souring. They'd all changed since that time. Tristan's curse was broken and though Aran had survived, he was colder than she remembered him from months ago. Maybe it was a fair sacrifice, but it didn't feel like it, dampening her mood. "Did you know him? I mean, you're almost as old as he is."

Tiryn gave her a pained chuckle, raking a hand through red hair. "Not well, and no. That's a story for a different day, I think."

Maybe it was but Susannah couldn't help a lingering bit of curiosity all the same. There was so little she still knew about the Greek hunter or her own obligations. At least she wouldn't be alone in it. There was always her boyfriend for company. She wouldn't have to face the future and decades to come alone.

SNEAK PREVIEW
OF
EVE

MARK JONATHAN RUNTE'S
NEXT RELEASE

Prologue

July 10th, 2008—Somewhere, Arizona
The mattress was thin, barely worth the name and the blanket was worse, threadbare and full of holes. She batted at one of the bugs, knocking it out of the air and crushed it beneath a too flat pillow. It was one less insect to shit on her at night when she was trying to sleep.

She stood, pacing out the confines of the small room. Eight feet by six. Six by eight. It was roomy for a prison cell holding one person—with a few 'comforts' included. A bookshelf with three battered paperbacks on it. A toilet hidden behind a curtain. They called her a patient, but the word was nothing more than a lie. She was an unwilling prisoner, and they weren't doctors.

All these butchers wanted from her was her blood and hair. If that failed them, then they'd take her apart piece by piece for what she carried inside her.

She swept matted brown hair over her shoulder, glancing towards the only window in her cell. Set too high up and too small for an easy escape. She'd tried already, only to find that the bars at the front of her cage were coated with silver. Someone, whoever they were had planned this for a while, and well. Escape was nearly impossible.

They'd even made the effort to put something in her food and water after she'd torn the IV line from her arm. Whatever it was, dulled her senses and slowed her thoughts without putting her into sleep. No one had invented a medicine to stop her from dreaming though, even if it was only in snatched fragments. Her brother, her... sister, and the hot sun overhead. The scent of asphalt. And the screech of tires as a beige colored lorry skidded to a halt. Somewhere, something more dreamlike —a wolf calling out for her.

Sleep would have been kinder. She paced the confines of her cell again, picking at the raw skin on her forearm until it bled. They wouldn't like to see their precious pet hurt herself and this would be sure to draw them. All she had to do was wait and watch as droplets of bright red spotted her blanket.

Food came, delivered on a metal tray shoved through a slot at the bottom of her prison and she dropped to her knees in front of it. Old bread, and slightly moldy in appearance and smell. A slice of fruit that was just days away from overripe and rotting. The only thing that could be remotely called fresh was the meat, delivered on a separate dish. She went for it first, ignoring the plastic utensils wrapped in a paper napkin. It would give her strength that the bread and fruit wouldn't. And tasted better for the coppery tang of blood in the back of her mouth.

In the early days, they had tried to cook it—only for her to throw the meal uneaten at the warden when he'd come to check on her. They'd since learned her preferences.

She sat back, tucking her legs beneath her body as she wiped the juice away, smearing it across the back of her arm. Say what they could about her mouth and throat, the thin white hospital shift was only stained at the collar.

The tray was collected once more by a woman in navy blue scrub top and pants before the man scent filled her nose. She drew back, snarling softly as the keys rattled in the lock. He was seldom alone, and lead would kill as easily as silver if enough of it was put into her back. Silver only burned; bullets were more dangerous despite their size.

His hand struck the side of her face, leaving a reddened mark behind as his guards leveled their weapons at her. She shrank back, seeing the danger and bowed her head as she stepped out of the cage. For now she'd play quiet and submissive, showing the side of her throat to him like she was the lowest ranked wolf in the pack.

She was many things but suicidal wasn't one of them. He gave her an approving look and turned away without a word, striding for the metal door at the far end of the corridor. The guards were a step or two behind her, she could smell the faintly acrid scent of their fear even if their faces didn't betray it. They would shoot to kill if given the slightest advantage and only their fear of the white clad 'doctor' kept them from going to their weapons.

She suppressed the low growl and stepped across the threshold into the room. It smelled like bleach and antiseptic, stinging in her nose. Nothing natural or pleasant in the stink. The thin lines between the floor tile beneath her bare feet were reddish brown. They had offered her slippers once when she'd first come to this place. She had thrown them at her keeper, cursing his name.

The lessons in... obedience had been hard ones to learn. She bowed her head, seating herself on the bed, nails tearing little lines into the paper as he slipped the syringe into her arm and drew the plunger back on it, filling the little plastic tube with bright red. For the sake of the child curving her stomach, she would cooperate. It was more than her life at stake here.

She closed her eyes as the IV needle was placed in her arm and its sleeping power dripped through the tube connecting it. Faith was something hard come by but she'd found it in small prayers to the mother of darkness who came to her in her dreams of late.

The dream goddess's mate would come for her and then she'd be free of this den and its cruelty. Free to take her natural form.

*   *   *

Sweat burned her eyes as she tried to rub it from her face. The sun scorched overhead, blinding against the pale sand as she put one foot in front of the other. For the sake of her child, she had to go on. If her mouth didn't taste like dust and the ache behind her eyes didn't threaten to send her to her knees. The only thing that was wet besides the dampness of her hair was between her legs. She went to her knees, pressing one arm against her stomach as the spasm came again. Harder, stronger than it had been.

She dug her nails into the palm of her hand, drawing blood and squeezed her eyes shut tight against the sun and pain, refusing the whimper that threatened to escape. The contraction came again as she wrapped her free hand around a sharp-edged rock. The pain from the cuts focused her scattered thoughts as she drew a breath in and pushed, arching her back at the effort.

Her child was early but there was no point in delaying it when the boy wanted to come now. Feeding him would have to wait until they found a sheltered place and pool of water to drink from. Or if some kind human stopped for the woman dressed in a stained hospital shift.

One more hard push and a shriek of her own before the child emerged squalling onto the sand. She crouched, panting as she cut through the cord and pulled her shift off, swaddling the gray furred bundle in it. The boy's eyes were closed above the small muzzle but when they opened, they would be blue for a time before starting to darken to amber.

*   *   *

The highway river stretched out in front of her, vanishing into the distance as she held a hand out, hoping to attract someone willing to give her a ride towards the faint smudge on the horizon. She cradled her pup in her other arm, keeping the small ball of fluff hidden out of sight. Her first prospect slowed his vehicle, blanched and took off again, leaving her retching into the sand at the shoulder of the road from the exhaust fumes. The next driver was less particular or unable to see her as anything but a twelve-year-old girl with a furry ball cradled in her arms. Odd, but likely harmless in his view.

MARK RUNTE is a transmasculine writer who likes exploring the realms of folklore and mythology in his stories. He currently lives at home with a shih tzu bichon mix and a black Havanese.

www.ingramcontent.com/pod-product-compliance
Lightning Source LLC
Chambersburg PA
CBHW030638020726
47493CB00006B/1777